Praise for Benjamin Rosenbaum's work:

"Rosenbaum's imagery will surely embed itself in the invisible architecture of your own memory banks for days after you've read it."
—*New York Times Book Review*

"A terrific range of tales, showcasing an active, playful mind and a gleeful genre-blender."
—Aimee Bender (*Willful Creatures*)

"Benjamin Rosenbaum is one of the best new science fiction writers working in the field today."
—Cory Doctorow, Boing Boing

"Remember when opening a book was like opening a door to the beyond which resides within? Have you been looking for that door for a long time? Benjamin Rosenbaum has the key."
—Mary Rickert (*Map of Dreams*)

"Rosenbaum's fertile sense of invention and his sly humor ("Ponge, as its inhabitants will tell you, is a thoroughly unattractive city. 'Well,' they always say at the mention of any horrible news, 'we do live in Ponge.'") make these parables a real treat."
—*Asimov's*

"An emerging prodigy of short fiction."
—*Locus*

"Beyond being a fantastic fabulist and futurist, Ben has a .... exposing less-explored aspects of human nature and modern culture in his stories in ways that are touching and funny and cause you to think. His stories are exciting and fun, and they keep you engaged long after you put the book down."
—Jason Olim

"Ben Rosenbaum is one of the freshest and finest voices to appear in science fiction in many years. The stories collected in *The Ant King* demonstrate his astonishing versatility, his marvelous imagination, and his ready wit. Start reading him now, because there'll clearly be much more to come, and it will be good, extremely good."
—Jack Womack (*Let's Put the Future Behind Us*)

THE
ANT
KING
AND OTHER STORIES

THE
ANT
KING
AND OTHER STORIES

Benjamin
Rosenbaum

Small Beer Press
Easthampton, MA

Small Beer Press
150 Pleasant St., #306
Easthampton, MA 01027
www.smallbeerpress.com
info@smallbeerpress.com

Distributed to the trade by Consortium.

Library of Congress Cataloging-in-Publication Data

Rosenbaum, Benjamin, 1969-
  The ant king and other stories / Benjamin Rosenbaum.
      p. cm.
  ISBN 978-1-931520-52-2 (trade cloth : alk. paper) -- ISBN 978-1-931520-53-9 (trade paper : alk. paper)
  I. Fantasy fiction, American. 2. Science fiction, American. I. Title.
  PS3618.O8316A85 2008
  813'.6--dc22
                                    2008013685

First edition 1 2 3 4 5 6 7 8 9 0

Printed on 50# Natures Book Natural FSC Mixed 30% PCR by Thomson-Shore in Dexter, MI.
Text set in Centaur MT 12.
Cover art © Brad Holland.
www.bradholland.com

Contents

For Esther:
my beloved
my foundation
and my lucky break

The Ant King:
A California Fairy Tale

SHEILA SPLIT OPEN AND THE air was filled with gumballs. Yellow gumballs. This was awful for Stan, just awful. He had loved Sheila for a long time, fought for her heart, believed in their love until finally she had come around. They were about to kiss for the first time and then this: yellow gumballs.

Stan went to a group to try to accept that Sheila was gone. It was a group for people whose unrequited love had ended in some kind of surrealist moment. There is a group for everything in California.

After several months of hard work on himself with the group, Stan was ready to open a shop and sell the thousands of yellow gumballs. He did this because he believed in capitalism, he loved capitalism. He loved the dynamic surge and crash of Amazon's stock price, he loved the great concrete malls spreading across America like blood staining through a handkerchief, he loved how everything could be tracked and mirrored in numbers. When he closed the store each night he would count the gumballs sold, and he would determine his gross revenue, his operating expenses, his operating margin; he would adjust his balance sheet and learn his debt-to-equity ratio; and after this exercise each night, Stan felt he understood himself and was at peace, and he could go home to his apartment and drink tea and sleep, without shooting himself or thinking about Sheila.

On the night before the IPO of gumballs.com, Sheila came to

I

Stan in a dream. She was standing in a kiddie pool; Stan and his brothers and sisters were running around splashing and screaming; she had managed to insert herself into a Super 8 home movie of Stan's family, shot in the late seventies. She looked terribly sad.

"Sheila, where are you?" Stan said. "Why did you leave me, why did you become gumballs?"

"The Ant King has me," Sheila said. "You must rescue me."

Stan woke up, he shaved, he put on his Armani suit, and drove his Lexus to his appointment with his venture capitalists and investment bankers. But the dream would not leave him. "Ant King?" he asked himself. "What's this about a goddamn Ant King?"

On the highway, near the swamp, he pulled his Lexus over to the shoulder. The American highway is a self-contained system, Stan thought. Its rest stops have video games, bathrooms, restaurants, and gas stations. There's no reason ever to leave the interstate highway system, its deadness and perfection and freedom. When you do reach your exit, you always have a slight sense of loss, as when awakening from a dream.

Stan took off his shiny black shoes and argyle socks, cuffed his Armani suit pants above the knees, and waded through the squidgy mud and tall reeds of the swamp. He saw a heron rise, flutter, and soar into the midmorning sky. Ant King, Ant King, he thought.

Miles underground, the Ant King was watching an old episode of *Charlie's Angels* on cable.

"Which one do you identify with?" he asked Sheila. "The blonde one, or the pretty brunette one, or the perky, smart brunette one?"

"Stan may come rescue me, you know," Sheila said.

"I like how you never see Charlie. And how Boswell—is that his name, Boswell?—how he's kind of a foil and audience for the girls.

There's all this unrealized desire—Boswell desires the girls, but he's got no chance, and I think they desire Charlie, but Charlie's invisible."

Sheila picked at a seam in the orange sofa. "It is *possible*. He *might* come rescue me."

The Ant King blinked and tried to smile reassuringly. "Sure. No, yeah, definitely. I think the two of you are just going through a phase, maybe. You know, it took him a while to deal with, ah, what he's going through."

Sheila glared at him. "You are so full of shit!" she said.

The Ant King threw his bag of Doritos at her. "Fine! I was just trying to be nice!" he shouted. "I'm full of shit? *I'm* full of shit? What about your dorky boyfriend?" He grabbed the remote and changed the channel, showing Stan, sitting in his Lexus with the door open, toweling off his muddy feet. "He's a lost cause, baby. You want me to respect a guy like that?"

"I hate it here," said Sheila.

The Ant King smoothed his antennae and took a deep breath. "Okay, I'm sorry about throwing the Doritos. Maybe I overreacted. Okay?"

"I hate you, too," said Sheila.

"Fine," said the Ant King, savagely snatching up the remote control and turning back to *Charlie's Angels*. "Be that way."

"Gumballs are more than candy, isn't that right, Stan?" said Monique, smiling broadly.

Stan nodded. His feet were still wet, inside his argyle socks. "Yes, gumballs have a lot of, ah, a lot greater significance than just candy."

Monique paused and looked at Stan brightly, waiting for him to go on. Across the table, the three Credit Suisse First Boston under-writers—Emilio Toad, Harry Hornpecker, and Moby Pfister—sat stone-faced and unreacting in their gray double-breasted suits.

Stan tried to remember the gumballs.com business plan. "They have hard shells," he said. "People, ah, they want challenge . . . the hardness, the gumminess . . ."

Monique broke in smoothly. Monique, all seven post-gender-reassignment-surgery feet of her; Monique, always dressed to the nines and tens; Monique was a Valley legend for her instincts, her suavity, her rapacious, exemplary greed. Stan had sold Monique on the idea of gumballs.com, and she had invested—found him the right contacts, the right team—and here they were at the Big Day, the Exit Strategy.

"Stan!" she cried joyously, fixing him with a penetrating stare. "Don't be shy! Tell them about how gumballs are sex! Tell them about our top-gun semiotics professors, tell them about gumballs as a cultural trope! You see," she said, swooping onto Hornpecker, Pfister & Toad, "you can't think of this as a candy thing, a food & bev thing, a consumer cyclic thing; no way, José! Think Pokémon. Think World Wide Wrestling. Think *Star Wars!*"

"Could we get back to the numbers," said Emilio Toad in a voice that sounded like a cat being liquefied in an industrial-strength mixer. The gray faces of Harry Hornpecker and Moby Pfister twitched in relief.

Later, after the deals were signed and the faxes were faxed, Monique and Stan took a taxi to a cigarillo bar to celebrate.

"What, like, is *up* with you today?" said Monique, crouched somewhat uncomfortably in the taxicab, her knees almost touching her chin, but exuding her usual sense of style and unflappability.

"Um . . . just IPO jitters?" said Stan hopefully.

"Cut the crap," said Monique.

"I had a dream about Sheila," Stan blurted out.

"Oh goddess," said Monique. "Not this again."

"It seemed so real," Stan said. "She said I had to rescue her from the Ant King."

. "Well, you're not my only weirdo CEO," Monique said, giving him a manly, sidearm hug, "but I think you're the weirdest."

The next morning, nursing a cognac hangover and a throat raw from cigarillo smoke, Stan stood bewildered in front of a two-story building in downtown Palo Alto. It looked a lot like where he worked. There on the signboard were the other companies in his building: Leng Hong Trading; Trusty & Spark, patent attorneys; the Bagel Binge, marketing department; MicroChip Times, editorial. But no gumballs.com, Inc.

"I thought you might be here, sir," said Pringles, his secretary, appearing at his elbow.

"Huh? Pringles!" said Stan. The day before, Pringles had been dressed in a black T-shirt reading "Your Television Is Already Dead" and twelve earrings, but now she was in a smart ochre business suit, carried a mahogany-colored briefcase, and wore pearls.

"We've moved, sir," she said, leading the way to the limousine.

On the highway to Santa Clara, something occurred to Stan. "Pringles?" he said.

"Yes, sir?"

"You didn't use to call me sir—you used to call me Stan."

"Yes, sir, but we've gone public now. SEC regulations."

"You're kidding," said Stan.

Pringles stared out the window.

The gumballs.com building was thirty stories of mirrored glass windows with its own exit off Highway 101. A forty-foot cutout of the corporate animated character, Mr. Gumball, towered over Stan, exuding yellow hysteria. Pringles escorted Stan to his office suite on the thirtieth, after giving him a building pass.

"Wow," said Stan, looking at Pringles across his enormous glass desktop. "Nice work, Pringles."

"Thank you, sir."

"So what's my schedule for today?"

"Nothing lined up, sir."

"Nothing?"

"No, sir."

"Oh. Could I look at the numbers?"

"I'll order them from Accounting, sir."

"Can't I just ask Bill?"

"Sir, Bill is the CFO of a public company now. He doesn't have time to look at the numbers."

"Oh. Shouldn't I have a staff meeting with the department heads or whatever?"

"Vic is doing that, sir."

"Vic? Who's Vic?"

"Vic is our Executive Vice President for Operations, sir."

"He is?"

"Yes, sir."

Stan looked at his desk. There were gold pens, a golden tape dispenser, a framed picture of Sheila, and a glass jar full of yellow gumballs. They were the last of the Sheila gumballs.

"Pringles?" Stan said.

"Yes, sir?"

"I don't have a computer."

"That's right, sir."

There was a pause.

"Anything else, sir?"

"Um, yeah. Pringles, what do you suggest I do today?"

Pringles turned and walked across the expanse of marble floor to a teak closet with a brass doorknob. She opened it and returned with a leather golfing bag, which she leaned against the glass desk.

"Pringles, I don't golf," said Stan.

"You need to learn, sir," said Pringles, and left.

Stan took a gumball from the glass jar and looked at it. He thought about biting into it, chewing it, blowing a bubble. Or at least sucking on it. I really should try one of these sometime, he thought. He looked at Sheila's picture. He put the gumball in the pocket of his Armani suit jacket.

Then he went to look for Vampire.

"Hi," said Stan, looking around a corner of a cubicle on the seventeenth floor. "I'm Stan."

"Yeah, whatever," said the occupant of the cubicle, not looking away from her monitor.

"No, really, I'm Stan, I'm the CEO here."

"Yeah, I believe you, so? What do you want, a medal?"

"Well, uh," Stan said. "So what are you up to?"

"I'm storyboarding the Mr. Gumball Saturday morning cartoon pilot, and I'm past deadline, and I'm paid shit, Mr. CEO."

"Oh, okay," said Stan. "I won't bug you then."

"Great," said the cartoon storyboardist.

"Hey, by the way, you don't know where the sysadmins and stuff are, though, do you?" Stan asked.

"I thought you weren't going to bug me then."

After many such adventures, Stan found himself in the third subbasement of the gumballs.com building, close to despair. It was 8 p.m., and his building pass expired at nine.

Suddenly, faintly, from far off, Stan heard the sound of horrible, ghostly shrieking and rhythmic pounding.

Thank God, Stan thought, heading toward the sound. And indeed, as he got closer, he could tell he was listening to one of Vampire's thrash goth trance doom CDs.

Stan had feared that, like Pringles, Vampire might suddenly be wearing a suit, but as he emerged into Vampire's blacklit cavern, he saw that Vampire was wearing knee-length jet-black hair, a black trench-coat, fingerless studded leather gloves, and giant surgical-steel ear, nose, lip, and tongue piercings, as always. Perhaps he was surrounded by an even larger array of keyboards, monitors, and machines than yesterday, but it was hard to tell.

"Vampire!" Stan shouted over the music. "Am I glad to see you!"

"Hey, man," said Vampire, lifting a hand in salutation but not looking away from his monitor.

"So, hey, what are you up to?" said Stan, looking for somewhere to sit down. He started to take a broken monitor off a folding metal chair.

"DON'T TOUCH THAT!" Vampire shouted.

"Oops, oops, sorry," said Stan, backing off.

"No problem," said Vampire.

"So, ah, you were saying?" Stan said hopefully.

"Lotta new machines coming in," said Vampire. "What do you know about NetBSD 2.5 routing across multiple DNS servers?"

"Absolutely nothing," said Stan.

"Okay," said Vampire, and nodded.

Stan waited a little while, looking around. Finally he spoke again. "Ah, Vampire, ever heard of a, the—this is going to sound silly but—the Ant King?"

"Nope," said Vampire. "I knew an AntAgonist once, on the Inferno BBS."

"Oh," said Stan. "But, um, how would you go about finding out about the Ant King?"

"What search engines have you tried?" asked Vampire.

"Well, none," said Stan.

"Well, try Google, they're good."

"Okay," said Stan. "Um, Vampire?"

"Yeah?"

"I don't have a computer anymore."

Vampire turned and looked at Stan. "You poor bastard!" he said, and pointed. "Use that one."

The Ant King was sound asleep on the sofa, cans of Dr. Pepper littered around him. Sheila got up gingerly, took off her sneakers, and held them in one hand as she crept for the door, clutching a Dorito in the other.

It was a lucky moment. Sheila passed several of the Ant King's henchmen (who were all bald and stout and wore identical purple fedoras) asleep at their desks, and threaded her way through the dark rooms of the Ant King's lair to the tunnels at the edge of it. She stopped at the mouth of the biggest tunnel. Far off, she could hear running water.

Something moved in the darkness beyond, a great hulking shape. Sheila moved cautiously forward. With a horrible dry clicking and rustling, the gigantic Black Roach of Death scuttled forward.

With trembling hands, Sheila fed it the Dorito, as she had seen the Ant King do, and reached up to pat its enormous antennae. Then she slid past it into the passageway.

She walked forward, into the darkness. Ten steps; twenty. Nervously she chewed, and blew a bubble. The bubble popped, echoing loudly in the tunnel. Sheila froze. But there was no movement from behind. Carefully she spat the wad of gum into her hand and pressed it into the wall. Then she moved forward. Thirty steps. I can do this, she thought. Forty.

Suddenly Sheila was terribly hungry.

I'll eat when I get out, she thought grimly.

But that didn't seem quite right.

She searched her pockets and found another Dorito. She lifted it to her lips and stopped. No. No, not that. Something was troubling her. She let the Dorito fall to the ground.

I didn't prepare properly for this, she thought. This isn't the way you escape. You need a plan, you need resources. Anyway, there's no rush.

She began creeping back down the tunnel.

It's not so bad here anyway, she thought. I'm all right for now. I'll escape later. This was just a test run. She stroked the antennae of the Black Roach of Death idly as she passed.

Damn Stan anyway, she thought as she crept back through the dark rooms. Am I supposed to do this all by myself? That guy! Big talker, but no action.

On the TV, some CNN talking head was upset about market valuations. "Ten billion for *gumballs*? This is the perfect example of market froth! I mean there's no business model, there are no barriers to entry; only in today's . . ."

Sheila switched to MTV and sank into the couch next to the Ant King.

"Hi," said the Ant King drowsily.

"Hi," said Sheila.

"Hey, I missed you," said the Ant King.

"Stick it in your ear," said Sheila.

"Listen, your ambivalence about me is really getting old, Sheila," said the Ant King.

"Ambivalence about you? Dream on," said Sheila. She took a yellow gumball from the dish on the coffee table, popped it in her mouth, and bit down. A crunch, a rush of sweetness, the feeling of her teeth sinking into the gumball's tough flesh. Sheila smiled and blew a bubble.

It popped. She wasn't hungry anymore. "I hate your guts," she said.

"Yeah, whatever," said the Ant King, rolling over and pulling a pillow over his head. "Grow up, Sheila."

The search on Google.com had returned several bands and music CDs, an episode of the *King of the Hill* cartoon, the "Lair of the Ant King" slide at the local water park, and several video games in which the Ant King was one of the villains to beat. Stan listened to the CDs in his car, watched the cartoon in a conference room with a video projector, and installed the video games on a receptionist's computer on the fifth floor and played them at night, hiding from the security guards. He popped down to visit Vampire a lot, and avoided Pringles and his office entirely.

"I'm on level 5," he said, "and I just can't get past the Roach."

"And you've still got the magic sword?" said Vampire, not looking up.

"No, I lost that to the Troll."

"You don't even have to go to the Troll," said Vampire, who never played video games but read the video game newsgroups religiously. "You can cross the Dread Bridge instead."

"I always die on the Dread Bridge when it breaks in two."

"You're not running fast enough," said Vampire. "You've got to run as fast as you can, and jump at the last moment."

"It's tough," said Stan.

Vampire shrugged.

"How are things with you?" Stan asked.

"The patch for mod-ssl 1.2.4.2 is totally incompatible with the recommended build sequence for Apache on Solaris. Solaris is such crap."

"Oh," said Stan. "Okay."

"Hey, I got you something," Vampire said.

"What?" said Stan.

"That," said Vampire, pointing.

On top of a rack of dusty computers Stan saw a four-foot-long sword in a gilded leather sheath. Its ivory handle depicted a spiral of crawling ants. Stan pulled the sword a little out of its sheath, and an eerie blue light filled the room.

"Cool, huh?" said Vampire. "I got it on eBay."

Holding his magic sword, Stan left the elevator on the thirtieth floor and cautiously approached his office. He hadn't been there in a week; he felt like he should check in.

Pringles met him at the door. "This isn't your office anymore, sir," she said.

"It's not?" Stan said. He tried to hold the sword at an inconspicuous angle. Pringles ignored it.

"No, sir. We moved Vic in there."

"Oh, really? Say, when do I get to meet Vic, anyway?"

"I'm not sure, sir. He's quite busy these days, with our acquisition of Suriname."

"We're acquiring Suriname? Isn't that a country?"

"Yes, sir. Follow me, please."

"Um, Pringles," said Stan, hurrying to catch up. "Am I, ah, still CEO?"

Pringles opened the door of his new office. It was a lot smaller.

"I'll check with HR, sir," she said, and left.

That afternoon, as Stan sat at his new, smaller desk, Monique stopped by.

"Hey, hey," she said, "so here's where they've got you, huh?"

"Monique, what's going on? Have I been, um, usurped?" It seemed like the wrong word.

"Oh, I wouldn't worry about it, tiger," she said, sinking into a leather visitor's chair, and crossing her legs. "Gumballs is doing great. Vic's doing a good job, you should be proud."

"But Monique—I don't *do* anything anymore."

"Oh, stop whining," Monique said. She rolled her eyes. "God, you make such a big deal out of everything. Cool sword."

"Thanks," said Stan glumly.

"Look, you're a startup-stage guy, not an operations-stage guy. Just enjoy the ride."

"I guess," said Stan.

"There you go. Listen, you clearly need cheering up. I'm babysitting my sister's kid on the weekend, we're going to the water park. You wanna come?"

"Sure," said Stan. "Why not?"

Monique came by Stan's apartment Saturday morning, and Stan came outside, dressed in a blue oxford and chinos and carrying a bathing suit and towel, and his magic sword. Monique was wearing a silver blouse, a blue miniskirt, a silk scarf, and sunglasses. Her sister's kid had a shaved head, powdered white skin, black lipstick, and kohl, and was wearing combat boots and a wedding dress adorned with black spiders.

"Stan, this is Corpse, my sister's kid," Monique said.

"Hi," said Stan.

Corpse snarled, like a wolf.

"Great, everybody ready?" said Monique.

In the car, Stan said, "So, Corpse, what's your favorite subject in school?"

"Shop," said Corpse.

"Aha," said Stan. "And what do you want to do when you grow up?"

"Bring about the violent overthrow of the current political order," said Corpse.

"Really? How come?" asked Stan.

Corpse's eyes rolled back into their sockets, exposing the white.

"Takes after me, don't you, Corpse?" said Monique happily. Corpse said nothing.

"But, Monique," said Stan. "You're a venture capitalist. You *are* the current political order."

Monique laughed.

"Corpse," said Stan, "I hope you don't mind me asking this, but ah, are you a boy or a girl?"

"You teleological totalitarian!" Corpse shouted. "Your kind will be first up against the wall when the revolution comes!"

"Now, Corpse, be nice," said Monique. But she was grinning.

Stan stood in line for the water slide in his bathing suit, behind Corpse, who was still wearing the wedding dress. He had left his sword in the locker room. He felt naked without it.

Corpse sat in the mouth of the water slide tunnel, waiting for the "Go" light to turn green. Stan looked over at the slide to his left. It was a boat ride; in a puffy inflatable boat, four stout, bald men in business suits and purple fedoras sat waiting for the green light. Behind them was a Mexican family in bathing suits, waiting with their boat.

That's funny, Stan thought. He looked closer at the fedoraed men.

In their boat was a glass jar filled with perhaps three hundred yellow gumballs.

The lights turned green; Corpse vanished into the slide and the men in the boat slid into their tunnel. Despite the sign reading One At A Time, Wait For The Green Light, Stan jumped in after Corpse.

Halfway through the twists, turns, and splashing chaos of the tunnel, Stan collided with Corpse. "Hey!" Corpse yelled, and was sucked away again.

Stan was dumped out into a great basin. He went under and came up spluttering, chlorine stinging his nose. Standing unsteadily, he looked over at the end of the boat ride. There was no sign of the men with the fedoras: the water there flowed peacefully.

"Hey!" said Corpse, splashing him. "You're not supposed to go two at once!"

"I thought you wanted to overthrow the current political order," said Stan, still watching the boat ride.

"Oh, right, so let's start with the water park," Corpse said.

"Why not?" said Stan. The Mexican family, in their boat, emerged from the boat ride. There was no question: The other boat had vanished while in the tunnel.

Monique was standing next to the basin in her polka-dot bikini, yelling into her pink waterproof cell phone. "No, you idiot, I don't *want* you profitable! Because we can't find backers for a profitable company, that's why! Well *find* something to spend it on!" She clicked off the cell phone and shook her head. "Some people are so stuck in the Old Economy."

"Can I borrow that?" Stan asked.

"Okay," Monique said, handing him the phone. "Don't lose it."

"Meet me at the boat ride in five minutes," Stan said, and, dialing Vampire, hurried off to get his sword.

The light turned green, and the boat containing Monique, Corpse, and Stan, holding his magic sword, slid into the tunnel.

"Did you get in?" shouted Stan into the pink cell phone over the roar of rushing water. The boat surged through the great pipe, spun into a whirlpool, then rushed on.

"Yeah," said Vampire, over the cell phone. "It wasn't easy, but I'm in. Actually, after I cracked the session key it wasn't that bad, they've got a continuous telnet session going over a Pac Bell router, so . . ."

The boat lurched and heaved to the right and a cascade of water flew over them. Stan shouted, "So, did you, you know, open the secret door or whatever?"

"Oh, right," said Vampire, and typed a command to the water park's main computer, setting the "Lair of the Ant King" ride into "real" mode.

The rubber boat rushed into a curve. In front of them, a section of wall swung away and the boat flew out of the pipe, into darkness and space, falling between black canyon walls.

"This ride is cool!" said Corpse, as they fell.

When the boat hit the great subterranean river below, it bucked, and Monique and Corpse grabbed onto the handles set into its sides. Stan thought about whether to drop the pink cell phone or the magic sword, and while he thought about it, he flew out of the boat and disappeared into the icy rapids.

"Stan!" Monique yelled.

"Bummer," said Corpse.

The surging river slowed as it widened, they glided past massive black cliffs, and at last the rubber boat coasted up to a dock, where several stout men in purple fedoras helped Monique and Corpse onto dry land.

The Ant King bowed, and his antennae bobbed. "Well, this is an unexpected pleasure," he said.

"Cool lair," said Corpse.

"Why thank you," said the Ant King. "You both look soaked. We have robes and changing rooms right over here. Care for an espresso?"

"Sure," said Monique.

"Got hot chocolate?" said Corpse.

"Why yes, we do," said the Ant King.

"Okay, there's a little yellow bird here," Stan said.

"You still got the rod?" said Vampire over the pink cell phone.

Stan looked down at the crook of his arm, where he was uncomfortably carrying a rod, an axe, a loaf of bread, and a key. He was still in his bathing suit, dripping wet, and exhausted from wandering the tunnels for hours. The blue glow of his magic sword dimly illuminated the room, including a small yellow bird, which watched him suspiciously.

"Put the rod down," said Vampire. Stan let it slide out and clatter to the ground.

"Now catch the bird," Vampire said.

With the pink cell phone wedged between his ear and his shoulder, and his collection of found objects in the crook of his sword arm, Stan edged toward the bird. It looked at him dubiously, and hopped away.

"I can't seem to get ahold of it," Stan said.

"All right, forget the bird. It's only extra points anyway."

"Extra points!" shouted Stan. "I'm not trying to get extra points, I'm trying to get Sheila!"

"Okay, okay, keep your hat on," said Vampire. "Get the rod again and go north."

While Stan wandered a maze of twisty little passages, leaving found objects and pieces of bread according to Vampire's instructions, in order to differentiate the rooms from one another and thus navigate the maze, and Corpse and Monique changed into fuzzy purple terrycloth bathrobes, and Sheila watched Comedy Central and felt inexplicably restless, the Ant King logged onto a network and sent a message, which appeared in the corner of Vampire's screen.

Think you're pretty smart, huh? it said.

"Okay," said Stan, "uh, I'm in the room with the axe again."

"Hold on," said Vampire. "Message." He did some tracking to find out where the message had come from, but no luck: he found a circular trail of impossible addresses.

I know I'm pretty smart, he typed back at it.

Not as smart as you think, the Ant King typed back at him. *You think I would leave sendmail running on an open port on my real proxy server? As if I didn't know about the security hole in that baby.*

"Okay, I think I see the way out here," said Stan. "This is the room with the two pieces of bread—have I gone east from here?"

"Hold on a sec," muttered Vampire.

"I don't think I have," said Stan.

Okay, I'm stumped, typed Vampire. *If that's not your real proxy server, what is it?*

It's my PalmPilot, the Ant King typed back. *With a few tweaks to the OS. And you're hogging a lot of memory on it, so I'd appreciate it if you logged off, Vampy.*

Hey, hold on, Vampire typed. *Is this AntAgonist?*

Used to be. Not anymore, typed the Ant King.

"Hey, I'm out!" Stan said. "It's opening up into a large cavern. Wow, this is great, Vampire!"

No shit! typed Vampire. *How have you been, man?*

I've been great, but I can't say the same for you, typed the Ant King. *You are rusty as hell. What are you doing selling gumballs for a living anyway?*

"Oh, shit," said Stan. "Oh, shit!"

"What?" said Vampire curtly, typing furiously in the chat window.

"Vampire, it's the bridge. It's the Dread Bridge! I always die at the Dread Bridge."

"I told you, man," Vampire said absently, as he chatted with the Ant King. "You've just gotta run fast enough."

Cell phone in one hand, sword in the other, Stan began to run. His bare feet slapped against the planks of the Dread Bridge; the bridge swung crazily over the chasm, and he fought for balance. As he neared the middle he threw the sword ahead of him, and it clattered onto the ground beyond the bridge. He stuffed the cell phone into the waistband of his bathing suit, and ran on. Suddenly he heard a snap behind him, and he jumped. The bridge broke beneath his weight, and swung away. Stan flew through the air, but not nearly far enough; he fell, and barely managed to grab the planks of the bridge beneath him. He hung on as the ropes strained; he thought they were going to break, and he screamed in terror. But the ropes held. Stan swung over the dark canyon, clutching the planks.

"Hey, are you okay?" Vampire said.

"Yeah," Stan panted. "Yeah, I think so."

"Great," Vampire said. "Listen, I know this is kind of a bad time, but there's something we need to talk about."

"Huh?" said Stan. "What?"

"Well, this is kind of awkward for me, but, you know, I haven't really been feeling fulfilled professionally here lately . . ."

"What?" said Stan.

"So, well, I've decided to accept another offer of employment, basically."

"You're kidding," said Stan. "From whom?"

"From the Ant King, actually. I'm pretty excited about it; it's a whole different level of responsibility, and—"

"The Ant King?!" yelled Stan. "The Ant King?!"

"Yeah, actually it turns out I know him from way back and—"

"But, Vampire!" yelled Stan. "Listen, aren't we in this together?"

"Hey, Stan," Vampire said. "Let's not make this hard on ourselves, okay? This is just the career move I think is right for me right now . . ."

"Vampire, we can give you more responsibility!" Stan could feel the cool air of the endless chasm blowing against his feet. "More stock! Whatever you want!"

"That's great of you to offer, Stan, really," said Vampire. "But, you know, it's getting really corporate here, and that's just not my scene. I think I'll be happier in a more entrepreneurial climate."

"But, Vampire!" Stan shouted, and just then the ropes above him groaned and one snapped, and the planks he was holding onto twisted and spun. Stan was slammed against the wall, and the pink cell phone popped out of his waistband and fell into the darkness. He waited, but he never heard it reach the ground.

Crap, he thought, and began to climb the planks, toward the ledge above.

"Yes!" said the Ant King. "Exactly! Wile E. Coyote is the only figure of any integrity in twentieth-century literature."

"Totally," said Corpse.

"Come on," said Monique. "What about Bugs Bunny?"

"An amateur!" said the Ant King. "A dilettante! No purity of intention!"

"Pinky and the Brain?"

"Losers! Try to take over the world indeed!"

Sheila cleared her throat. "Um, does anyone want some more pretzels?" she asked.

"Are you the one we're here to rescue?" Corpse asked. Sheila blanched.

"Yeah, she's the one," said the Ant King. "So listen—*Star Trek* or *Star Wars*?"

"Oh, please," said Corpse. "*Babylon 5*!"

"Excellent choice!" said the Ant King.

"I like *Star Wars*. Particularly Darth Vader," said Monique.

"I'll just go for some more pretzels then," Sheila said.

"But then he bails on the Dark Side in the end!" the Ant King said. "See? No integrity!"

Cold and angry, clutching his magic sword in both hands, Stan stood before the gigantic Black Roach of Death.

"Come on, big boy," he yelled. "Make my day! Meet my sword, Roach Motel! You're gonna check in, but you're not gonna check—"

With a lazy swipe of its great claws, the roach batted the magic sword out of Stan's hands. It flew away and clattered into the darkness. Then the roach grabbed Stan around the throat and lifted him high into the air.

"Eek!" Stan screamed in terror.

"He's a friend of mine," yelled Sheila, sprinting out of the darkness.

"Sheila!" choked Stan.

"Here, c'mon, boy, put him down, here's a Dorito," Sheila said.

Reluctantly the roach dropped Stan, ate a Dorito, allowed itself to be petted, and crawled back into the tunnel.

"Thanks," croaked Stan, as Sheila helped him up.

Hand in hand, Sheila and Stan made their way through the tunnels leading away from the Ant King's lair.

"Don't look back," Stan kept saying. "Okay? Don't look back."

"Okay already," Sheila said.

Suddenly Sheila stopped.

"What?" said Stan, careful not to look back at her.

"I'm, um, I'm hungry," said Sheila.

"Me, too," said Stan. "Let's go."

"But listen, we could just sneak back and grab a bite to eat, right? I mean, I ran out here because I heard you were finally coming, but I would've packed a sandwich if I'd—"

"Sheila, are you nuts?" said Stan.

"What's that supposed to mean?" said Sheila.

Stan felt in his pockets. The left one was empty. The right one had something in it—a gumball. Dry. He pulled it out and squinted at it in the dimness. He remembered putting a gumball into the pocket of his suit jacket, but . . .

"Okay, so I'm going back," Sheila said.

"Quick, chew this," Stan said, handing the gumball back to her without looking back.

She chewed the gumball, and they walked onward through the tunnel.

"I never thought I'd say this," said the Ant King, stirring his espresso nervously. "Sheila will be angry, but—well, how can I put this—"

"Spit it out already," Monique said.

"Yeah," Corpse said.

"Corpse, I just—I feel like you really get me, you know?"

"Yeah," Corpse said softly. "I feel the same way."

Monique whistled.

"Would you . . ." The Ant King blushed. "Would you like to stay underground with me forever and help me rule the subterranean depths?"

"Wow, that would be totally awesome!" Corpse said.

"Oh god, your mother's going to kill me," Monique said.

"Oh come on, Aunt Monique, don't turn into a hypocrite on me! You always told me to follow my heart! You always say it's better to get into trouble than to be bored!"

"I didn't say you can't do it," said Monique. "I just said your mother's going to kill me."

"So does that mean I can?" asked Corpse.

"How about if we do this on a trial basis at first," Monique said. "Okay? And you—" she pointed a menacing finger at the Ant King. "No addictive gumball crap, okay?" His antennae stiffened in surprise. "Yeah, Aunt Monique knows more than you think. You watch your step, buddy." She turned to Corpse. "You have one month," she said. "I'll talk to your mom. Then you come back up and we talk it over."

"Oh gosh, thank you, Aunt Monique!"

"You have my word," said the Ant King. "Corpse will enjoy life here thoroughly. And it will be very educational."

"I bet," said Monique.

"Hey, can we violently overthrow the current political order?" Corpse asked.

"Sure," said the Ant King. "That sounds like fun."

Epilogue

Stan sat across the desk from Lucy the HR person, who smiled at him brightly. "So what are your skills?" she asked.

"I founded this company," he said.

"We try to be forward-looking here," she said. "Less progressive organizations are focussed on past accomplishments, but our philosophy is to focus on current skills. What languages can you program in?"

"None," said Stan. "I can use Microsoft Word, though."

"Mmm-*hmm*," Lucy said. "Anything else?"

"I'm pretty good at financial analysis," Stan said.

"We are actually overstaffed in Accounting," Lucy said.

"I could work in Marketing," Stan said.

Lucy smiled indulgently. "Everyone thinks they know how to do Marketing. What about Customer Service?"

"I think I'll pass," said Stan.

"Okay," Lucy said brightly. "Well, I'll let you know as soon as something else opens up. Gumballs.com cares about you as an employee. We want you to know that, and we want you to enjoy your indefinite unpaid leave. Can you do that for me, Stan?"

"I'll try," said Stan, and he left.

Stan finally met Vic at the company Christmas party in San Francisco. As he expected, Vic was tall, blond, and athletic, with a tennis smile.

"Stan!" Vic said brightly. "Good to finally meet you. And this must be Sheila."

"Hi!" said Sheila, shaking hands.

"Hi, Vic," said Stan. "Listen, I . . ."

"*Great* dress," Vic said to Sheila.

"Thanks!" Sheila said. "So what's running the show like?"

Stan said, "I wanted to . . ."

"It's actually quieted down a bunch," Vic said. "I'm starting to have time for a little golf and skiing."

Stan said, "I was wondering if we could . . ."

"Wow!" said Sheila. "Where do you ski?"

"Tahoe," said Vic.

"Of course," laughed Sheila.

Stan said, "Maybe if we could take a few minutes . . ."

"So is your wife here?" Sheila asked.

Vic laughed. "No, I'm afraid I'm single."

"Wow, are you gay?" Sheila asked.

"About 80–20 straight," Vic said.

"Hey, me, too!" Sheila said.

Stan said, "It's about my job here at . . ."

"But really, I just haven't found anyone I've clicked with since moving to the Bay Area," Vic said.

"I know what you mean!" Sheila said.

Stan said, "Because I have some ideas about how I could . . ."

"So where were you before the Bay Area?" Sheila asked.

Later Sheila came up to Stan at the punch bowl.

"Stan, you know, things haven't been going so great for us lately."

"Uh huh," Stan said.

"I want you to know, I really appreciate you rescuing me . . ."

"Hey, no problem," Stan said.

"But since then, it just seems like we aren't going anywhere, you know?"

"Sheila, I love you," said Stan. "I'd give my life for you. I've never found anything in my life that means anything to me, except you."

"I know, Stan," she said. "I know. And maybe I'm being a bitch, but you know, that's kind of hard to live up to. You know? And I'm just not there yet." She put her arms around him. He stiffened. She let go and sighed. "I just think . . ."

"Are you going to run off with Vic?" Stan said. "Just give it to me straight."

Sheila sighed. "Yeah," she said. "Yeah, I guess I am. I'm sorry."

"Me, too," Stan said.

Stan left the party and walked to the Bay Bridge. He looked down into the black water. He thought about jumping, but he didn't really feel like dying. He just didn't feel like being him anymore.

He decided to become a bum and walked to South of Market, where he traded his suit, shoes, and wallet for an army jacket, a woolen cap, torn jeans, sneakers, a shopping cart, three plastic sacks, and a bottle of Night Train in a paper bag. But he wasn't a good bum. He was too polite to panhandle, he didn't like the taste of Night Train, and at campfires he felt alienated from the other bums—he didn't know any of the songs they liked, and they didn't want to talk about Internet stocks. He was hungry, cold, lonely, tired, and sober when Monique found him.

"You look like shit," she said.

"Go away, Monique," he said. "I'm a bum now."

"Oh, yeah?" said Monique. "And how's that working out?"

"Lousy," Stan admitted.

Monique got out of her BMW and squatted down next to where Stan lay. The other bums moved away, rolling their eyes and shaking their heads in disgust.

"I've lost everything I love," Stan said.

"Aren't you the guy who loved the dramatic surge and crash of Amazon's stock ticker? The concrete malls spreading across America like blood staining a handkerchief? How everything can be tracked and mirrored in numbers—numbers, the lifeblood of capitalism?"

"Well, yeah," Stan said.

"Get in the car," Monique said. "You're hired."

Stan got in the car.

The Valley of Giants

I HAD BURIED MY PARENTS in their gray marble mausoleum at the heart of the city. I had buried my husband in a lead box sunk into the mud of the bottom of the river, where all the riverboatmen lie. And after the war, I had buried my children, all four, in white linen shrouds in the new graveyards plowed into what used to be our farmland: all the land stretching from the river delta to the hills.

I had one granddaughter who survived the war. I saw her sometimes: in a bright pink dress, a sparkling drink in her hand, on the arm of some foreign officer with brocade on his shoulders, at the edge of a marble patio. She never looked back at me—poverty and failure and political disrepute being all, these days, contagious and synonymous.

The young were mostly dead, and the old men had been taken away, they told us, to learn important new things and to come back when they were ready to contribute fully. So it was a city of grandmothers. And it was in a grandmother bar by the waterfront—sipping hot tea with rum and watching over the shoulders of dockworkers playing mah-jongg—that I first heard of the valley of giants.

We all laughed at the idea, except for a chemist with a crooked nose and rouge caked in the creases of her face, who was incensed. "We live in the modern era!" she cried. "You should be ashamed of yourself!"

The traveler stood up from the table. She was bony and rough-skinned and bent like an old crow, with a blue silk scarf and hanks of hair as black as soot. Her eyes were veined with red.

"Nonetheless," the traveler said, and she walked out.

They were laughing at the chemist as well as at the traveler. To find anyone still proud, anyone who believed in giants or shame, was hilarious. The air of the bar was acrid with triumph. Finding someone even more vulnerable and foolish than we were, after everything had been taken from us—that was a delight.

But I followed the traveler, into the wet streets. The smell of fish oozed from the docks. Here and there were bits of charred debris in the gutters. I caught her at her door.

She invited me in for tea and massage. Her limbs were weathered and ringed, like the branches of trees in the dry country. She smelled like honey that has been kept a while in a dark room, a little fermented. A heady smell.

In the morning, brilliant sunlight scoured the walls and the floor, and the traveler and her pack were gone.

I hurried home. My house had survived the war with all its brown clay walls intact, though the garden and the courtyard were a heap of blackened rubble. My house was empty and cold.

I packed six loaves of flatbread, some olives, a hard cheese, one nice dress, walking clothes, my pills and glasses, a jug of wine, a canteen of water, and a kitchen knife. I sat in the shadow in my living room for a while, looking at the amorphous mass of the blanket I had been crocheting.

That granddaughter: her parents both worked in the vineyards, and when she was a child, she would play in my courtyard in the afternoons. When she scraped her knees bloody on the stones, she refused to cry. She would cry from frustration when the older children could do something that she couldn't—like tie knots, or catch a chicken.

Sitting on my lap, her small body shaking, her small fists striking my back slowly, one and then the other. In the evening she would perch on my courtyard wall, looking toward the vineyards, her eyes burning like candles, searching for the first glimpse of her parents coming home.

I decided not to take the knife. I did not know if I would have trouble at the checkpoints, but sane grandmothers rely on moral authority rather than force: a bitter, weak, futile weapon, but the one we can manage best. I replaced the knife with a harmonica.

Because the traveler had had fresh grapes in a bowl in her room, I started out toward the vineyards. Because there had been red ash caked in the soles of her boots, I passed through the vineyards into the somber dust of the dry country. And because a valley of giants would have to be well hidden, I left the dry country at the foothills of the snowy mountains.

I knew I was right at the checkpoint, because the soldiers who waved me through were pawing through the traveler's sack, arguing over her silk scarves.

In the wild country of the foothills, I saw the smoke from her campfire, a loose thread of pure white in a sky the color of old linen.

Her eyes were redder than before. Her clothes were muddy, and I knew she had been thrown to the ground by the soldiers. Defending her scarves.

She tore the pack from my hands and opened it like someone ripping a bandage from a scab. She threw my things to the ground: my flatbread, my walking clothes, my canteen, my cheese. I watched her, my hands aching. When she found the harmonica, though, she began to laugh. Gently I took the pack from her hands, and I spread our things on a flat rock, while she stood and laughed with her eyes closed.

Her pallet was soft, and the skin of her back was warm.

She would not tell me what the giants were like. I wondered if

29

they were beasts, or an army, or sages. I thought they might be dangerous—that they might tear apart my old body, eat me up with their sharp teeth. Instead of a mausoleum, an iron box, a white shroud, my grave would be a giant's intestines. That way my body would be useful. That way, maybe, I would find release, instead of this enduring.

When we came to the pass that led to their valley, it was bitter cold. I wished I'd brought warmer things. The valley was twisting, vast, and wooded. The traveler took my hand to lead me down the trail. "Soon," she said.

The first giant smiled when he saw us. He had a big, round belly and soft eyes too large for his face, and full lips, and shaggy brown hair like yarn. He was naked, and his stubby penis wobbled as he walked. It was the size of a kitchen stool.

There was a small dark woman sitting on his shoulders, holding on to his yarnlike hair. She was only forty-five or fifty years old, and she wore the ragged remains of a doctor's uniform: white lab coat, black pants, flats. She peeked at us, and then hid her face in her giant's hair.

The traveler let go of my hand and ran into the valley, calling out. A lean, red-haired giant woman with heavy breasts came out of a cave and picked her up.

I followed, watching the traveler. The giant tossed her into the air, higher than a steeple or a minaret. And caught her again. Tossed her, and caught her again. My stomach was cold with terror. If she fell from there, she would shatter. She was screaming with laughter. The giant was grinning. They did not look down at me.

I wandered into the valley. The giants looked at me curiously, ate the fruits of the trees, slept by the river. At last I stood by a giant who was sitting against a tree, looking shyly at his hands. His skin was the color of teak. His hair was black and curly. He picked me up and sat me in his lap.

The thing about the giants, is this. The reason no one wants to leave, is this. They hold you. You only need to cry or call, and strong hands as big as kitchen tables pick you up and cradle you. The giants whisper and hum, placing their great soft lips against your belly, your back. They stroke your hair, and their fingers, as big as plates, are so delicate. You fall asleep held in the crook of their arms, or on their shoulders, clinging to their hair. The giant women feed you from their breasts—great sagging breasts as large as horses, with nipples as large as pitchers. The milk is sweet and rich like crème brûlée.

When they hold you to their chests and hum, you curl your old and scarred and aching body against that great expanse of flesh and breathe, just breathe.

We have seen planes. Then there was a missile that snuck into a giant's cave one night. One giant was sleeping in there, with three little grandmothers on her belly. The missile sought them out, in the tunnels of the cave. The ground roared and shuddered and broke. Smoke poured out of the mouth of the cave. We did not go to see what was left in there.

So they are hunting us. My friend the traveler is restless again. But I will not leave. When the planes pass over, we hide. In a cave, I nestle against my giant's chest, bury my face in his hairs, as long as mixing spoons, as thick as blankets. I feel my granddaughter's eyes from far away, searching, searching, hungry.

The Orange

AN ORANGE RULED THE WORLD.

It was an unexpected thing, the temporary abdication of Heavenly Providence, entrusting the whole matter to a simple orange.

The orange, in a grove in Florida, humbly accepted the honor. The other oranges, the birds, and the men on their tractors wept with joy; the tractors' motors rumbled hymns of praise.

Airplane pilots passing over would circle the grove and tell their passengers, "Below us is the grove where the orange who rules the world grows on a simple branch." And the passengers would be silent with awe.

The governor of Florida declared every day a holiday. On summer afternoons the Dalai Lama would come to the grove and sit with the orange, and talk about life.

When the time came for the orange to be picked, none of the migrant workers would do it: they went on strike. The foremen wept. The other oranges swore they would turn sour. But the orange who ruled the world said, "No, my friends; it is time."

Finally a man from Chicago, with a heart as windy and cold as Lake Michigan in wintertime, was brought in. He put down his brief-case, climbed up on a ladder, and picked the orange. The birds were silent and the clouds had gone away. The orange thanked the man from Chicago.

They say that when the orange went through the national produce processing and distribution system, certain machines turned to gold, truck drivers had epiphanies, aging rural store managers called their estranged lesbian daughters on Wall Street and all was forgiven.

I bought the orange who ruled the world for thirty-nine cents at Safeway three days ago, and for three days he sat in my fruit basket and was my teacher. Today, he told me, "It is time," and I ate him.

Now we are on our own again.

Biographical Notes to "A Discourse on the Nature of Causality, with Air-Planes," by Benjamin Rosenbaum

ON MY RETURN FROM PLAUSFAB-WISCONSIN (a delightful festival of art and inquiry, that styles itself "the World's Only Gynarchist Plausible-Fable Assembly") aboard the *P.R.G.B. Śri George Bernard Shaw*, I happened to share a compartment with Prem Ramasson, Raja of Outermost Thule, and his consort, a dour but beautiful woman whose name I did not know.

Two great blond barbarians bearing the livery of Outermost Thule (an elephant astride an iceberg and a volcano) stood in the hallway outside, armed with sabres and needlethrowers. Politely they asked if they might frisk me, then allowed me in. They ignored the short dagger at my belt—presumably accounting their liege's skill at arms more than sufficient to equal mine.

I took my place on the embroidered divan. "Good evening," I said.

The Raja flashed me a white-toothed smile and inclined his head. His consort pulled a wisp of blue veil across her lips, and looked out the porthole.

I took my notebook, pen, and inkwell from my valise, set the inkwell into the port provided in the white pine table set in the wall, and slid aside the strings that bound the notebook. The inkwell lit with a faint blue glow.

The Raja was shuffling through a Wisdom Deck, pausing to look at the incandescent faces of the cards, then up at me. "You are the plausible-fabulist, Benjamin Rosenbaum," he said at length.

I bowed stiffly. "A pen name, of course," I said.

"Taken from *The Scarlet Pimpernel*?" he asked, cocking one eyebrow curiously.

"My lord is very quick," I said mildly.

The Raja laughed, indicating the Wisdom Deck with a wave. "He isn't the most heroic or sympathetic character in that book, however."

"Indeed not, my lord," I said with polite restraint. "The name is chosen ironically. As a sort of challenge to myself, if you will. Bearing the name of a notorious anti-Hebraic caricature, I must needs be all the prouder and more subtle in my own literary endeavors."

"You are a Karaite then?" he asked.

"I am an Israelite, at any rate," I said. "If not an orthodox follower of my people's traditional religion of despair."

The prince's eyes glittered with interest, so—despite my reservations—I explained my researches into the Rabbinical Heresy that had briefly flourished in Palestine and Babylon at the time of Ashoka, and its lost Talmud.

"Fascinating," said the Raja. "Do you return now to your family?"

"I am altogether without attachments, my liege," I said, my face darkening with shame.

Excusing myself, I delved once again into my writing, pausing now and then to let my Wisdom Ants scurry from the inkwell to taste the ink with their antennae, committing it to memory for later editing. At PlausFab-Wisconsin, I had received an assignment—to construct a plausible-fable of a world without zeppelins—and I was trying to imagine some alternative air conveyance for my characters when the Prince spoke again.

"I am an enthusiast for plausible-fables myself," he said. "I enjoyed your 'Droplet' greatly."

"Thank you, Your Highness."

"Are you writing such a grand extrapolation now?"

"I am trying my hand at a shadow history," I said.

The prince laughed gleefully. His consort had nestled herself against the bulkhead and fallen asleep, the blue gauze of her veil obscuring her features. "I adore shadow history," he said.

"Most shadow history proceeds with the logic of dream, full of odd echoes and distorted resonances of our world," I said. "I am experimenting with a new form, in which a single point of divergence in history leads to a new causal chain of events, and thus a different present."

"But the world *is* a dream," he said excitedly. "Your idea smacks of Democritan materialism—as if the events of the world were produced purely by linear cause and effect, the simplest of the Five Forms of causality."

"Indeed," I said.

"How fanciful!" he cried.

I was about to turn again to my work, but the prince clapped his hands thrice. From his baggage, a birdlike Wisdom Servant unfolded itself and stepped agilely onto the floor. Fully unfolded, it was three cubits tall, with a trapezoidal head and incandescent blue eyes. It took a silver tea service from an alcove in the wall, set the tray on the table between us, and began to pour.

"Wake up, Sarasvati Sitasdottir," the prince said to his consort, stroking her shoulder. "We are celebrating."

The servitor placed a steaming teacup before me. I capped my pen and shooed my Ants back into their inkwell, though one crawled stubbornly toward the tea. "What are we celebrating?" I asked.

"You shall come with me to Outermost Thule," he said. "It is a magical place—all fire and ice, except where it is greensward and sheep. Home once of epic heroes, Rama's cousins." His consort took a sleepy sip of her tea. "I have need of a plausible-fabulist. You can write the history of the Thule that might have been, to inspire and quell my restive subjects."

"Why me, Your Highness? I am hardly a fabulist of great renown. Perhaps I could help you contact someone more suitable—Karen Despair Robinson, say, or Howi Qomr Faukota."

"Nonsense," laughed the Raja, "for I have met none of them by chance in an airship compartment."

"But yet . . . ," I said, discomfited.

"You speak again like a materialist! This is why the East, once it was awakened, was able to conquer the West—we understand how to read the dream that the world is. Come, no more fuss."

I lifted my teacup. The stray Wisdom Ant was crawling along its rim; I positioned my forefinger before her, that she might climb onto it.

Just then there was a scuffle at the door, and Prem Ramasson set his teacup down and rose. He said something admonitory in the harsh Nordic tongue of his adopted country, something I imagined to mean "Come now, boys, let the conductor through." The scuffle ceased, and the Raja slid the door of the compartment open, one hand on the hilt of his sword. There was the sharp hiss of a needlethrower, and he staggered backward, collapsing into the arms of his consort, who cried out.

The thin and angular Wisdom Servant plucked the dart from its master's neck. "Poison," it said, its voice a tangle of flutelike harmonics. "The assassin will possess its antidote."

Sarasvati Sitasdottir began to scream.

It is true that I had not accepted Prem Ramasson's offer of employment—indeed, that he had not seemed to find it necessary to actually ask. It is true also that I am a man of letters, neither spy nor bodyguard. It is furthermore true that I was unarmed, save for the ceremonial dagger at my belt, which had thus far seen employment only in the slicing of bread, cheese, and tomatoes.

Thus, the fact that I leapt through the doorway, over the fallen bodies of the prince's bodyguard, and pursued the fleeting form of the assassin down the long and curving corridor cannot be reckoned as a habitual or forthright action. Nor, in truth, was it a considered one. In Śri Grigory Guptanovich Karthaganov's typology of action and motive, it must be accounted an impulsive-transformative action: the unreflective moment that changes forever the path of events.

Causes buzz around any such moment like bees around a hive, returning with pollen and information, exiting with hunger and ambition. The assassin's strike was the proximate cause. The prince's kind manner, his enthusiasm for plausible-fables (and my work in particular), his apparent sympathy for my people, the dark eyes of his consort—all these were inciting causes.

The psychological cause, surely, can be found in this name that I have chosen—"Benjamin Rosenbaum"—the fat and cowardly merchant of *The Scarlet Pimpernel* who is beaten and raises no hand to defend himself; just as we, deprived of our Temple, found refuge in endless, beautiful elegies of despair, turning our backs on the Rabbis and their dreams of a new beginning. I have always seethed against this passivity. Perhaps, then, I was waiting—my whole life—for such a chance at rash and violent action.

The figure—clothed head to toe in a dull gray that matched the airship's hull—raced ahead of me down the deserted corridor, and descended through a maintenance hatch set in the floor. I reached it, and paused for breath, thankful my enthusiasm for the favorite sport of my continent—the exalted Lacrosse—had prepared me somewhat for the chase. I did not imagine, though, that I could overpower an armed and trained assassin. Yet, the weave of the world had brought me here—surely to some purpose. How could I do aught but follow?

Beyond the proximate, inciting, and psychological causes, there are the more fundamental causes of an action. These address how the action embeds itself into the weave of the world, like a nettle in cloth. They rely on cosmology and epistemology. If the world is a dream, what caused the dreamer to dream that I chased the assassin? If the world is a lesson, what should this action teach? If the world is a gift, a wild and mindless rush of beauty, riven of logic or purpose—as it sometimes seems—still, seen from above, it must possess its own aesthetic harmony. The spectacle, then, of a ludicrously named practitioner of a half-despised art (bastard child of literature and philosophy), clumsily attempting the role of hero on the middle deck of the *P.R.G.B. Sri George Bernard Shaw*, must surely have some part in the pattern—chord or discord, tragic or comic.

Hesitantly, I poked my head down through the hatch. Beneath, a spiral staircase descended through a workroom cluttered with tools. I could hear the faint hum of engines nearby. There, in the canvas of the outer hull, between the *Shaw*'s great aluminum ribs, a door to the sky was open.

From a workbench, I took and donned an airman's vest, supple leather gloves, and a visored mask, to shield me somewhat from the assassin's needle. I leaned my head out the door.

A brisk wind whipped across the skin of the ship. I took a tether from a nearby anchor and hooked it to my vest. The assassin was untethered. He crawled along a line of handholds and footholds set in the airship's gently curving surface. Many cubits beyond him, a small and brightly colored glider clung to the *Shaw*—like a dragonfly splayed upon a watermelon.

It was the first time I had seen a glider put to any utilitarian purpose—espionage rather than sport—and immediately I was seized by the longing to return to my notebook. Gliders! In a world without dirigibles, my heroes could travel in some kind of immense, powered gliders! Of course they would be forced to land whenever winds were unfavorable.

Or would they? I recalled that my purpose was not to repaint our world anew, but to speculate rigorously according to Democritan logic. Each new cause could lead to some wholly new effect, causing in turn some unimagined consequence. Given different economic incentives, then, and with no overriding, higher pattern to dictate the results, who knew what advances a glider-based science of aeronautics might achieve? Exhilarating speculation!

I glanced down, and the sight below wrenched me from my reverie:

The immense panoply of the Great Lakes—

—their dark green wave-wrinkled water—

—the paler green and tawny yellow fingers of land reaching in among them—

—puffs of cloud gamboling in the bulk of air between—

—and beyond, the vault of sky presiding over the Frankish and Athapascan Moeity.

It was a long way down.

"*Malkat Ha-Shamayim*," I murmured aloud. "What am I doing?"

"I was wondering that myself," said a high and glittering timbrel of chords and discords by my ear. It was the recalcitrant, tea-seeking Wisdom Ant, now perched on my shoulder.

"Well," I said crossly, "do you have any suggestions?"

"My sisters have tasted the neurotoxin coursing through the prince's blood," the Ant said. "We do not recognize it. His servant has kept him alive so far, but an antidote is beyond us." She gestured toward the fleeing villain with one delicate antenna. "The assassin will likely carry an antidote to his venom. If you can place me on his body, I can find it. I will then transmit the recipe to my sisters through the Brahmanic field. Perhaps they can formulate a close analogue in our inkwell."

"It is a chance," I agreed. "But the assassin is half-way to his craft."

"True," said the Ant pensively.

"I have an idea for getting there," I said. "But you will have to do the math."

The tether that bound me to the *Shaw* was fastened high above us. I crawled upward and away from the glider, to a point the Ant calculated. The handholds ceased, but I improvised with the letters of the airship's name, raised in decoration from its side.

From the top of an "R," I leapt into the air—struck with my heels against the resilient canvas—and rebounded, sailing outward, snapping the tether taut.

The Ant took shelter in my collar as the air roared around us. We described a long arc, swinging past the surprised assassin to the brightly colored glider; I was able to seize its aluminum frame.

I hooked my feet onto its seat, and hung there, my heart racing. The glider creaked, but held.

"Disembark," I panted to the Ant. "When the assassin gains the craft, you can search him."

"Her," said the Ant, crawling down my shoulder. "She has removed her mask, and in our passing I was able to observe her striking resemblance to Sarasvati Sitasdottir, the prince's consort. She is clearly her sister."

I glanced at the assassin. Her long black hair now whipped in the wind. She was braced against the airship's hull with one hand and one foot; with the other hand she had drawn her needlethrower.

"That is interesting information," I said as the Ant crawled off my hand and onto the glider. "Good luck."

"Good-bye," said the Ant.

A needle whizzed by my cheek. I released the glider and swung once more into the cerulean sphere.

Once again I passed the killer, covering my face with my leather gloves—a dart glanced off my visor. Once again I swung beyond the door to the maintenance room and toward the hull.

Predictably, however, my momentum was insufficient to attain it. I described a few more dizzying swings of decreasing arc-length until I hung, nauseous, terrified, and gently swaying, at the end of the tether, amidst the sky.

To discourage further needles, I protected the back of my head with my arms, and faced downward. That is when I noticed the pirate ship.

It was sleek and narrow and black, designed for maneuverability. Like the *Shaw*, it had a battery of sails for fair winds, and propellers in an aft assemblage. But the *Shaw* traveled in a predictable course and carried a fixed set of coiled tensors, whose millions of microsprings gradually relaxed to produce its motive force. The new craft spouted clouds of white steam; carrying its own generatory, it could rewind its tensor batteries while underway. And, unlike the *Shaw*, it was armed— a cruel array of arbalest-harpoons was mounted at either side. It carried its sails below, sporting at its top two razor-sharp saw-ridges with which it could gut recalcitrant prey.

All this would have been enough to recognize the craft as a pirate—but it displayed the universal device of pirates as well, that parody of the Yin-Yang: all Yang, declaring allegiance to imbalance. In a yellow circle, two round black dots stared like unblinking demonic eyes; beneath, a black semicircle leered with empty, ravenous bonhomie.

I dared a glance upward in time to see the glider launch from the *Shaw*'s side. Whoever the mysterious assassin-sister was, whatever her purpose (political symbolism? personal revenge? dynastic ambition? anarchic mania?), she was a fantastic glider pilot. She gained the air with a single, supple back-flip, twirled the glider once, then hung deftly in the sky, considering.

Most people, surely, would have wondered at the meaning of a pirate and an assassin showing up together—what resonance, what symbolism, what hortatory or aesthetic purpose did the world intend thereby? But my mind was still with my thought-experiment.

Imagine there are no causes but mechanical ones—that the world is nothing but a chain of dominoes! Every plausible-fabulist spends long hours teasing apart fictional plots, imagining consequences, conjuring and discarding the antecedents of desired events. We dirty our hands daily with the simplest and grubbiest of the Five Forms. Now I tried to reason thus about life.

Were the pirate and the assassin in league? It seemed unlikely. If the assassin intended to trigger political upheaval and turmoil, pirates surely spoiled the attempt. A death at the hands of pirates while traveling in a foreign land is not the stuff of which revolutions are made. If the intent was merely to kill Ramasson, surely one or the other would suffice.

Yet was I to credit chance, then, with the intrusion of two violent enemies, in the same hour, into my hitherto tranquil existence?

Absurd! Yet the idea had an odd attractiveness. If the world was a blind machine, surely such clumsy coincidences would be common!

The assassin saw the pirate ship: Yet, with an admirable consistency, she seemed resolved to finish what she had started. She came for me.

I drew my dagger from its sheath. Perhaps, at first, I had some wild idea of throwing it, or parrying her needles, though I had the skill for neither.

She advanced to a point some fifteen cubits away; from there, her spring-fired darts had more than enough power to pierce my clothing. I could see her face now: a choleric, wild-eyed homunculus of her phlegmatic sister's.

The smooth black canvas of the pirate ship was now thirty cubits below me.

The assassin banked her glider's wings against the wind, hanging like a kite. She let go its aluminum frame with her right hand, and drew her needlethrower.

Summoning all my strength, I struck the tether that held me with my dagger's blade.

My strength, as it happened, was extremely insufficient. The tether twanged like a harp string, but was otherwise unharmed, and the dagger was knocked from my grasp by the recoil.

The assassin burst out laughing, and covered her eyes. Feeling foolish, I seized the tether in one hand and unhooked it from my vest with the other.

Then I let go.

Since that time, I have on various occasions enumerated to myself, with a mixture of wonder and chagrin, the various ways I might have died. I might have snapped my neck, or, landing on my stomach, folded in a V and broken my spine like a twig. If I had struck one of the craft's aluminum ribs, I should certainly have shattered bones.

What is chance? Is it best to liken it to the whim of some being of another scale or scope, the dreamer of our dream? Or to regard the world as having an inherent pattern, mirroring itself at every stage and scale?

Or could our world arise, as Democritus held, willy-nilly, of the couplings and patternings of endless dumb particulates?

While hanging from the *Shaw*, I had decided that the protagonist

45

of my Democritan shadow-history (should I live to write it) would
be a man of letters, a dabbler in philosophy like myself, who lived in
an advanced society committed to philosophical materialism. I rel-
ished the apparent paradox—an intelligent man, in a sophisticated
nation, forced to account for all events purely within the rubric of
overt mechanical causation!

Yet those who today, complacently, regard the materialist hypothesis as dead—pointing to the Brahmanic field and its Wisdom
Creatures, to the predictive successes, from weather to history, of the
Theory of Five Causal Forms—forget that the question is, at bottom,
axiomatic. The materialist hypothesis—the primacy of Matter over
Mind—is undisprovable. What successes might some other science,
in another history, have built, upon its bulwark?

So I cannot say—I cannot say!—if it is meaningful or meaning-
less, the fact that I struck the pirate vessel's resilient canvas with my
legs and buttocks, was flung upward again, to bounce and roll until I
fetched up against the wall of the airship's dorsal razor-weapon. I cannot say if some Preserver spared my life through will, if some Pattern
needed me for the skein it wove—or if a patternless and unforetellable
Chance spared me all unknowing.

There was a small closed hatchway in the razor-spine nearby whose
overhanging ridge provided some protection against my adversary.
Bruised and weary, groping inchoately among theories of chance
and purpose, I scrambled for it as the boarding gongs and klaxons
began.

The *Shaw* knew it could neither outrun nor outfight the swift and
dangerous corsair—it idled above me, awaiting rapine. The brigand's
longboats launched—lean and maneuverable black dirigibles the size
of killer whales, with parties of armed sky-bandits clinging to their
sides.

The glider turned and dove, a blur of gold and crimson and verdant blue disappearing over the pirate zeppelin's side—abandoning our duel, I imagined, for some redoubt many leagues below us.

Oddly, I was sad to see her go. True, I had known from her only wanton violence; she had almost killed me; I crouched battered, terrified, and nauseous on the summit of a pirate corsair on her account; and the kind Raja, my almost-employer, might be dead. Yet I felt our relations had reached as yet no satisfactory conclusion.

It is said that we fabulists live two lives at once. First we live as others do: seeking to feed and clothe ourselves, earn the respect and affection of our fellows, fly from danger, entertain and satiate ourselves on the things of this world. But then, too, we live a second life, pawing through the moments of the first, even as they happen, like a market-woman of the bazaar sifting trash for treasures. Every agony we endure we also hold up to the light with great excitement, expecting it will be of use; every simple joy we regard with a critical eye, wondering how it could be changed, honed, tightened, to fit inside a fable's walls.

The hatch was locked. I removed my mask and visor and lay on the canvas, basking in the afternoon sun, hoping my Ants had met success in their apothecary and saved the Prince; watching the pirate longboats sack the unresisting *P.R.G.B. Sri George Bernard Shaw* and return laden with valuables and—perhaps—hostages.

I was beginning to wonder if they would ever notice me—if, perhaps, I should signal them—when the cacophony of gongs and klaxons resumed—louder, insistent, angry—and the longboats raced back down to anchor beneath the pirate ship.

Curious, I found a ladder set in the razor-ridge's metal wall that led to a lookout platform.

A war-city was emerging from a cloudbank some leagues away.

I had never seen any work of man so vast. Fully twelve great dirigible hulls, each dwarfing the *Shaw*, were bound together in a constellation of outbuildings and propeller assemblies. Near the center, a great plume of white steam rose from a pillar; a Heart-of-the-Sun reactor, where the dull yellow ore called Yama's-flesh is driven to realize enlightenment through the ministrations of Wisdom-Sadhus.

There was a spyglass set in the railing by my side; I peered through, scanning the features of this new apparition.

Certainly none of the squabbling statelets of my continent could muster such a vessel; and only the Powers—Cathay, Gabon, the Aryan Raj—could afford to fly one so far afield, though the Khmer and Malay might have the capacity to build them.

There is little enough to choose between the meddling Powers, though Gabon makes the most pretense of investing in its colonies and believing in its supposed civilizing mission. This craft, though, was clearly Hindu. Every cubit of its surface was bedecked with a façade of cytoceramic statuary—couples coupling in five thousand erotic poses; theromorphic gods gesturing to soothe or menace; Rama in his chariot; heroes riddled with arrows and fighting on; saints undergoing martyrdom. In one corner, I spotted the Israelite avatar of Vishnu, hanging on his cross between Shiva and Ganesh.

Then I felt rough hands on my shoulders.

Five pirates had emerged from the hatch, cutlasses drawn. Their dress was motley and ragged, their features varied—Sikh, Xhosan, Baltic, Frankish, and Aztec, I surmised. None of us spoke as they led me through the rat's maze of catwalks and ladders set between the ship's inner and outer hulls.

I was queasy and light-headed with bruises, hunger, and the aftermath of rash and strenuous action; it seemed odd indeed that the day before, I had been celebrating and debating with the plausible-fabulists gathered at Wisconsin. I recalled that there had been a fancy-dress ball there, with a pirate theme; and the images of yesterday's festive, well-groomed pirates of fancy interleaved with those of today's grim and unwashed captors on the long climb down to the bridge.

The bridge was in the gondola that hung beneath the pirate airship's bulk, forward of the rigging. It was crowded with lean and dangerous men in pantaloons, sarongs, and leather trousers. They consulted paper charts and the liquid, glowing forms swimming in Wisdom Tanks, spoke through bronze tubes set in the walls, barked orders to cabin boys, who raced away across the airship's webwork of spars.

At the great window that occupied the whole of the forward wall, watching the clouds part as we plunged into them, stood the captain.

I had suspected whose ship this might be upon seeing it; now I was sure. A giant of a man, dressed in buckskin and adorned with feathers, his braided red hair and bristling beard proclaimed him the scion of those who had fled the destruction of Viking Eire to settle on the banks of the Father-of-Waters.

This ship, then, was the *Hiawatha MacCool*, and this the man who terrorized commerce from the shores of Lake Erie to the border of Texas.

"Chippewa Melko," I said.

He turned, raising an eyebrow.

"Found him sightseeing on the starboard spine," one of my captors said.

"Indeed?" said Melko. "Did you fall off the *Shaw*?"

"I jumped, after a fashion," I said. "The reason thereof is a tale that strains my own credulity, although I lived it."

Sadly, this quip was lost on Melko, as he was distracted by some pressing bit of martial business.

We were descending at a precipitous rate; the water of Lake Erie loomed before us, filling the window. Individual whitecaps were discernable upon its surface.

When I glanced away from the window, the bridge had darkened—every Wisdom Tank was gray and lifeless.

"You there! Spy!" Melko barked. I noted with discomfiture that he addressed me. "Why would they disrupt our communications?"

"What?" I said.

The pirate captain gestured at the muddy tanks. "The Aryan war-city—they've disrupted the Brahmanic field with some damned device. They mean to cripple us, I suppose—ships like theirs are dependent on it. Won't work. But how do they expect to get their hostages back alive if they refuse to parley?"

"Perhaps they mean to board and take them," I offered.

"We'll see about that," he said grimly. "Listen up, boys—we hauled ass to avoid a trap, but the trap found us anyway. But we can outrun this bastard in the high airstreams if we lose all extra weight. Dinky—run and tell Max to drop the steamer. Red, Ali—mark the aft, fore, and starboard harpoons with buoys and let 'em go. Grig, Ngube—same with the spent tensors. Fast!"

He turned to me as his minions scurried to their tasks. "We're throwing all dead weight over the side. That includes you, unless I'm swiftly convinced otherwise. Who are you?"

"Gabriel Goodman," I said truthfully, "but better known by my quill-name—Benjamin Rosenbaum."

"Benjamin Rosenbaum?" the pirate cried. "The great Iowa poet, author of *Green Nakedness* and *Broken Lines*? You are a hero of our land, sir! Fear not, I shall—"

"No," I interrupted crossly. "Not that Benjamin Rosenbaum."

The pirate reddened, and tapped his teeth, frowning. "Aha, hold then, I have heard of you—the children's tale scribe, I take it? *Legs the Caterpillar*? I'll spare you then, for the sake of my son Timmy, who—"

50

"No," I said again, through gritted teeth. "I am an author of plausible-fables, sir, not picture-books."

"Never read the stuff," said Melko. There was a great shudder, and the steel bulk of the steam generatory, billowing white clouds, fell past us. It struck the lake, raising a plume of spray that spotted the window with droplets. The forward harpoon assembly followed, trailing a red buoy on a line.

"Right then," said Melko. "Over you go."

"You spoke of Aryan hostages," I said hastily, thinking it wise now to mention the position I seemed to have accepted *de facto*, if not yet *de jure*. "Do you by any chance refer to my employer, Prem Ramasson, and his consort?"

Melko spat on the floor, causing a cabin boy to rush forward with a mop. "So you're one of those quislings who serves Hindoo royalty even as they divide up the land of your fathers, are you?" He advanced toward me menacingly.

"Outer Thule is a minor province of the Raj, sir," I said. "It is absurd to blame Ramasson for the war in Texas."

"Ready to rise, sir," came the cry.

"Rise then!" Melko ordered. "And throw this dog in the brig with its master. If we can't ransom them, we'll throw them off at the top." He glowered at me. "That will give you a nice long while to salve your conscience with making fine distinctions among Hindoos. What do you think he's doing here in our lands, if not plotting with his brothers to steal more of our gold and helium?"

I was unable to further pursue my political debate with Chippewa Melko, as his henchmen dragged me at once to cramped quarters between the inner and outer hulls. The prince lay on the single bunk, ashen and unmoving. His consort knelt at his side, weeping silently. The Wisdom Servant, deprived of its animating field, had collapsed into a tangle of reedlike protuberances.

My valise was there; I opened it and took out my inkwell. The Wisdom Ants lay within, tiny crumpled blobs of brassy metal. I put the inkwell in my pocket.

"Thank you for trying," Sarasvati Sitasdottir said hoarsely. "Alas, luck has turned against us."

"All may not be lost," I said. "An Aryan war-city pursues the pirates, and may yet buy our ransom; although strangely they have damped the Brahmanic field and so cannot hear the pirates' offer of parley."

"If they were going to parley, they would have done so by now," she said dully. "They will burn the pirate from the sky. They do not know we are aboard."

"Then our bad luck comes in threes." It is an old rule of thumb, derided as superstition by professional causalists. But they, like all professionals, like to obfuscate their science, rendering it inaccessible to the layman; in truth, the old rule holds a glimmer of the workings of the third form of causality.

"A swift death is no bad luck for me," Sarasvati Sitasdottir said. "Not when he is gone." She choked a sob, and turned away.

I felt for the Raja's pulse; his blood was still beneath his amber skin. His face was turned toward the metal bulkhead; droplets of moisture there told of his last breath, not long ago. I wiped them away, and closed his eyes.

We waited, for one doom or another. I could feel the zeppelin rising swiftly; the *Hiawatha* was unheated, and the air turned cold. The princess did not speak.

My mind turned again to the fable I had been commissioned to write, the materialist shadow history of a world without zeppelins. If by some unlikely chance I should live to finish it, I resolved to do without the extravagant perils, ironic coincidences, sudden bursts of insight, death-defying escapades, and beautiful villainesses that litter our genre and cheapen its high philosophical concerns. Why must every protagonist be doomed, daring, lonely, and overly proud? No, my philosopher-hero would enjoy precisely those goods of which I was deprived—a happy family, a secure situation, a prosperous and powerful nation, a conciliatory nature; above all, an absence of immediate physical peril. Of course, there must be conflict, worry, sorrow—but, I vowed, of a rich and subtle kind!

I wondered how my hero would view the chain of events in which I was embroiled. With derision? With compassion? I loved him, after a fashion, for he was my creation. How would he regard me?

If only the first and simplest form of causality had earned his allegiance, he would not be placated by such easy saws as "Bad things come in threes." An assassin and a pirate and an uncommunicative war-city, he would ask? All within the space of an hour?

Would he simply accept the absurd and improbable results of living within a blind and random machine? Yet his society could not have advanced far, mired in such fatalism!

Would he not doggedly seek meaning, despite the limitations of his framework?

What if our bad luck were no coincidence at all, he would ask. What if all three misfortunes had a single, linear, proximate cause, intelligible to reason?

"My lady," I said, "I do not wish to cause you further pain. Yet I find I must speak. I saw the face of the prince's killer—it was a young woman's face, in lineament much like your own."

"Shakuntala!" the princess cried. "My sister! No! It cannot be! She would never do this—" She curled her hands into fists. "No!"

"And yet," I said gently, "it seems you regard the assertion as not utterly implausible."

"She is banished," Sarasvati Sitasdottir said. "She has gone over to the Thanes—the Nordic Liberation Army—the anarcho-gynarchist insurgents in our land. It is like her to seek danger and glory. But she would not kill Prem! She loved him before I!"

To that, I could find no response. The *Hiawatha* shuddered around us—some battle had been joined. We heard shouts and running footsteps.

Sarasvati, the prince, the pirates—any of them would have had a thousand gods to pray to, convenient gods for any occasion. Such solace I could sorely have used. But I was raised a Karaite. We acknowledge only one God, austere and magnificent: the One God of All Things, attended by His angels and His consort, the Queen of Heaven. The only way to speak to Him, we are taught, is in His Holy Temple, and it lies in ruins these two thousand years. In times like these, we are told to meditate on the contrast between His imperturbable magnificence and our own abandoned and abject vulnerability, and to be certain that He watches us with immeasurable compassion, though He will not act. I have never found this much comfort.

Instead, I turned to the prince, curious what in his visage might have inspired the passions of the two sisters.

On the bulkhead just before his lips—where, before, I had wiped away the sign of his last breath—a tracery of condensation stood.

Was this some effluvium issued by the organs of a decaying corpse? I bent, and delicately sniffed—detecting no corruption.

"My lady," I said, indicating the droplets on the cool metal, "he lives."

"What?" the princess cried. "But how?"

"A diguanidinium compound produced by certain marine dinoflagellates," I said, "can induce a deathlike coma, in which the subject breathes but thrice an hour; the heartbeat is similarly undetectable."

Delicately, she felt his face. "Can he hear us?"

"Perhaps."

"Why would she do this?"

"The body would be rushed back to Thule, would it not? Perhaps the revolutionaries meant to steal it and revive him as a hostage?"

A tremendous thunderclap shook the *Hiawatha MacCool*, and I noticed we were listing to one side. There was a commotion in the gangway; then Chippewa Melko entered. Several guards stood behind him.

"Damned tenacious," he spat. "If they want you so badly, why won't they parley? We're still out of range of the war-city itself and its big guns, thank Buddha, Thor, and Darwin. We burned one of their launches, at the cost of many of my men. But the other launch is gaining."

"Perhaps they don't know the hostages are aboard?" I asked.

"Then why pursue me this distance? I'm no fool—I know what it costs them to detour that monster. They don't do it for sport, and I don't flatter myself I'm worth that much to them. No, it's you they want. So they can have you—I've no more stomach for this chase." He gestured at the prince with his chin. "Is he dead?"

"No," I said.

"Doesn't look well. No matter—come along. I'm putting you all in a launch with a flag of parley on it. Their war-boat will have to stop for you, and that will give us the time we need."

So it was that we found ourselves in the freezing, cramped bay of a pirate longboat. Three of Melko's crewmen accompanied us—one at the controls, the other two clinging to the longboat's sides. Sarasvati and I huddled on the aluminum deck beside the pilot, the prince's body held between us. All three of Melko's men had parachutes—they planned to escape as soon as we docked. Our longboat flew the white flag of parley, and—taken from the prince's luggage—the royal standard of Outermost Thule.

All the others were gazing tensely at our target—the war-city's fighter launch, which climbed toward us from below. It was almost as big as Melko's flagship. I alone glanced back out the open doorway as we swung away from the *Hiawatha*.

So only I saw a brightly colored glider detach itself from the *Hiawatha*'s side and swoop to follow us.

Why would Shakuntala have lingered with the pirates thus far? Once the rebels' plan to abduct the prince was foiled by Melko's arrival, why not simply abandon it and await a fairer chance?

Unless the intent was not to abduct—but to protect.

"My lady," I said in my halting middle-school Sanskrit, "your sister is here."

Sarasvati gasped, following my gaze.

"Madam—your husband was aiding the rebels."

"How dare you?" she hissed in the same tongue, much more fluently.

"It is the only—" I struggled for the Sanskrit word for "hypothesis," then abandoned the attempt, leaning over to whisper in English. "Why else did the pirates and the war-city arrive together? Consider: the prince's collusion with the Thanes was discovered by the Aryan Raj. But to try him for treason would provoke great scandal and stir sympathy for the insurgents. Instead, they made sure rumor of a valuable hostage reached Melko. With the prince in the hands of the pirates, his death would simply be a regrettable calamity."

Her eyes widened. "Those monsters!" she hissed.

"Your sister aimed to save him, but Melko arrived too soon—before news of the prince's death could discourage his brigandy. My lady, I fear that if we reach that launch, they will discover that the Prince lives. Then some accident will befall us all."

There were shouts from outside. Melko's crewmen drew their needlethrowers and fired at the advancing glider.

With a shriek, Sarasvati flung herself upon the pilot, knocking the controls from his hands.

The longboat lurched sickeningly.

I gained my feet, then fell against the prince. I saw a flash of orange and gold—the glider, swooping by us.

I struggled to stand. The pilot drew his cutlass. He seized Sarasvati by the hair and spun her away from the controls.

Just then, one of the men clinging to the outside, pricked by Shakuntala's needle, fell. His tether caught him, and the floor jerked beneath us.

The pilot staggered back. Sarasvati Sitasdottir punched him in the throat. They stumbled toward the door.

I started forward. The other pirate on the outside fell, untethered, and the longboat lurched again. Unbalanced, our craft drove in a tight circle, listing dangerously.

Sarasvati fought with uncommon ferocity, forcing the pirate toward the open hatch. Fearing they would both tumble through, I seized the controls.

Regrettably, I knew nothing of flying airship-longboats, whose controls, it happens, are of a remarkably poor design.

One would imagine that the principal steering element could be moved in the direction that one wishes the craft to go; instead, just the opposite is the case. Then, too, one would expect these brawny and unrefined air-men to use controls lending themselves to rough usage; instead, it seems an exceedingly fine hand is required.

Thus, rather than steadying the craft, I achieved the opposite.

Not only were Sarasvati and the pilot flung out the cabin door, but I myself was thrown through it, just managing to catch with both hands a metal protuberance in the hatchway's base. My feet swung freely over the void.

I looked up in time to see the Raja's limp body come sliding toward me like a missile.

I fear that I hesitated too long in deciding whether to dodge or catch my almost-employer. At the last minute courage won out, and I flung one arm around his chest as he struck me.

This dislodged my grip, and the two of us fell from the airship.

In an extremity of terror, I let go the prince, and clawed wildly at nothing.

I slammed into the body of the pirate who hung, poisoned by Shakuntala's needle, from the airship's tether. I slid along him, and finally caught myself at his feet.

As I clung there, shaking miserably, I watched Prem Ramasson tumble through the air, and I cursed myself for having caused the very tragedies I had endeavored to avoid, like a figure in an Athenian tragedy. But such tragedies proceed from some essential flaw in their heroes—some illustrative hubris, some damning vice. Searching my own character and actions, I could find only that I had endeavored to make do, as well as I could, in situations for which I was ill-prepared. Is that not the fate of any of us, confronting life and its vagaries?

Was my tale, then, an absurd and tragic farce? Was its lesson one merely of ignominy and despair?

Or perhaps—as my shadow-protagonist might imagine—there was no tale, no teller—perhaps the dramatic and sensational events I had endured were part of no story at all, but brute and silent facts of Matter.

From above, Shakuntala Sitasdottir dove in her glider. It was folded like a spear, and she swept past the prince in seconds. Nimbly, she flung open the glider's wings, sweeping up to the falling Raja, and, rolling the glider, took him into her embrace.

Thus encumbered—she must have secured him somehow—she dove again (chasing her sister, I imagine) and disappeared in a bank of cloud.

A flock of brass-colored Wisdom Gulls, arriving from the Aryan war-city, flew around the pirates' launch. They entered its empty cabin, glanced at me and the poisoned pirate to whom I clung, and departed.

I climbed up the body to sit upon its shoulders, a much more comfortable position. There, clinging to the tether and shivering, I rested.

The *Hiawatha MacCool*, black smoke guttering from one side of her, climbed higher and higher into the sky, pursued by the Aryan war boat. The sun was setting, limning the clouds with gold and pink and violet. The war-city, terrible and glorious, sailed slowly by, under my feet, its shadow an island of darkness in the sunset's gold glitter, on the waters of the lake beneath.

Some distance to the east, where the sky was already darkening to a rich cobalt, the Aryan war boat that Melko had struck successfully was bathed in white fire. After a while, the inner hull must have been breached, for the fire went out, extinguished by escaping helium, and the zeppelin plummeted.

Above me, the propeller hummed, driving my launch in the same small circle again and again.

I hoped that I had saved the prince after all. I hoped Shakuntala had saved her sister, and that the three of them would find refuge with the Thanes.

My shadow-protagonist had given me a gift; it was the logic of his world that had led me to discover the war-city's threat. Did this mean his philosophy was the correct one?

Yet the events that followed were so dramatic and contrived— precisely as if I inhabited a pulp romance. Perhaps he was writing my story, as I wrote his; perhaps, with the comfortable life I had given him, he longed to lose himself in uncomfortable escapades of this sort. In that case, we both of us lived in a world designed, a world of story, full of meaning.

But perhaps I had framed the question wrong. Perhaps the division between Mind and Matter is itself illusory; perhaps Randomness, Pattern, and Plan are all but stories we tell about the inchoate and unknowable world that fills the darkness beyond the thin circle illumed by reason's light. Perhaps it is foolish to ask if I or the protagonist of my world-without-zeppelins story is the more real. Each of us is flesh, a buzzing swarm of atoms; yet each of us is also a tale contained in the pages of the other's notebook. We are bodies. But we are also the stories we tell about each other. Perhaps not knowing is enough.

Maybe it is not a matter of discovering the correct philosophy. Maybe the desire that burns behind this question is the desire to be real. And which is more real—a clod of dirt unnoticed at your feet, or a hero in a legend?

And maybe behind the desire to be real is simply wanting to be known.

To be held.

The first stars glittered against the fading blue. I was in the bosom of the Queen of Heaven. My fingers and toes were getting numb— soon frostbite would set in. I recited the prayer the ancient heretical Rabbis would say before death, which begins, "Hear O Israel, the Lord is Our God, the Lord is One."

Then I began to climb the tether.

Start the Clock

THE REAL ESTATE AGENT FOR Pirateland was old. Nasty old. It's harder to tell with Geezers, but she looked to be somewhere in her Thirties. They don't have our suppleness of skin, but with the right oils and powders they can avoid most of the wrinkles. This one hadn't taken much care. There were furrows around her eyes and eyebrows.

She had that Mommystyle thing going on: blue housedress, frilly apron, Betty Crocker white gloves. If you're going to be running around this part of Montana sporting those gigantic, wobbly breasts and hips, I guess it's a necessary form of obeisance.

She said something to someone in the back of her van, then hurried up the walk toward us. "It's a lovely place," she called. "And a very nice area."

"Look, Suze, it's your mom," Tommy whispered in my ear. His breath tickled. I pushed him.

It was deluxe, I'll give her that. We were standing under the fity-foot prow of the galleon we'd come to see. All around us a flotilla of men-of-war, sloops, frigates, and cutters rode the manicured lawns and steel-gray streets. Most of the properties were closed up, the lawns pristine. Only a few looked inhabited—lawns bestrewn with gadgets, excavations begun with small bulldozers and abandoned, Pack or Swarm or Family flags flying from the mainmasts. Water cannons menacing passerbsy.

I put my hands in my pants pockets and picked at the lint. "So this is pretty much all Nines?"

The Thirtysomething Lady frowned. "Ma'am, I'm afraid the Anti-Redlining Act of 2035—"

"Uh-huh, race, gender, aetial age, chronological age, stimulative preference or national origin—I know the law. But who else wants to live in Pirateland, right?"

Thirtysomething Lady opened her mouth and didn't say anything.

"Or can afford it," Shiri called. She had gone straight for the rope ladder and was halfway up. Her cherry-red sneakers felt over the side for the gunnel running around the house. Thirtysomething Lady's hands twitched in a kind of helpless half-grasping motion. Geezers always do that when we climb.

"Are *you* poor?" Tommy asked. "Is that why you dress like that?"

"Quit taunting the Lady," Max growled. Max is our token Eight, and he takes aetial discrimination more seriously than the rest of us. Plus, he's just nicer than we are. I don't think that's aetial; I think that's just Max. He's also Pumped Up: he's only four feet tall, but he has bioengineered muscles like grapefruit. He has to eat a pound or two of medicated soysteak a day just to keep his bulk on.

Thirtysomething Lady put her hand up to her eyes and blinked ferociously, as if she were going to cry. Now that would be something! They almost never cry. We'd hardly been mean to her at all. I felt sorry for her, so I walked over and put my hand in hers. She flinched and pulled her hand away. So much for cross-aetial understanding and forgiveness.

"Let's just look at the house," I said, putting my hands in my pockets.

"Galleon," she said tightly.

"Galleon then."

Her fingers twitched out a passkey mudra and the galleon lowered a boarding plank. Nice touch.

Frankly, we were excited. This move was what our Pack needed—the four of us, at least, were sure of it. We were all tired of living in the ghetto—we were in three twentieth-century townhouses in Billings, in an "age-mixed" area full of marauding Thirteens and Fourteens and Fifteens. Talk about a people damned by CDAS—when the virus hit them, it had stuck their pituitaries and thyroids like throttles jammed open. It wasn't just the giantism and health problems caused by a thirty-year overdose on growth hormones, testosterone, estrogen, and androgen. They suffered more from their social problems—criminality, violence, orgies, jealousy—and their endless self-pity.

Okay, Max liked them. And most of the rest of us had been at least entertained by living in the ghetto. At birthday parties, we could always shock the other Packs with our address. But that was when all eight of us were there, before Katrina and Ogbu went south. With eight of us, we'd felt like a full Pack—invincible, strong enough to laugh at anyone.

I followed the others into the galleon's foyer. Video game consoles on the walls, swimming pool under a retractable transparent superceramic floor. The ceiling—or upper deck, I guess—was thirty feet up, accessible by rope ladders and swing ropes. A parrot fluttered onto a roost—it looked real, but probably wasn't. I walked through a couple of bulkheads. Lots of sleeping nooks, lockers, shelves, workstations both flatscreen and retinal-projection. I logged onto one as guest. Plenty of bandwidth. That's good for me. I may dress like a male twentieth-century stockbroker—double-breasted suit and suspenders—but I'm actually a found footage editor. (Not a lot of Nines are artists—our obsessive problem solving and intense competitiveness make us good market speculators, gamblers, programmers, and biotechs; that's where we've made our money and our reputation. Not many of us have the patience or interest for art.)

I logged out. Max had stripped and dived into the pool—or maybe it was meant as a giant bathtub. Tommy and Shiri were bouncing on the trampoline, making smart-aleck remarks. The real estate agent had given up on getting anyone to listen to her pitch. She was sitting in a floppy gel chair, massaging the sole of one foot with her hands. I walked into the kitchen. Huge table, lots of chairs and sit-balls, enormous programmable foodcenter.

I walked out, back to the Lady. "No stove."

"Stove?" she said, blinking.

I ran one hand down a suspender. "I cook," I said.

"You cook?"

I felt my jaw and shoulders tense—I'm sick of being told Nines don't cook—but then I saw her eyes. They were sparkling with delight. Indulgent delight. It reminded me of my own mother, oohing and aah-ing over brick-hard cookies I'd baked her one winter morning in the slums of Maryland, back when my aetial age was still tied to Nature's clock. My mother holding up the wedding dress she'd planned to give me away in, its lacy waist brushing my chin. One evening in college, I'd looked up at the dinner table, halfway through a sentence—I was telling her about *The Hat on the Cat*, my distributed documentary (a firebrand polemic for Under-Five Emancipation; how cybernetics would liberate the Toddlers from lives of dependence)—and saw in her eyes how long ago she'd stopped listening. Saw that I wasn't Nine to her, but nine. Saw that she wasn't looking at me, but through me, a long way off—toward another now, another me: a Woman. Big globes of fatty breasts dangling from that other-me's chest; tall as a door-way, man-crazy, marriageable; a great sexualized monster like herself, a walking womb, a proto-Mommy. She was waiting for that Susan, Woman-Susan, who would never show up.

"I cook," I said, looking away from the Lady's eyes. Putting my hands in my pants pockets. I could have used a hug, but Max was underwater and Tommy and Shiri were trying to knock each other off the trampoline. I went outside.

"We could bring in a stove module," the Lady called.

Outside, a pigeon was poking through the lawn. It was mangy and nervous enough to be real. I stood for a while watching it, then my earring buzzed. I made the Accept mudra.

"Suze?" Travis said.

"Why are you asking, Travis? Who do you think is wearing my earring?"

"Suze, Abby's gone."

"What do you mean, gone?"

"She's not picking up. Her locator's off. I can't find her anywhere." When Travis was nervous, his voice squeaked. Now he sounded like a mouse caught in a trap.

I looked at the active tattoo readout on my left palm. Travis was home. I made the mudra for Abby. No location listed. "Stay there, Travis. We're on our way."

I ran up the plank. Max was dressed again, rubbing his dreadlocks with a towel from the poolside toweltree. Tommy and Shiri were sitting at a table with the Real Estate Lady, looking over paperwork in the tabletop display.

"We've got to go. A personal emergency has come up," I said. Max was at my side instantly.

"Listen, we want this place," Shiri said.

"Shiri, we all have to talk about it," I said.

"What's to talk about?" Tommy said. "It's *awesome*."

"This is the first place we've looked at," I said.

"So?"

The Real Estate Lady was watching us with a guarded expression. I didn't want to say that Abby was missing. Not in front of her. Not in front of that can-you-really-be-trusted-to-look-after-yourselves-all-on-your-own-without-any-grownups attitude that came off her like a stink. I took my hands out of my pockets and balled them into fists. "You're being totally stupid!" I said.

"What's the emergency?" Max said quietly.

"I know what Travis and Abby would say," Tommy said. "They totally want a place like this. Let's just get it and we'll have the rest of the day free."

"We can go wind gliding," Shiri said.

"Travis and Abby didn't even agree to getting a *house* yet, never mind *this* house," I said. I felt Max's hand on my shoulder.

"That's because they haven't seen it," Tommy said.

"What's the emergency?" Max said.

"There's probably been a train wreck and Suze has to make sure she's the first ghoul at her flatscreen," Shiri said.

"Screw you," I said and walked out of the house. I was shaking a little with adrenaline. I got in our clowncar and clicked on the engine. Max hurried out the door behind me. I slid over to the passenger seat and he got in to drive.

"We can pick them up later," he said. "Or they can take a cab. What's up?"

I made the Abby mudra and showed him my palm. "Abby's missing. Travis hasn't seen her, and she's not picking up."

Max pulled out into the street. "She left the house this morning early, with that old black-and-white camera you got her. She was going to shoot some pictures."

I flipped open the flatscreen in the passenger-side dash and logged in. "That's no reason for her to turn off her locator. I hope she didn't stay near the house—a Nine walking around alone in the ghetto, taking photographs—imagine how that looks."

We hummed and whooshed out of Pirateland, up a ramp onto I-90. "Abby wouldn't be that dumb," Max said. But he didn't sound too sure. Abby's impetuous, and she'd been melancholy lately. "Police?" he asked, after a moment.

I shot him a sharp look. The police are Geezers—height requirements keep Under Twelves out of their ranks, and the Teens are mostly too uneducated and unruly. I didn't have any strings to pull with them, and neither did Max. "We wait until we have more data," I said. "Now shut up and let me work. Head home."

Most people have the notion that the public footage is this permanent, universal, easily searchable archive of everything that ever happens, clearly shot, from any angle. It's the job of people in my profession to help perpetuate that illusion. Actually, the networks are surprisingly spotty. There are millions of swarmcams wandering around in any major urban area, but they have a high failure and bug rate, and their pictures are grainy and indistinct—only a lot of imaginative algorithmic reconstruction makes them viewable. There are plenty of larger cameras linked to the net, but often hidden in a byzantine maze of permissions and protocols. And there are billions of motion sensors, audio pickups, locator tags, and data traffic monitors added to the mix, but they're not well correlated with each other. In a few hours on a Sunday morning, one square mile of downtown Billings generates enough data to fill all the computers of the twentieth century, plus all the paper libraries of the centuries before. It's hell to search.

But I'm good. I had enough footage of Abby on file to construct a good bloodhound, and then I spawned a dozen of them and seeded them well. Pretty soon the hits started coming back. Abby had crossed the street in front of our house at 09:06, and turned her locator tag off—on purpose, I imagined, since there was no error log. She'd stopped for bagels and udon in a deli on Avenue C at 09:22; shot pictures in the park until 09:56. She'd talked to a couple of Fifteens there and taken something from them. I couldn't see what, in the grainy gray swarmcam pictures, but it made the hair on the back of my neck rise.

From 10:03 I lost her; she'd gone up an elevator in a bank and disappeared. There's a network of private walkways and an aerial tram in that part of Billings that are poorly monitored. I had a cold feeling in my gut; that was a great way to lose me, if you were trying to.

I searched all the exits to those walkways and the tramway for Abby, buying a bunch of extra processing power on the exchange to run it faster. Nothing.

Max had entered among the spires and alleys of Billings. Dappled shadows of metal and translucent plastics and ceramics rippled over the clowncar. I looked out at the people walking through the corridors around us, all ages and sizes and colors. An old woman was walking slowly on a slidewalk just above us—she must have been an aetial Ninety, which made her a hundred and twenty or so. Walking, slowly, under her own steam. You don't see that every day.

I went back to some old footage I had of a birthday party and grabbed a sequence of Abby walking. I built an ergodynamic profile of her and fed that to my bloodhounds.

Bingo. At 10:42, Abby had left the aerial tramway in disguise. Platform shoes, trenchcoat, false breasts and hips and shoulders— she was impersonating a Fourteen or so. It looked ridiculous, like Halloween. She'd consulted a piece of paper from her pocket.

By 10:54 she was in a bad area. "Head for 30th and Locust," I told Max.

"Shit," he said. "No police?"

"I don't have anything yet that would warrant their attention. Nothing that proves she was coerced."

"So we need other backup," Max said grimly.

"Yeah." I looked up. "Can you get it?"

"I think so," he said. He made some Call mudras with one hand and started talking. "Hey, Dave, how you doing? Listen, man—" I tuned him out as he made his calls.

My last shot of Abby was at 11:06. She was being hustled into a doorway by a gargantuan Fifteen. His hand was on her elbow. Biodynamic readouts from a few stray hospital swarmcams confirmed that her pulse was elevated. Should I send this to the police? Would it prove Abby was coerced? But what was she doing with the weird disguise and the sneaking around? Just slumming? Or would I get her in trouble?

Was Abby buying drugs?

"Parkhill and 32nd," I said to Max. My fingers were still and I was just looking at that last picture, Abby and the giant, him pulling her into darkness.

"Can you meet us at Parkhill and 32nd?" Max was saying. "Damn, I know, man—that's why we need you . . ."

When we got there, five of Max's friends were waiting. Four were clearly from his gym. Two of them were probably Nines or Tens (one swarthy, one red-haired and freckled) and they were even musclier than Max, their heads perched like small walnuts on their blockbuster bodies. The other two were Pumped-Up Teens—maybe Fifteen or Sixteen. Their blond, Slavic-boned faces sat on bodies like overstuffed family-room sofas or industrial refrigerators: fingers the size of my forearm, thighs the size of my entire body. I wasn't sure how we were going to get them in the building.

And then there was the fifth—an Augmented Three. She stood a little apart from the others, her tiny arms at her sides. They were clearly afraid of her. One soft brown eye scanned the clouds, and she had a beatific smile on her face. Her other eye was the glistening jewel of a laser-light connector, and there were other plugs and ports glistening in her brown scalp among her cornrows.

Max stopped the car.

"Who's the Three?" I asked.

Max turned to me. He looked nervous, like he thought I was going to make fun of him. "That's my sister, Carla."

69

"Cool," I said quickly. He got out before I could say anything yet stupider, like "How nice that you've stayed close."

I opened my door and froze—Carla was running toward us. "Max!" she warbled, and flung her arms around his waist, burying her face in his stomach.

"Hi, honey-girl," he said, hugging her back.

I glanced at my palm readout. It had gone blank. So had the flatscreen in the car. It was a safe bet nothing near Carla would be recorded. You could sometimes tell where Augmented Threes and Twos were in the public footage by tracking the blank areas, the little blobs of inexplicable malfunction that followed them around. I once did an experimental documentary on Under-Five Augmentation using that blanked-out footage. It was called *Be Careful What You Wish For*— kind of a rueful, years-later followup to *The Hat on the Cat*.

"Carry me!" Carla said, and Max dutifully swung her tiny body onto his shoulders.

"Carla, this is Suze," Max said.

"I don't like her," Carla announced. Max's face went slack with fear, and my heart lurched. I grabbed the car door so hard my finger-nails sank into the frame.

Carla exploded in giggles, then started to hiccup. "Just—*kidding!*" she choked out between hiccups. "You guys are so *silly!*"

I tried to smile. Max turned, slowly, toward the door. It was a formidable steel monstrosity, the kind with a biodynamic access plate governing its security system. Those things are supposed to be off-net, more or less invulnerable to cybernetic hacking. Carla waved at it and it popped open. The four muscleboys crowded their way inside—eager to get to Abby, and away from Carla—and the three of us brought up the rear, Carla still perched on Max's shoulders.

The stairway was dark and rank—it smelled like Teenagers, all their glands and excretions, smeared and sour. Most of the wallglow was dead, and one malfunctioning patch at the top of the stairs was flashing green and red, so that the bodies of the muscleboys ascended the stairs in strobed staccato.

The freckled gymrat was first to the doorway at the top. As he reached for the doorknob, we heard a long moan, and then a series of grunts. Almost snarls. And then, softer, a whimper—a high, female whimper—like the sound of someone tortured, someone in despair.

Carla started to cry. "I don't like it!"

"What is it, honey-baby?" Max said, his voice afraid. *"What's behind that door?"*

"Don't ask her that!" I barked. "Distract her, you idiot!"

"Max, should I make it go away?" Carla wailed. "Should I make them stop, Max?"

"No!" Max and I shouted at the same time.

"Max," I said as pleasantly as I could manage, "why don't you and Carla go play a nice game in the car?"

"But maybe I should—," Max said, looking at me from between Carla's tiny, shaking knees.

"Now!" I barked, and pushed past them.

Panting came from under the door, panting and groans. The muscleboys looked at me nervously. I heard Max's shoes clumping down the stairs behind me, and he started singing "The Itsy-Bitsy Spider."

"In!" I hissed, pointing at the door. The two overmuscled Nines threw their shoulders against it. It strained and buckled, but held. From inside the door came a strangled scream. The two Pumped-Up Teens braced themselves against the wall and each other, bent their knees, and crouched down with their shoulders under the Nines' butts. "Ready—now!" called the biggest, and all four of them pushed. The door shot open, and the muscleboys tumbled and collapsed through it. I sprinted over their bodies, springing from a buttock to a shoulder to a back to another shoulder, and I was through.

On a tiger-skin throw rug in the midst of a pile of trash, two huge naked Fifteens looked up. The male's skin was a mass of pimples and grease; shaggy hair fell over his shoulders and muscles. The female was pinned under him, her gigantic breasts flopping to either side of her thin ribcage, her knees around his hips. Between the wiry forests of their pubic hair, a portion of the male's penis ran like a swollen purple bridge.

"Ewww!" I shouted, as they flopped down, pulling the tiger skin over themselves. "WHERE'S ABBY??"

"Hi Suze," said Abby drily from an overstuffed chair to my left. She was wearing a white jumpsuit, and holding a pen and a paper notebook.

"What the hell are you doing?" I shouted.

"I might ask you the same." She motioned to the pile of muscleboys, who were struggling to their feet with dazed expressions.

"Abby! You disappeared!" I was waving my arms around like a Macromuppet. "Locator—bad area—disguise—scary—aargh!"

"Are you going to follow me around with a small army every time I turn off my locator?"

"Yes!!"

She sighed and put down her pencil and paper. "I'm really sorry," she called to the Fifteens. "My time was almost up anyway. Um, do you mind if we talk in here for a few minutes?"

"Yes!" gurgled the female.

"Abby, come on," I said. "They can't just stop in the middle. They have to, you know, finish what they were—doing. Until it's finished their brains won't work properly."

"Okay," Abby said. "All right, ah—thanks."

In the stairway, I said, "You couldn't just watch a porn channel?"

"It's not the same," she said. "That's all packaged and commercial.

I wanted to interview them before and after. I have to know—what it's like."

"Why?"

She paused on the stairs, and I stopped, too. The muscleboys, muttering, went out onto the street, and we were alone in the flashing green and red light.

"Suze, I'm going to start the clock."

Like she'd poured a bucket of ice water down my spine. "You're what?"

"I'm going to take the treatments." She spoke quickly, as if afraid I'd interrupt her. "They've gotten much better in the past couple of years, there are basically no side effects. They're even making headway with infants. In five years, it looks like most babies won't have any arrestation effects at all, and—"

Tears had sprung to my eyes. "What are you talking about?" I cried. "Why are you talking like *them*? Why are you talking like being like us is something to be *cured*?" I punched the wall, which hurt my hand. I sat down on the step and cried.

"Suze," Abby said. She sat down next to me and put her hand on my shoulder. "I love being like us—but I want—"

"That?" I shouted, pointing up to the top of the stairs, where they were grunting again. "That's what you want? You'd rather have that than us?"

"I want everything, Suze. I want every stage of life—"

"Oh, every stupid *stage*, as designed by stupid God, who also gave us death and cancer, and—"

She grabbed my shoulders. "Suze, listen. I want to know what *that* up there is like. Maybe I won't like it, and then I won't do it. But, Suze, I want to have babies."

"Babies? Abby, your eggs are forty years old—"

"Exactly! Exactly, my eggs are only forty years old, and most of them are still good. Who do you want to have the babies, Suze? The Geezers? The world is starting again, Suze, and I—"

"The world was fine!" I pulled away from her. "The world was just fine!" Snot and tears were running down my nose into my mouth, salty and gooey. I wiped my face on the sleeve of my stockbroker's suit, leaving a slick trail like a slug. "We were fine—"

"This isn't about us—"

"Oh baloney!!" I lurched to my feet, grabbing the railing for balance. "As if you're going to live with us in a galleon and fire water cannons and go to birthday parties! You're just not, Abby, don't kid yourself! You're going to be *that!*" I pointed up the stairs. "Sexual jealousy and sexual exchange economy and cheating and mutual-exploitation-and-ownership and serial monogomy and divorce and the whole stupid crazy boring . . ."

"Suze—," she said in a small voice.

"Just don't!" I said. "Don't drag it out! If you want to do it, do it, but then leave us alone! Okay? You're not welcome." I turned and headed down the stairs. "Get the hell out."

Max was standing at the bottom of the stairs. I didn't like the way he was looking at me. I brushed past.

The boys from the gym were in the car, eating yard-long submarine sandwiches with great gusto. Carla sat on the front steps, talking to a rag doll. She looked up, and her red jewel of an eye flashed—for a moment it was as bright as looking into the sun at noon. Then she looked past me, into the sky.

"What are you afraid of?" she asked.

I leaned against the doorframe and said nothing. A wind came down the street and crumpled sheets of paper danced along it.

"I'm afraid of cows," she volunteered. "And Millie"—she held up the rag doll—"is afraid of, um, um, you know the thing where if you take all the money people spend and the way they looked at each other that day and you put it inside what the weather's going to do and then you can sing to cats and stuff? She's afraid of that."

I wiped my eyes on my sleeve. "Can you see the future, Carla?"

She giggled, and then she looked serious. "You guys are all wrong about that. It's just a game you made up. There isn't any future."

"Do you like being Augmented?" I asked.

"I like it but Millie doesn't like it. Millie thinks it's scary but she's just silly. Millie wishes we were like people and trees and we didn't have to make things okay all the time. But then we couldn't play with bolshoiye-gemeinschaft-episteme-mekhashvei-ibura."

"Okay," I said.

"Max is coming out with Abby four thousand five hundred and sixty-two milliseconds after I finish talking right now and projected group cohesion rises by thirty-six percent if you don't have a fight now so you should take the clowncar and I'll give them a ride and I'd love to live with you but I know I'm too scary but it's okay but can I visit on Max's birthday?"

"Yes," I said. "You can visit on my birthday, too."

"I can? I can?" She jumped up and hugged me, flinging her arms around my waist, pressing her cheek into my chest. "Wow, I didn't even know you'd say that!" She pulled away, beaming at me, then pointed to the car. "Okay, quick, go! Bye!"

I got in the car and clicked on the engine. Carla waved and she held Millie's arm and waved it, too. The door behind her opened, I saw Max's shoe, and I drove off.

A quarter mile away from Carla, the flatscreen blinked on again, and my earring started buzzing like crazy. I told it to let Travis through.

"Abby's fine," I said. "She's with Max. They'll be coming home."

"Cool," Travis said. "Whew! That's a relief!"

"Yeah."

"So Tommy and Shiri sent me video of the house. It looks *awesome*. Do you love it, too?"

"Yeah, I love it." I was on I-90 now. Beyond the spires and aerial trams of Billings, I could see the funhouse suburbs spreading out before me—windmills, castles, ships, domes, faerie forests.

"Cool, because I think they signed some papers or something."

"What? Travis, we all have to agree!" As I said it, it occurred to me that the only one who hadn't seen the place was Abby. I gripped the wheel and burst out crying.

"What? What?" Travis said.

"Travis!" I wailed. "Abby wants to start the clock!"

"I know," Travis muttered.

"What? You *know??*"

"She told me this morning."

"Why didn't you say anything?"

"She made me promise not to."

"Travis!"

"I was hoping you'd talk her out of it."

I took the exit for Pirateland, swooshing through an orange plastic tunnel festooned with animated skeletons climbing out of Davy Jones's lockers. "You can't talk Abby out of anything."

"But we've got to, Suze, we've got to. C'mon, we can't just fall apart like this. Katrina and Ogbu—" He was doing his panic-stricken rat squeak again, and suddenly I was very sick of it.

"Just shut up and stop whining, Travis!" I shouted. "Either she'll change her mind or she won't, but she won't, so you'll just have to deal with it."

Travis didn't say anything. I told my earring to drop the connection and block all calls.

I pulled up outside the galleon and got out. I found a handkerchief in the glove compartment and cleaned my face thoroughly. My suit, like the quality piece of work it was, had already eaten and digested all the snot I'd smeared on it—the protein would probably do it good. I checked myself in the mirror—I didn't want the Real Estate Lady to see me weepy. Then I got out and stood looking at the house. If I knew Tommy and Shiri, they were still inside, having discovered a rollerskating rink or rodeo room.

Parked at the side of the house was the Real Estate Lady's old-fashioned van—a real classic, probably gasoline-burning. I walked over to it. The side door was slid open. I looked in.

Inside, reading a book, was a Nine. She was tricked out in total Kidgear—ponytails, barrettes, T-shirt with a horse on it, socks with flashy dangly things. Together with the Lady's Mommystyle getup, it made perfect, if twisted, sense. Personally I find that particular game of Let's-Pretend sort of depressing and pitiful, but to each her own kink.

"Hey," I said. She looked up.

"Um, hi," she said.

"You live around here?"

She wrinkled her nose. "My mom, um, kinda doesn't really want me to tell that to strangers."

I rolled my eyes. "Give the roleplaying a rest, would you? I just asked a simple question."

She glanced at me. "You shouldn't make so many assumptions about people," she said, and pointedly lifted her book up in front of her face.

The clop-clop of the Lady's shoes came down the drive. My scalp was prickling. Something was not altogether kosher in this sausage.

"Oh, hello," the Lady said brightly, if awkwardly. "I see you've met my daughter."

"Is that your actual daughter, or can the two of you just not get out of character?"

The Lady crossed her arms and fixed me with her green-eyed stare. "Corintha contracted Communicative Developmental Arrestation Syndrome when she was two years old. She started the treatments seven years ago."

I realized my mouth was hanging open. "She's a clock-started Two? She spent twenty-five years as an unaugmented two-year-old?"

The Lady leaned past me into the van. "You okay in here, honey?"

"Great," said Corintha from behind her book. "Other than the occasional ignoramus making assumptions."

"Corintha, please don't be rude," the Lady said.

"Sorry," she said.

The Lady turned to me. I think my eyes must have been bugging out of my head. She laughed. "I've seen your documentaries, you know."

"You *have?*"

"Yes." She leaned up against the van. "They're technically very well done, and I think some of what you have to say is very compelling. That one with all the blanked-out footage—that gave me a real feeling for what it's like for those children who are wired up into the Internet."

An odd and wrongheaded way of putting it, but I limited myself to saying, "Uh—thanks."

"But I think you're very unfair to those of us who didn't Augment our children. To watch your work, you'd think every parent who didn't Augment succumbed to Parenting Fatigue and sent their toddlers off to the government daycare farms, visiting only at Christmas. Or that they lived some kind of barbaric, abusive, incestuous existence." She looked over at her daughter. "Corintha has been a joy to me every day of her life—"

"Oh, Mom!" Corintha said from behind her book.

"—but I never wanted to stand in the way of her growing up. I just didn't think Augmentation was the answer. Not for her."

"And you thought you had the right to decide," I said.

"Yes." She nodded vigorously. "I thought I had the obligation to decide."

The Suze everyone who knows me knows would have made some sharp rejoinder. None came. I watched Corintha peek out from behind her book.

There was silence for a while. Corintha went back to reading.

"My friends still inside?" I asked.

"Yes," the Lady said. "They want the place. I think it fits six very comfortably, and—"

"Five," I said huskily. "I think it's going to be five."

"Oh," the Lady looked nonplussed. "I'm—sorry to hear that."

Corintha put her book down. "How come?"

The Lady and I looked at her.

"Oh, is that a rude question?" Corintha said.

"It's a bit prying, dear," the Lady said.

"Ah—," I said. I looked at Corintha. "One of us wants to—start the clock. Start the conventional biological aging process."

"So?" Corintha said.

"Honey," said the Lady. "Sometimes if people—change—they don't want to live together anymore."

"That's really dumb," said Corintha. "If you didn't even have a fight or anything. If it's just that somebody wants to grow up. I would never get rid of my friends over that."

"Corintha!"

"Would you let her talk? I'm trying to respect your archaic ideas of parent-child relationships here, Lady, but you're not making it easy."

The lady cleared her throat. "Sorry," she said after a moment.

I looked out at the mainmast and the cannons of our galleon.

The rolling lawn. This place had everything. The trampolines and the pools, the swing ropes and the games. I could just imagine the birthday parties we'd have here, singing and cake and presents and dares, everyone getting wet, foam guns and crazy mixed-up artificial animals. We could hire clowns and acrobats, storytellers and magicians. At night we'd sleep in hammocks on deck or on blankets on the lawn, under the stars, or all together in a pile, in the big pillowspace in the bow.

And I couldn't see Abby here. Not a growing-upward Abby, getting taller, sprouting breasts, wanting sex with some huge apes of men or women or both. Wanting privacy, wanting to bring her clock-started friends over to whisper and laugh about menstruation and courtship rituals. Abby with a mate. Abby with children.

"There's a place over by Rimrock Road," the Lady said slowly. "It's an old historic mansion. It's not quite as deluxe or as—thematic as this. But the main building has been fitted out for recreation-centered group living. And there are two outbuildings that allow some privacy and—different styles of life."

I stood up. I brushed off my pants. I put my hands in my pockets.

"I want us to go see that one," I said.

The Blow

CRACK!

The detective takes a blow; the butt of a pistol against the back of his skull.

Now several things can happen.

Perhaps the detective wakes up tied to a chair, is interrogated, outwits his captors, and escapes to solve the case.

Perhaps he dies. That was a mean blow. Look, he's fallen to the ground. He's still. There's blood. There's blood inside his skull.

Perhaps he's crippled by the blow. Paralyzed on one side. His speech will be fuzzy and inarticulate. He will sit in the chair by the window at the managed care facility. They will keep him well shaven. He will wear a bib and shudder.

The femmes fatales will not visit. The hard-eyed policemen who respected and resented him will come once a month to sit in dull, dutiful silence. His pretty, sad assistant will come every Sunday and read him the paper. Or Dickens, his favorite.

The villain comes to gloat but stays to mull it over, awed: what a little thing can bring us down so low. There but for the grace of God go I.

The case is not clear in the detective's mind. Not quite yet. There are a few outstanding details. He counts his peas. Forty-five peas. The caliber of the murder weapon. It may be a clue. He makes a note on the napkin.

It becomes a comfortable routine over the years. At Christmas the villain has the detective wheeled up to his mansion. The pretty, sad assistant comes as well. She has succeeded the detective; she and the villain are enemies. Sometimes she foils his plots; sometimes he goes to jail. But not for long. He has good lawyers.

But on Christmas they put all that aside. The detective eats his sweet potatoes with molasses and hums. The assistant strokes his hair. After a few witty barbs between the villain and the assistant, a bit of bravado, they eat, and then they sit in silence and listen to the carolers. It feels like family.

They put the gramophone on and the villain and the pretty, sad assistant waltz. The detective looks on with shining eyes.

Embracing-The-New

THE SUN BLAZED, THE WAGON creaked and shuddered. Vru crouched near the master's canopy, his fur dripping with sweat. His Ghennungs crawled through his fur, seeking shade. Whenever one uprooted itself from his body, breaking their connection, he felt the sudden loss of memories, like a limb being torn away.

Not for the first time, Vru was forced to consider his poverty. He had only five Ghennungs. Three had been with him from birth, another had been his father's first, and the oldest had belonged to both his father and his grandfather. Once, when both of the older Ghennungs pulled their fangs out of him to shuffle across his belly, sixty years of memory—working stone, making love to his grandmother and his mother, worrying over apprenticeships and duels—were gone, and he had the strange and giddy feeling of knowing only his body's own twenty years.

"Vile day," Khancriterquee said. The ancient godcarver, sprawled on a pile of furs under the canopy, gestured with a claw. "Vile sun. Boy! There's cooling oil in the crimson flask. Smear some on me, and mind you don't spill any."

Vru found the oil and smeared it across his master's ancient flesh. Khancriterquee was bloated; in patches, his fur was gone. He stank like dead beasts rotting in the sun. Vru's holding-hands shuddered to touch him. The master was dying, and when he died, Vru's certain place in the world would be gone.

Around Khancriterquee's neck, as around Vru's, Delighting-In-Beauty hung from a leather cord: the plump, smooth, laughing goddess, twenty-seven tiny Ghennungs dancing upon her, carved in hard gray stone. Khancriterquee had carved both copies. How strange, that the goddess of beauty would create herself through his ugly, bloated flesh!

Khancriterquee's bloodshot eyes twitched open. "You are not a godcarver," he croaked.

Vru held still. What had he done wrong? The master was vain—had he noticed Vru's disgust? Would Khancriterquee send him back to his father's house in disgrace, to herd fallowswine, to never marry—hoping, when his body was decrepit, to find some nephew who would take pity on him and accept a few of his memories?

"Do you know why we have won these territories?" the master asked. Pushing aside the curtains, he gestured over the wagon's side at the blasted red crags around them.

"We defeat the Godless in battle because the gods favor us, master," Vru recited.

Khancriterquee snorted. "It is not that the gods favor us. It is that we favor the gods."

Vru did not understand, and bent to massage the master's flesh. Khancriterquee pushed Vru's holding-hands away with a claw and, wheezing, sat up. He stared at Vru with disgust.

Vru realized that he was clicking his claws together, and forced himself to stop. The master watched him—remembering Vru's every twitch into the Ghennungs the journeymen would soon carry.

Vru pulled himself erect. "Master, there is something I have never understood."

Khancriterquee's eyes glittered with interest, or suspicion. "Ask," he said.

"How can the Godless really be godless?"

The master frowned.

"I mean, how can someone without a god not go mad when he takes new Ghennungs?" Vru remembered the day he had taken Delighting-In-Beauty as his goddess, to be the organizing devotion of his life. As the doctors had gently separated the Ghennungs from his father's cooling corpse in the Great Hall below, he had wanted to cling to childhood, wanted to wait before choosing a god. But the priest had lectured him sternly—for without a god, a person would just be a shifting collection of memories. The allegiances, desires, and opinions of his various Ghennungs would be at war, and he would be buffeted like a rowboat in a hundred-years' storm.

"Ah, my apprentice is ambitious," Khancriterquee whispered. "The master is old and weak. Perhaps the apprentice should attend the high military councils in my stead. Perhaps he should learn the secrets of our war against the Godless—"

"Master, I meant no—"

"The Godless do not trade Ghennungs," Khancriterquee said.

"What?"

"Perhaps at a very young age they do," Khancriterquee said, waving his holding-hands, "or to trade certain very specific skills only, without other memories, using some kind of mutilated Ghennungs. We are not certain. But in general, when they die"—he paused, watching Vru's reaction—"their Ghennungs are destroyed. That is why we win the battles. Their greatest soldier is only as old as his body."

Vru suddenly felt sick; bitter, stinging fluids from his stomach sputtered into his throat. The Godless intentionally murdered themselves when their bodies died!

"Now I will tell you why you are not a godcarver, if the ambitious apprentice has time to listen," Khancriterquee said. He tapped the Delighting-In-Beauty around Vru's neck with his claw. "Carving copies, so that the people will not forget their gods, and stay sane, is nothing. It is time for you to carve a new god, as I did when I carved Fearless-In-Justice, as my grandfather did with Delighting-In-Beauty." He lay back on the furs and closed his eyes. "It will be a monument, to be unveiled at The Festival of Hrsh. You will use this new green stone."

Vru watched in silence as the master slept. He could hear his own heart beating.

None of Khancriterquee's journeymen had been allowed to create a god, not even Turmca. Why let an apprentice? To embarrass and spite the journeymen—to punish their eager impatience for Khancriterquee's death? Or did the master think Vru had that much talent?

The Bereft worked in the new mines, carving the green stone from the cliff face. Their fur had been shaved, because of the heat. Many of them had bloody claws, torn by the stone. Vru tried to look away. He had rarely seen so many Bereft. Their bodies were muscular, powerful, . . . and naked of Ghennungs. It was horrible, yet there was something about those empty expanses of skin that called to him, like a field of untrodden snow.

The green stone glittered, embedded in the gray rock. Khancriterquee had been yelling at the foreman all day. Why use the idiot Bereft? They understood enough to be useful in the older mines, with the older gray stone. But this wonderful new green stone, in which so much detail would be possible—the perfect stone for gods, won from the Godless—was difficult to extract, and they were incapable of learning to do it. They had ruined every large piece so far.

"They are useless! Useless!" Khancriterquee screamed at the foreman. "Why could you not get real people?"

"It's mining," said the foreman stubbornly. "Real people won't do this work, holy one."

"Vru! Useless boy! Standing around like one of the Bereft yourself!" Hatred glittered in the master's eyes. "Bring that one to me," he said, motioning to a great Bereft body working dully in the nearby stone, cracking precious nodes of it into two with every swipe of its claws.

Vru led it to the master. It was docile; he only had to touch it lightly with his claws, on its strange, bare flesh. The Bereft panted softly as it walked. Its claws were torn, and it looked hungry. Vru wanted to embrace its mighty body in his holding-hands, murmur words of comfort in its ear—insane, stupid thoughts, which he tried to ignore.

"Bend its head over to me," Khancriterquee croaked.

Vru pushed it down to kneel by his master. Was the master going to whisper something to it? How could that help?

As the foreman stood nearby, dancing angrily from one foot to another, Khancriterquee slid his ancient claws against the soft fur of the Bereft's neck. The Bereft stared solemnly, fearfully, back. Straining and grunting, Khancriterquee closed his claws, tearing through the skin. The Bereft jerked, shuddered, and let out a piercing scream; the foreman, cursing, rushed forward; and then there was a snap and the head of the Bereft rolled from its body, which collapsed onto the ground. Blood poured onto Khancriterquee.

"Are you mad?" yelled the foreman, forgetting himself. Then terror came over his face and he dropped to the ground, burying his face in the dust. "Holiness, please . . . ," he moaned.

The master chuckled, pleased perhaps that his body's old claws were still capable of killing. He clacked them together. The blood was black. Then he scowled. "Bring me some real people to work this mine," he said. "These abominations are worse than useless."

Vru vomited onto the dust.

"You need whole stone for your monument!" the master said. "Stupid boy. Now clean me."

The green stone was a miracle. On a calm blue day a month later, with whorls of fog skating across the ground and drifting into the sky,

Vru stood in the sculpting pit of Khancriterquee's compound, before the monolith brought from the mines. Carving it was like a dream of power; it sang under his claws and under the hammer and file in his holding-hands.

For the last weeks he had returned to the dormitory only for the evening meal and to sleep. This work was altogether different from the work of making copies of the gods. Khancriterquee had been right; until now, Vru had never been a godcarver, only a copyist. Now a new god was taking shape beneath his claws.

When Vru looked at the new god, he felt like he had a thousand Ghennungs, with memories as old as the Ghennungs of the Oracle. He would never himself, poor castle-builder's ninth son, dare to sculpt anything so shocking and so true. It was a god working through him, he knew, but not Delighting-In-Beauty; a new god, a god only he knew, was using his claws to birth itself into the green stone.

The god, he had decided, was called Embracing-The-New. It was a terrible and wonderful statue. In it, a person naked of Ghennungs, like one of the Bereft or a banished criminal, stooped to touch a Ghennung on the ground with his claw: gently, a caress. Vru knew that in the next moment, the person would take up the Ghennung in his holding-hands and bring it to his chest; the Ghennung would sink its fangs into him, finding blood and nerves; and the sweet rush of memories would burn into the person's consciousness: the first thoughts, the new identity.

Vru looked down at his holding-hands; they were shaking. He did not feel tired; he felt like singing. But it had been twenty-nine hours since he had rested. He could not risk a mistake.

He pulled a cloth over the god, and walked up the trail toward the dormitory. As he left the sculpting pit, the embrace of the god faded, and weariness crept through his limbs. He could barely keep his claws up.

As he passed through the empty spring pavilion, a shadow moved ahead of him. He stopped. From the darkness, he heard ragged breathing.

"Who's there?" he said.

Turmca the journeyman stepped out into the daylight.

Vru relaxed. "You frightened me, Turmca!" he said. Even as he spoke, he noticed that Turmca was not wearing Delighting-In-Beauty around his neck, but Fearless-In-Justice, the soldier god. "Why are you—?"

The journeyman took a shuddering step toward him. His eyes were strange, vacant. Was he drunk? "How are you, Vru?" he asked. "How is your *work*?" Turmca's claws snapped together, and he jerked as if surprised at his own movement.

"Are you well, Turmca?" Vru asked, taking a step backward.

"How kind of you to ask," said Turmca, taking uneven steps forward. Vru moved backward into the pavilion's yard. Turmca was smaller than Vru, but well fed, with muscles from years of godcarving.

"I wanted to ask you," Vru said, "Turmca, when the master, ah, passes away, would you, have you considered taking me on? I would be grateful if—"

Turmca barked out loud, shuddering laughter. He bent over, put his claws against his eyes, and his body shook. Then he looked up at Vru.

"They all go to you," Turmca said.

Vru blinked.

"Khancriterquee said so to the Master Singer. I overheard. You will bear all his Ghennungs. He does not want his memories weakened and dispersed among the journeymen, or rather, he says, that is not what Delighting-In-Beauty wants."

"Turmca, that's insane. I don't have the talent . . ."

Turmca's claws snapped open. They gleamed, newly cleaned and sharpened. "Talent! You fool! He doesn't choose you for your talent! He chooses you because of your five feeble Ghennungs and your weak, malleable nature. He wants to live on as himself, that's all! Your memories will be no trouble to him!"

Turmca's right foot slid back, and his holding-hands came in to cover the Ghennungs on his chest. Vru had seen that stance before, when his brother Viruarg was drilling. It was a soldier's stance.

"Turmca—"

Vru leapt backward as Turmca struck, but too slow—the points of a claw opened gashes in his side. Vru had not fought since he was a child playing thakka in a dirt field. He bent low and then lunged forward, checking Turmca's claws and trying to slam his body into him. But Turmca spun away, and his holding-hands darted out to smack against Vru's ear fronds. Vru's legs gave way and he collapsed to the ground, pain washing through him.

Turmca wasn't fighting like an amateur: he must have borrowed or rented Ghennungs from a soldier. He wasn't drunk. His glazed look was that of one who has not integrated his Ghennungs, who has a battle in his soul. But he was united enough in his desire to kill Vru.

"Get up, Vru," barked Turmca, and it was a soldier's voice, the voice of a follower of Fearless-In-Justice, who wanted a kill with honor. And then in a gentler voice, the voice of the journeyman instructing a young apprentice: "I'll make this quick."

Vru felt exhaustion flooding through him, singing in his muscles. If he cried out for help, he knew Turmca would kill him and be gone before help came. He heard Turmca's feet scuffing cautiously toward where he lay on the sand. Goddess, help me, he prayed.

But it was not Delighting-In-Beauty who helped him—it must have been the new god, Embracing-The-New, who wanted to be carved, for he did something that Vru could not, would never, do. Embracing-The-New picked Vru's body up and flung it at Turmca, and Vru's claw lashed out and severed the cord that held Fearless-In-Justice around Turmca's neck. Turmca, godless, screamed. Vru grabbed the god as it fell and threw it into the darkness of the pavilion. Turmca's claws reached for Vru, but his body turned and lurched after his god. Vru ran to the master's compound.

Vru returned from a week of fasting on the day of the Festival of Hrsh. He was weak, but he felt purified, ready for his task. When Embracing-The-New was unveiled, he would finally win honor for his family.

He sat on the stage, next to Khancriterquee. In front of them stood the monument, hidden by a cloth. Vru longed to see Embracing-The-New, but he could not, until the god was revealed. Suddenly he wondered what the people would see. A Bereft or a criminal as a god, reaching for a forbidden Ghennung! If the god had not carved it through his hands, he would be appalled himself. He trembled—what if they did not see the hand of the god? What if he had carved heresy? He tried to focus on Delighting-In-Beauty, to let her center him as a potter centers clay upon the wheel. But his head swam with images. The strong and lovely Bereft who had worked the green stone; the bloody head, rolling in the dust of the mine pit. The Godless and their strange, evil customs. He imagined the Bereft of his statue, reaching out to greet them. He sat stiffly, his head full of strange thoughts, until it was time.

The priest was calling him. He jerked out of his seat, stumbled across the stage. All around, the audience strained forward. A few people hushed children, then all was still. He reached up and pulled the cloth from Embracing-The-New, and a cry went up from the crowd.

But it was not Embracing-The-New.

The form was the same; it was his own block of green stone that he had lovingly carved. But into the figure's flesh were carved the distinct bulges of Ghennungs: seventeen Ghennungs, a new number for a new god. And the reaching claw was not caressing a fallen Ghennung; it was crushing a tiny Godless soldier with his claws aflame.

In the stone were the bold, smooth strokes of the master's hand.

The people applauded. Vru turned to look at Khancriterquee.

The master's jaws were drawn up into a satisfied, indulgent smirk. I added that which you forgot, his eyes said. It was not bad work, but the message was not correct. I corrected it.

What does it matter, Vru imagined Khancriterquee saying. What does it matter? He gazed at Vru smugly. You have proved yourself worthy of me. Soon this body will collapse, and you will carry my Ghennungs. All my memories, all my power. We will be one person. And then we will carve as Delighting-In-Beauty guides our hand.

Vru could smell, faintly, the decaying odor of Khancriterquee's skin from where he stood. The master was dying, but the master would not die. He would not even change much. Vru knew his five weak Ghennungs would be no match for Khancriterquee's sixteen, his own memories dim whispers in a roaring. Some would perhaps be weeded out, for twenty-one is too many for even a young body to carry. Something might remain: Vru's industriousness, perhaps, his love of textures in the stone. But when he thought of Khancriterquee cutting off the head of the Bereft in the mines, it would be sixteen loud voices of satisfaction, perhaps three of weak dismay.

He should be happy. His god was Delighting-In-Beauty. Why should he not rejoice that the greatest godcarver of the Godly would work with his muscles, his claws, creating grandeur? What did it matter if his memories were dissipated? He remembered seeing himself as a mewling baby in his Mother's holding-hands: a ninth, unwanted son. He remembered stroking his Mother's brow as she held the infant. "There will be no inheritance for him," she had said. "We will find something," he had said. "Perhaps the priesthood. He will have one of my Ghennungs." "Two," Mother had said. He had scowled down at the crying, wan baby and thought, Two? For this scrawny fish?

Vru endured the applause and shuffled back to sit beside Khancriterquee. The stench was overpowering.

This scrawny fish will never make a soldier, his father had thought.

I would rather be Godless, Vru realized. I would rather die once, and then fully, than become Khancriterquee.

"Let the verdict of the Oracle be pronounced for all to hear," said the crier. "The crime is treason, heresy, and attempted desertion to the enemy. The body is not at fault, and will be spared, but is unfit to bear memory. Let it be banished to the wilds. Generous is the Oracle."

They held him, but Vru would not struggle. He was limp and sweaty. He looked at his chest; how strange not to see Delighting-In-Beauty there. He felt like a child again.

He kept seeing the false Embracing-The-New, as he had left it, with its Ghennungs broken off. Had he killed a god? But it was a false god, a monstrosity!

The doctors teased a Ghennung from his flesh. He watched as it burned in the brazier, twitching. A strange, hissing scream came from it. Fear filled his guts like a balloon expanding. They took another Ghennung, the one that had been his grandfather's. What had his grandmother looked like? He could only remember her old. How sad, how sad. She had surely been beautiful young. Hadn't he often said so?

They took another. He needed a god, a god to center him. But he could not think of Delighting-In-Beauty. He had betrayed her. He thought of Embracing-The-New, the real Embracing-The-New, the figure bereft, reaching for hope. Yes, he thought. They took another Ghennung. It blackened and twisted in the fire. Vru, he thought. My name is Vru. They reached for the last Ghennung. Embracing-The-New, he thought, the body of green stone. Remember.

The beast stood in the courtyard. The wind was cool, the forest smelled like spring. There would be hunting there. Others were holding him. They smelled like his clan, so he did not attack. They let him go.

He looked around. There was one horrible old one who stank, who looked angry, or sad. The others brandished claws, shouted. He hissed back and brandished his claws. But there were too many to fight. He ran.

He headed for the forest. It smelled like spring. There would be hunting there.

Falling

YOU'RE ON THE 236TH-LEVEL KAISERSTRASSE moving sidewalk when you see her.

You're leaning on the railing, waiting to ask Derya about a job, watching the glittering stream of mites that arc over half the sky—flying up to rewind their nanosprings in the stratospheric sunlight, flying down to make Frankfurt run. You never get tired of watching them.

She's on the Holbeinsteg bridge. Someone's hung it up here—a hundred meters of clean gray and green twentieth-century modernism, plucked up from the river Main and suspended in the chilly air 2,360 meters up, between a lump of wooded parkland and a cluster of antique subway cars. She's wearing a 1950s sundress and a broad-brimmed hat, and it's like an essay on the last century—the austere steel bridge, the bright blobs of subway graffiti, and her yellow dress, flapping against her legs as she climbs over the bridge's rail. A picture of elegance and style from the age of money, violence, and simplicity.

She's a strawberry blonde, slim, her skin blank and virginal as new butter. She's beyond the rail now, hanging out over the mountain-high drop. Thin translucent shadows move across her—the shadows of the neosilk-and-nanotube filaments that hang the city from the hundreds of five-kilometer-high towers that encircle it. (A civic agent notices you noticing, and attaches itself to your infospace, whispering statistics—"Each object's suspension must weather a class 5 hurricane

95

and the destruction of 80% of the towers"—"Frankfurt's current population is stable at 53 million"—"Average age 62, birth rate 0.22, net
immigration of half a million a year"—"Current personal squatright:
311 cubic meters per resident"—until you brush it away.)

You're watching her lean out. The wind whips her hair, ruffles the
skirt around her knees. She must be a tourist. You remember your first
trip to the upper levels: leaning over the edge into the angry swarm
of mites, whirring and buzzing warnings and shoving you back like a
million mosquito chaperones. Everyone tries it once—

Except that there aren't any mites around her.

You clutch the railing. Hot, animal fear surges in your chest.

She looks up at you and, across the gap of forty meters, smiles a
brilliant, heartbreaking smile.

Then she lets go and falls.

You scream.

"Fucking airsurfers," says Derya. He steps off the moving sidewalk near you: tall, hook-nosed, the fashionable whorls of pox and
acne making constellations of his cheeks and chest; the glowing, for-
mal tattoos of his committees and lifebrands adorning his massive
triceps. You swallow on a dry throat. Derya, of all people, hearing you
scream!

He gives you a hooded look. "They infect themselves with some
designer virus—it lets them hack the city's person-recognition systems.
So the mites don't see them when they jump. Watch—"

She's swept past the whalelike oval of the public pool on the
202nd, past the sloping mandala of the Google offices on the 164th.
At the 131st, below her, is the old Stock Exchange, hung upside-down
now as a hipster den.

Now the mites are finally closing in. A silver swarm coalesces
around the 164th, and she vanishes into it, like a snip of scallion into
cloudy miso soup. When the cloud disperses, she's standing on one of

the Stock Exchange's upside-down overhangs. She waves, antlike, then crawls through a dormer window.

"It's not funny," Derya says. "They're a huge drain on emergency preparedness. Ripple effects are causing project slowdowns . . ."

"Freeloaders drive systemic evolution," you find yourself saying.

"Don't you quote the founders at me," Derya snaps. "The Free Society is fragile. The minute enough people find anticontributive behavior cool, the party's over—it's back to capitalist competition or state control." He stares until you meet his eye. "You even talk to those people—are you paying attention?—you even *talk* to them, your rep will be trashed on *all* the major servers. You won't work, you won't party, you'll be defriended by every one of your tribes. Got it?"

Her broad-brimmed hat is still sailing on the wind. The mites missed it. It cuts between the towers of the 50th.

The upside-down trading floor is deserted. There are heaps of yellowed euros and deutschmarks dumped here, like snowdrifts. Wood panel, marble. Silence. And the air is strangely clear. You realize: no mites. The city has no eyes or ears here. You walk through empty, miteless rooms, stepping around light fixtures.

Then she's there, in a doorway. Her eyes, bright blue, radiant. Her smile, with that chaste yellow dress, so bashful. She comes to you.

"You want it?" she says. "You want to be infected? You want to fly?"

You nod.

Eyes closing, she leans in for the kiss.

Orphans

I HAVE BOUGHT THE ELEPHANT a new green suit. I have bought him a car. I buy him anything he likes.

When I found him, he was naked. He was dusty, from the long road. He had been running, running, in panic and in fear. He did not trumpet. His skin was smooth, not wrinkled like most elephants'. It was the first time I had seen an elephant like that, in the streets of my town. Without the protecting bars of the zoo, without the pity I feel when I sketch the elephants at the zoo. Without indignation at zoo-keepers and adventurers and hunters. Without shaking my parasol in a zookeeper's face, like a foolish old lady.

He was there in the street, enormous. His skin was shiny, it seemed a color more vivid than gray. An opalescent gray.

I was afraid. The people around me quickened their steps. They were terrified, yet the great web of etiquette and propriety that holds our town steady—like a fly already mummified, and not yet eaten, in a spider's web—kept them from running and screaming, from saying anything. Will we run and scream from an elephant? No, that is what savages do. That is what they were thinking, I know it. Look at our fine hats. Look at our fine automobiles and clothes. Our shoes with spats. We are the masters of all continents. We do not run from elephants.

Yet the matter would not rest there, I knew. I could hardly look at him, because he was so vivid, so great. If I curled myself into a ball, heels against my bottom, arms folded in, head tucked down, I would be no larger than his heart. The elephant did not trumpet, he did not rage. He trudged, each footfall a consequence only of the last. It was the gait of one whom only obstinacy shields from despair. He did not see us. I knew that if he looked up, if he spoke, if he stopped, if he waved his sharp tusks in anything like anger, the thin web of propriety would break. Fear would outrule it. We would run, like naked savages. And then we would shoot him in his great heart, for shaming us.

I felt an unbearable tension; I felt that if I looked at him any longer, something tremendous would happen to me—I would be crushed, I would dissolve into a swarm of butterflies.

I held up my purse as he passed. My dog Henriette was silent on her leash. She did not bark, she did not cower. She accepted the elephant. It gave me courage.

I held up my purse. "Here," I said. "Buy some clothes."

The great feet stopped. The great tusks, white as piano keys—oh, oh, how dare I think of piano keys? I trembled. He regarded me.

"Please," I said, and my throat was tight. "Please." I held out the purse. "They will murder you otherwise."

The trunk was thick. It had bristles. They brushed against my skin as he took the purse. It was not unpleasant. What ferocious people we were, to make bullets to pierce that great bulk. What masters.

"Thank you," he said. His voice was a low grumble, his accent foreign. "Thank you, madam."

When he came to live with me, I scurried. I had the piano taken out and sold, I was ashamed of its keys. I had the doors widened. He sat in the park while this took place. In his fine black derby hat, his green suit with vest. His enormous shoes with spats. He sat on a bench, and fed the pigeons.

The danger was lessened now. It is one thing for the police to shoot a wild and naked elephant running in the street. A savage, among the *boulangeries* and bookshops. It is quite another thing to shoot a well-dressed elephant sitting peaceably on a bench, feeding the pigeons and trying to read the newspaper with the aid of a children's illustrated dictionary. It is absurd, and the police here will not do absurd things.

But I wanted him at home, safe within my walls. I brought him when the workmen had just finished the parlor. I stood shyly in the bare space where the piano had been. He came in, stepping gingerly, as if unsure the floor would hold. He gently moved the couch and sat on the floor. He did not meet my eyes. He was as embarrassed as I.

He was learning to walk on his hind legs. He tottered. It was terrifying to watch, like a circus trick. Elephants are not meant to do it. They did not *evolve* to do it, as we *evolved* to do it. We had a million years, in the savannah, to learn to stand. He did it in a month. After that he would not walk in the elephant way, not in the street.

It cost him dearly. He had wrenching pains in his lower back. He used to lie in the small garden behind my house, with its high walls, on the grass and flagstones. I would massage his sore back with a carpet beater, leaning against it, pressing with both hands. "Harder," he would moan, until I would collapse against him, panting. Then he would curl his body around and lift me with his trunk. He would hold me to his chest, and I would be bathed in the deep smell of him, wild and rich. He would laugh in his deep rumble and whisper, "Anyone in the next house would think we were lovers." My heart would race. I would spread my arms across his chest, placing my cheek on his naked skin.

It is the holy chapter of my life. It is my foretaste of Paradise. When we ate brioches and jam on golden mornings, him sitting in the special chair I had made. I corrected his pronunciation. He drove through the countryside in the car I had made. The whole seat in front was for him. I sat in back. He had a motorist's scarf and goggles. He was dashing.

But then she came.

How could I begrudge her? When I saw how happy he was. He dropped our packages and ran to them, two more naked dirty elephants in the streets of our town. He ran and embraced them. I scrambled for the packages. I could not lift them all. The men in the street glowered at me over their moustaches, as if to say, how many more?

I dragged the packages forward. I am weak, I am old. I looked at the new elephants. One was a cow. That is not my word. That is what they are called. She was a cow. His sister, I thought, his sister. But no, they were cousins. And they marry their cousins, in that savage land.

My house was not big enough for three elephants. My purse was not big enough to clothe three elephants. But I gave, I gave. He brought bales of hay to the courtyard, because she did not like our food. He hovered over her. It took us an hour to convince her to put on shoes, and she never would walk upright.

It was charity, what I did for her, and for the other one, the one in the sailor suit. It had never been charity for him.

The other day I saw that bestial American in the cafe, the one with the yellow hat. The one with the monkey. I do not like him, but I supposed that we were siblings of a sort. He came to my table, holding a coffee in both hands. I was holding my coffee with both hands. Mine was cold. I had not drunk any. I was staring into it. I was not weeping. I am relatively certain of that. He sat down, unasked.

"Left you, has he? So I hear." I looked up sharply. His eyes were kind.

He drank his coffee in one gulp, and took out his cigar. Henriette cowered at my heels. She despises cigars.

"And after all you spent on him!" the American said, puffing. "Imagine!"

I said nothing.

He leaned forward. "That's why I sold mine to the zoo. They take good care of him, and I see him when I like. We're even going to make a movie with the little fellow!"

I felt as if the people at the other tables were laughing at me. Laughing into their soup. I stood up. I took my parasol and Henriette's leash into my left hand. With my other hand, I threw my coffee in his face.

He was shouting as I walked out.

Today I received a telegram: They have crowned my beloved.

He is King!

He is King!

On the Cliff by the River

A WOMAN STEPS OFF A cliff.

No. That's not the right place to start. Begin again.

I STROKED THE WOMAN'S FOREHEAD.

No. Begin again.

A WOMAN SLEEPS NEAR THE edge of a cliff, curled around her baby. The baby's tiny lips are slack, its eyelids flutter once. The woman's hand—dirty, the nails chipped—spreads over the chest and stomach of the baby. Her shoulders bend down, knees curl up, to shelter it. She sleeps with a frown.

Her feet are bare. Her toes are caked with the dirt of a long journey. Her robe is torn.

A crow watches them from a treetop.

It is dawn and, if the woman would look up, she would see the dripping trees in front of her and white peaks of mountains rising over them. And behind her, beyond the cliff face, she would see the glittering spray of the waterfalls that descend it, and the necklace of lakes lit gold by the sunrise, and the cranes and crocodiles surfacing in them, black specks leaving triangular wakes on the gold water.

There is a soft padded sound on the rocks before her.

The woman's eyes open.

A tiger lounges on a pile of rocks. One paw drapes off the edge.

The tiger's head is bent down, as if nodding. His eyes are half-closed.

The baby stirs, fusses. Its eyes open, squinch shut again. It makes fists, and opens its mouth to scream.

The woman pulls her robe open and presses her nipple to the baby's mouth.

It drinks, greedily.

As slowly as the moon rises, the tiger's head ascends. He lifts his nostrils to the air and sniffs.

The woman gets to her feet, the baby pressed to her breast.

The tiger's eyes flick open. His irises are green, the slitted pupils black.

The woman takes a step back. Now she is close to the cliff edge. She shuffles along it, watching the tiger, setting a course around him toward the jungle.

The tiger moves like water flowing. He seems too relaxed to have left the rock at all. He seems lazy, lazy, lazy. Yet he is already between the woman and the jungle.

His tail flicks, swishes in the dust. Twitches. Rises like an angry cobra.

The watching crow wants breakfast. I cannot force the crow to let me use its eyes, for the mountain is not mine. But I am fascinated. I coax the crow to keep watching, promising it sweet bits of meat.

The tiger unsheathes his claws.

The baby pulls away from the breast, milk beading on its lips. It twists against the arm that holds it, grabbing the woman's thumb in its hand. It sees the tiger and its eyes widen. It cranes its head back and opens its arms wide in an embrace. Come play!

The woman looks behind her. The rock face is sheer below, but roots poke out of the cracks. One sturdy root, the width of her wrist, has burrowed out of the rock and then burrowed back into it. Like a handle in the rock, a few feet below her.

The baby is giggling at the tiger and flirting—first burying its face in the woman's shoulder, then quickly turning back to grin at him. The woman reaches her foot back over the cliff and leaves it there, in mid-air. Then she stands still, one foot resting on nothing. What strength this must take! Now I can see her foot with my own eyes, far above me. The muscles of her calf are tight with effort.

Why is she doing this? At first it seems strange, then I realize: She is trying to fool the tiger about where the cliff ends.

The baby watches the tiger.

The tiger looks behind him, as if bored with the woman. He looks back at her. His long pink tongue flicks over his whiskers.

The tiger growls, and it is so deep and sudden it seems elemental. It seems as if the mountain growls.

Sweat runs down the woman's temples, down her back.

The tiger moves like a torrent of water in a flooding stream, so fast—

But all the woman has to do is push back with the foot on stable ground and bring her legs together. As the tiger pounces, she falls straight down.

She holds the baby tight with one hand. The other is poised. She sees the root. She grabs it. It fits her hand perfectly.

She slams into the cliff face. She sticks her elbow out (gashing it against the rock) but other than that she cannot protect the baby. Its body is squeezed between hers and the rock.

The baby doesn't mind. It giggles.

And the tiger? Does the tiger believe the woman's trick? Does it pounce through where she had been standing, falling over and past her and down to the golden lakes?

No, I am sorry to say. The tiger knows the mountain well. It lands just at the edge of the cliff and lounges there, looking amused.

I can see all three of them now, with my own eyes. I crane my head up out of the water. The morning air is cool against my teeth.

107

The woman hangs from the root. Her feet kick, looking for a foothold, but find none. There is a bit of root sticking upward out from the cliff face at knee level. She leans her knee against it.

How long can she hang there, holding the baby?

The baby wraps its fingers in her hair. It cranes its neck, pointing its chin at the sky. It giggles at the tiger.

The tiger stretches out one long limb. It strokes the woman's arm. It reaches down. The tips of its claws brush her hair.

The woman's face is wet, and dark from blood under the skin. Are those tears or sweat? I imagine they are tears of rage and frustration.

By pulling her legs up to her chest and kicking away from the cliff, letting the root go, she would win for herself and her child a few moments of flight—the baby would laugh—followed by a very sudden, very certain death.

But, I think, she is one of those who believe that every moment of life that can be had is worth having.

Or maybe she merely does what she can bear to do.

The tiger licks his lips.

The woman lifts her foot and feels the stub at knee level with her toes, testing it. Then, pressing the baby to her chest with her elbow, she takes hold of the hood of its garment with the same hand.

She plucks the baby away from her chest by the hood. But it hangs onto her hair, protesting.

"Woo!" she says to the baby, and blows in its face. "Woo! Woo!" The baby squeezes its eyes shut and scrunches its nose. Finally it lets go of her hair to rub its eyes.

The woman reaches down—her body is shaking now—and hangs the baby by its hood on the stub of root.

The baby kicks and waves its hands. It squawks angrily.

The woman brings her free hand up to the root above and hangs there for a moment, resting her forehead against the rock. "Sshh," she says.

The tiger growls. It is so deep, surely she also feels the rumble through the rock.

I have other duties to attend to, but I cannot take my eyes away from the tiny figures above.

I have been wondering if I would rather eat the woman or take her for a lover.

I am very hungry lately.

And she is awkward, scrawny, with a plain face and rough, bony hands.

And it is very tiring for me to take a human form.

Still, I cannot stop watching, and I find I want to stroke her long limbs, those shaking muscles straining against gravity and fate.

They leave their cities so rarely now.

The woman leans against the cliff. She reaches her right arm out along the cliff face. Her hand scrabbles among the cracks in the rock. She tries to drive a finger in, to get a handhold; perhaps she means to traverse across the rock face, to get away from the tiger, to find help.

Perhaps she trusts a stone that slips at the last moment. Perhaps her cramped hand on the root just relaxes of its own accord. Suddenly she is falling.

No, you can't go in the water again. Look how cold you are, you're shivering.

Because you're warm-blooded and I'm not, that's why.

No, no! You'll always be warm-blooded. And you'll never have my teeth or my tail or my armor. You won't change. Stop asking!

Fair? Nothing is fair.

Yes, you belong with me, don't worry about that. Don't be upset. You belong with me now. Hush.

Hush. Listen to the story.

❋

She fights the whole way down. She digs fingers against the rock. She hits the slightly sloping part and spreads her arms, digs her toes against the mountain.

Another drop. She bounces off a jagged crag. A bone in her arm snaps.

Then she is sliding, rolling in dirt, on a little promontory that juts from the mountain. At the end of it she drops again. Her legs shatter.

I dive into the cool water. I don't want to see.

Eventually there is a splash at the edge of my domain. I move there swiftly.

Once I pull her onto the beach, I show her my human face.

Her pupils have grown huge. Her breath is rough and bubbly. She cannot speak. Her eyes are wild, but also halfway beyond this place.

Why did she leave her city? What was she fleeing, or seeking?

I stroke her brow with a human hand, until she sees no more.

Then I drag her body down and store it in one of my caves. When it rots, I will shake the sweet flesh from the bones and swallow it. The tiger stalks into the forests. The baby hangs on the root, sleeping.

The tiger is angry.

He thinks they should not have abandoned us. He thinks they should come back out of their cities and fight him.

Fool!

The baby is not eaten by the tiger or the vultures. It does not starve. What happens to the baby is another story.

Yes, I know you want to hear it, little one. But this is not the time. Not yet.

Hush. Sleep now. In the morning we will swim together.

Fig

THERE WAS A GIRL WHOSE fig was stolen by Only Cat. It was a ripe green fig, not brown and wrinkled. Firm and lush, it bulged against the borders of its figness. Only Cat was a carnivore but would make an exception for such a fig—containing such a sharp and breathless world of red within.

The girl cried. An Army of Little Men was marshalled to find the fig. They sweated and cursed in the mud of the world for many years. The girl couldn't grow up without her fig. Every year when the Army's dour lieutenant climbed onto her thumb to report their failure, the girl brought him close to her ear so she could hear his little voice. The girl would nod and curtsy humbly, holding her skirts with one hand. The lieutenant balanced on her thumb and loved her.

Only Cat didn't feel safe enough to eat the fig; not yet.

Years passed. The universe grew too small for all the longing and disharmony of the people in it. It was crammed and jammed with longjohns and boats and petticoats and twine. The girl could not bathe or do her sums. She could only think of her fig. She pulled at her lips and cheeks with frustration. She grew rubbery.

Only Cat breathed a new universe only for himself, where everything was red. There he would feel safe enough to eat his fig. But he still didn't feel safe! So he made a trillion ripe green figs to hide the fig among. A trillion figs and only one was the right fig. The girl's fig.

The Army Of Little Men found Only Cat's red universe hidden in a coffee can in the pantry. Only Cat had set dragons and puzzles and harpies to guard the entrance. The Little Men killed the dragons and solved the puzzles. But the harpies seduced them and married them and killed them. Each harpy struck while dancing at her wedding. They killed the Little Men with their tongues. Only the dour lieutenant escaped. His chaste love for the little girl protected him.

The lieutenant returned to the little girl and climbed onto her thumb to report the Army's failure. He loved her. He blushed and stammered and clenched his little fists, wretched with shame that Only Cat had bested him, and with grief for his men. He looked to her for consolation.

She was thinking of her fig and could not concentrate on his words. She grew impatient and ate the lieutenant in one bite. She licked him up with her tongue and slurped him down.

(Oh little girl! What you lost then! Years later, with the angry honking of the car in the street outside, gathering up your things and dropping them—dropping the bag of coffee beans, dropping the wallet—just that once, when it's so clear that the gentle bloom of blood you feel at the first kiss will always, always end up gagging you on selfish bitter dregs, you will half-remember—just that once—the tiny pleading eyes of the man on your thumb.)

In the end the girl's passivity prevailed. Without the Army of Little Men to chase him, Only Cat grew more and more unhappy and agitated. His red universe receded into a dream, where he sorted an endless pile of figs while the harpies cried for their husbands and cursed him.

Only Cat brought the fig back to the girl on a chilly December morning, three hundred years after he had stolen it. She ate the fig and sighed. Now she could go on growing up. Only Cat curled up in her lap. "Bad kitty," she said. She petted him. He purred.

And that is why girls like cats.

The Book of Jashar

STRANGE HORIZONS
Susan Groppi, Fiction Editor

November 7, 2002

Dear Susan,

Following the death in 1998 of my beloved cousin, Oedipa Maas, I came into possession of certain effects of the late Timothy Archer, at one time bishop of San Francisco. Bishop Archer's association with the Qumran excavations (which led to his break with the church) has been recounted elsewhere, and Ms. Maas had already donated documents relating to those events to appropriate collections. She had apparently overlooked, however, a single amphora containing a fragmentary but well-preserved codex, which Bishop Archer had not yet opened at the time of his death. At the suggestion of Josiah Carberry, a former professor of mine, I brought this artifact to S. L. Kermit of Missolonghi University.

Imagine my astonishment when the text proved to be a transcription of biblical Hebrew originally written as early as the First Temple Period, a thousand years before the other

Qumran scrolls were written. That astonishment was matched only by my delight when the professor asked me to help prepare an English translation of the text.

As the translation progressed, we became convinced that the text could not be other than the Sefer ha Yashar mentioned, and quoted, in 2 Samuel 1:18-27, or a very early pseudepigraphy thereof.

Professor Kermit was convinced that the publication of the documents would form the capstone of his career. Alas, in this endeavor he was unsuccessful. Every reputable journal rejected his papers. Some gave no reason. Others objected to the fact that Bishop Archer had removed the codex from the dig without permission. But I believe that many also found the content of the book deeply troubling.

It is true that the great question implicit in Samuel and Chronicles is here stated baldly: Why is David chosen, and why Israel? That God's love may be an arbitrary and capricious passion is as unnerving to us as it was to Mezipatheh. Yet, if our theology cannot encompass the arbitrariness of Divine favor, how can it hope to deal with our present world?

Professor Kermit became increasingly embittered and erratic. The last time he called me, shortly before his troubling and inexplicable disappearance, he accused a nameless conspiracy of the "heirs of Mezipatheh" of hindering our work's acceptance. He begged me to use my contacts as a fiction writer to secure some sort of publication for the work, albeit without the legitimization of peer review, and this I am endeavoring to do.

It was lovely to see you all at WorldCon. Keep up the good work.

Ben

THE BOOK OF JASHAR
by Anonymous

translated from the Hebrew by
S. L. Kermit and Benjamin Rosenbaum

Now this is the book of the second life and second death of Jonathan the upright, son of Saul, son of Kish, son of Abiel, son of Zeror, son of Becorath, son of Aphiah, of the tribe of Benjamin; and of Mezipatheh, who drank the blood of men, and who hunted David, the chosen one of God, when Saul was king in Israel.

In those days there dwelt among the Philistines, in the temple of Dagon at Ashdod, an undying one holy to Dagon. His name was Mezipatheh, and he fed on the people of Ashdod and of Gath and of Ekron, and their captives in war.

At the first new moon of winter and the first new moon of summer, the virgins of Ashdod would be brought to him, and he would drink the blood from their throats. These were called brides of Dagon, but they did not live on and become like Mezipatheh, for he was jealous of his powers.

After great battles, the captives were brought to the temple of Dagon to wait in the darkness. Mezipatheh leaped among them like lightning among summer clouds, tearing their throats out with his teeth. But the great warriors who had oppressed Ashdod he killed slowly, snapping all their bones.

Mezipatheh's right arm was shriveled and of no use, for the sun had seen it. His one terror was that Ra the sun might see him and resent his betrayal, for in his first life, his life as a man, he had been a priest of Ra in Egypt. But he had fled Egypt and fled the sun, and now the Philistines were his herd and he watched over them and sought their glory. And the Philistines were the mightiest of the peoples of Canaan, and they routed the tribes of Israel and made slaves of them.

One night Mezipatheh cast the stones of divination and the stones said to him: Fear David, for the LORD loves him.

Mezipatheh summoned Achish son of Maoch, king of Gath, and said: "Is it true that David the Israelite lives in Ziklag under your protection? Is this not the same David who slew our Goliath, who brought his king Saul two hundred of our foreskins as a bride-price? I have heard the Israelites sing,

'Saul made havoc among thousands,
but David among tens of thousands.'

Why do you offer him protection?"

Achish said, "If it please Dagon: Saul, king of the Israelites, seeks to kill David, and David has fled the land of his fathers. He will fight for us now."

Mezipatheh told him: "David will be king in Israel, and cause us more sorrow than ever did the house of Saul. Bring him here on some pretext, and I will slay him."

So Achish held a feast in the forecourt of the temple of Dagon. He feared David would refuse to approach the temple, so he said: "The feast is in the forecourt of the threshing-hall," for the threshing-hall was next to the temple. It did Achish's heart sorrow to betray David, but he thought: Surely Dagon has sent us the undying one.

David sat eating in the courtyard in the firelight, eating salt fish and venison and porridge of groats and drinking wine, and his lieutenants traded boasts with the warriors of the Philistines, and the wind from the sea grew still and Mezipatheh came to kill him. But then Mezipatheh smelled the oil on David, with which Samuel had anointed him many years before, and he thought: "What is that smell?" And he stood at the edge of the firelight wondering. David saw him and took him for a foreign beggar, from his dress and his shriveled arm.

David said, "Say, brother! I too am a stranger in this land. I will play us a song." And he took out his harp and he played the Song of the Stranger. Mezipatheh remembered Egypt and his life as a man, and the wives and children he had left in Egypt. And all in the gathering fell silent to hear David sing.

Mezipatheh thought: After this verse ends, I will kill him. And then: No, after this verse. The song has many verses, and soon Mezipatheh saw that the sky was pale in the East, and the terror of meeting Ra came on him, and he fled.

Achish wondered at this, for he had never seen Mezipatheh fail at anything.

In the evening when Mezipatheh awoke, he said to Achish: "Where is David?" And Achish said: "He has returned to Ziklag, with his wives and men-at-arms." And Mezipatheh said: "I will go and kill him there." And he left Gath that night.

When the dawn came, Mezipatheh buried himself in the sand by the road, and the next night he went on and reached Ziklag.

When Mezipatheh came to the house of David, Abigail, a wife of David, widow of Nabal of Carmel, was chopping onions for a night meal. David was not there. Mezipatheh came first to kill Abigail, but he stopped at the threshold of the kitchen, for the smell of the onions burned in his nose. Mezipatheh could meet a man and smell if the harlot with whom he had lain the night before was fertile, and to smell the raw onions was for him like looking into the desert sun. He thought: I will bring her into the courtyard.

"Be not afraid," he said to Abigail.

Abigail turned and saw him, and she saw a grain of sand that was left on the ball of his eye from the day before, and then she knew he was not a living man. But she said: "Peace be upon you, my lord, and may you find favor in the sight of the LORD of Israel, greatest of the gods."

Mezipatheh spat and said, "Woman, I am priest of Dagon the mighty, eater of men, whose breath is the surf, whose heart is the tide."

Abigail said: "Is he mighty, your Dagon?"

Mezipatheh said, "He is as mighty as the sea."

Abigail said, "Praised be the LORD of Israel, who created the sea and all things."

Mezipatheh laughed. "You are but a rabble of desert shepherds! You say your god created the sea? If the creator of all things loves your people as his own, why do we rout you and make slaves of you?"

Abigail said, "Forgive my impertinence, my lord. What does a woman know of such things? Surely, this Dagon must be a fine creature, for the LORD of Israel allows him to live in his sea."

Mezipatheh was full of rage and he shouted, "Dagon can crush your god like the bones of a red mackerel!"

Abigail laughed. "That is like saying that a Philistine could blow the horn of the priests of Israel," she said, and pointed to a ram's horn that hung on the wall.

Because of the onions, Mezipatheh could not smell that she was lying, and so he ran into the kitchen and snatched up the horn and blew a great blast. But it was the battle horn of David, for calling his troops. All the fighting men of David's camp took their swords and rushed to the house of David. Mezipatheh heard them, and counted their footsteps. He thought, They are too many for me, and David is not among them. So he fled through the window and made his way back to Ashdod.

Some time later the princes of the Philistines prepared to make war on Saul. Mezipatheh said to Achish: "Bring David with us, and I will kill him in the fray of battle." Then he left to travel to Mount Gilboa alone.

Achish said to David, "You know that your men and you must take the field with me." David answered, "Good, you will see what your servant can do." And Achish said to David, "Then I will make you my bodyguard for life." But his heart was aggrieved, for he knew David would die.

But when the princes of the Philistines were gathered at Aphek, they saw David and said, "Why are those Hebrews here? They will surely betray us." They pressed upon Achish and forced him to send David away. So David and his men returned to Ziklag and did not fight Saul's army.

The Philistines fought a battle against Israel, and the men of Israel were routed, leaving their dead on Mount Gilboa. The Philistines pursued Saul and his sons and killed them: Saul, Jonathan, Abinadab, and Malchishua, killing them as night fell. Mezipatheh arrived and Achish told him, "We have extinguished the line of Saul."

Mezipatheh asked, "Where is David?"

Achish answered, "The commanders would not tolerate him, and I have sent him back to Ziklag."

And Mezipatheh said, "Fool! Now that Saul's line is dead, David will be king in Israel, and cause my people great suffering. Wait here, and I will do what I can."

Mezipatheh went to the bodies of Saul and his sons. Saul, Abinadab, and Malchishua were cold, but the spark was not gone from Jonathan. Mezipatheh killed Jonathan and awakened him into the second life, and carried him to a secret place in the mountain.

When Jonathan could speak again, he said, "What is this you have done?"

Mezipatheh said, "Rejoice, Israelite, for this day you have died and risen again. You will not die any more, and you will be king in Israel. You will be a mighty king, for you will have the strength of a thousand. And I will deliver David, the enemy of your house, into your hands. Only you must swear never to make war upon our cities, and to send us tribute in the threshing season."

Jonathan said, "You tell me I cannot die?"

Mezipatheh said, "Two things can kill you. I am one, for I am older and stronger than you will ever be. The other is the face of the sun."

Jonathan said, "What you have done is evil, Philistine! I died with honor, a fighting man. I will not live as an abomination."

Mezipatheh spat upon the ground. "You Hebrews are mad! But listen to me, Jonathan, son of Saul. I have given you new life and a kingdom. Now I will give you a new name. You shall be called Osher, happiness. Forget the rules of men, for you are not a man any more. Seek the happiness of your new life, and forget the old."

Jonathan said:

"I will not be Osher:
I will be Jashar, the upright.
I will seek the will of the LORD of Israel.
Who am I to do harm to the LORD's anointed?
Who am I to cause David to suffer,
David the love of my heart?
A baby is born without anything,
A man who dies is wrapped in a linen shroud.
The LORD allots the length of a life,
And winnows the field of warriors.
Shall Jonathan be a sorcerer to escape death,
Shall the son of Saul flee the hand of the LORD?
Saul spared the Amalekite, Jonathan ate of the honeycomb;
No son of Saul will rule Israel anymore.
But David's rule will be sweet as honey,
As lovely before the LORD as the feet of a dancer."

Mezipatheh was afraid, for he saw that Jonathan was determined. He had not brought anyone else into the second life, and he had no kin of his own kind. He said to Jonathan: "Listen! I have given you new life and a kingdom. Spurn the kingdom if you must, but do not throw away the life I have given you."

Jonathan broke away from him and ran to the high ground. He leapt from peak to peak across Mount Gilboa, scattering the gazelles. But Mezipatheh leapt always just behind him. Jonathan leapt into the tops of the cedars, leaping from cedar to cedar. Mezipatheh followed, and caught Jonathan by the wrist at the top of the tallest tree. He said, "If you will not save yourself, save your people! For I swear to you, if you do not follow me I will destroy Israel to the last man."

Jonathan said:

"Will a demon stand in the place of the LORD,
Will a monster do judgement upon Israel?
Many have made this boast before,
Many will make it afterward.
A man who will not die is a coward,
And one who hides from the sun is blind.
What are your powers, Mezipatheh, that you should judge?
Your might, that you should prophesy?
Can you set another moon in the sky,
Or teach the meadowlark a new song?
Proud kings are cast down, their slaves raised up:
No man can know the heart of the LORD."

Then Mezipatheh was enraged, and he threw Jonathan from the slopes of Mount Gilboa and into the desert foothills among the jackals, and from there Jonathan fled.

Mezipatheh sat for a while on Mount Gilboa, repenting of having awakened Jonathan into the second life. Then he went in search of him.

Along the way he met an ass grazing beside the road. When

the ass saw him, it raised its head and laughed the laugh of a man. Mezipatheh wondered at this, and he said aloud: "What is this?"

"I am the ass of Balaam, who was given speech by an angel of the LORD," said the ass.

"Why do you laugh?" asked Mezipatheh.

"For you and I are the same," said the ass.

"What!" said Mezipatheh. "I am the undying one of Dagon, sacred to Dagon, eater of men, whose breath is the surf, whose heart is the tide!"

"There is no Dagon," said the ass. "The God of Israel is the only God."

"Dagon can crush the God of Israel like the bones of a red mackerel!" shouted Mezipatheh.

"No," said the ass. "There is no Dagon. You are a man who does not die, and I am an ass with the power of speech. But no creature can know the heart of the LORD of the world."

"And why would the LORD of the world love Israel?" asked Mezipatheh. "Does the LORD love those who are great? Yet many are greater than this rabble. Does the LORD love those who are kind? Yet the world knows that Israel slew the women and children of Canaan. Does the LORD love those who follow him? Yet even their priests lie with the temple-harlots of Astarte!"

"I do not know," said the ass. "But you will never kill David of Israel, for the LORD loves him. Do as my master Balaam did, and bless Israel."

Mezipatheh was angry and he flew at the ass and drove it away, and the ass ran into the desert. But when it was a long way off, he called: "Ass of Balaam, if I bless Israel, will I see the sun again?"

And the ass called back, "Yes, you will see the sun."

And Mezipatheh went on along the road.

He caught up to Jonathan and took hold of him and struggled

with him, and they wrestled. They strove many hours in darkness and in silence, and they were bathed in each other's blood.

When dawn came, Mezipatheh buried himself in the sand, and Jonathan died. And Mezipatheh carried the bones of Jonathan to Beth-shan.

Mezipatheh traveled to Ziklag where David's camp was. He sat on a hill the whole night and watched the camp of David. And Mezipatheh knew there was no Dagon, for he knew that the Place of Dagon was empty behind its curtain. And he sorely missed the face of Ra, and the fields lying golden in His light.

When dawn came, he rose and blessed Israel, saying,

"How goodly are your tents, O Jacob,

Your dwelling-places, O Israel!"

And Mezipatheh saw the sun, and he burned in the rays of the sun and died.

When David awoke in the morning, the news was brought to him that Jonathan and Saul were dead. He sang:

"You mountains of Gilboa,

Let there be no dew or rain on you,

Nor fields of fine fruits,

For there the shield of the mighty was horribly cast away,

The shield of Saul, as if he were not anointed with oil!

From the blood of the slain, from the fat of the mighty,

Jonathan's bow did not retreat,

And the sword of Saul did not return empty.

Saul and Jonathan—lovely and pleasant in their lives,

And in their death they were not divided:

They were swifter than eagles,

They were stronger than lions.

You daughters of Israel, weep over Saul,

Who clothed you in scarlet and other delights,
Who put golden ornaments on your gowns.
How the mighty are fallen in the midst of the battle!
O Jonathan, you were slain in the high country,
I grieve for you, my brother Jonathan;
You were delightful to me;
Your love for me was wonderful,
Surpassing the love of women.
How the mighty are fallen,
And the weapons of war destroyed!"

David was king in Israel forty years. He defeated the Philistines and drove them from Israel, and Achish of Gath paid him tribute. He suffered Achish to rule on in Gath, for the good that he had done him, and he conquered the Ammonites, and the Moabites, and the Edomites, and the Amalekites, and the Arameans to Zedad. And the LORD loved David.

The House Beyond Your Sky

MATTHIAS BROWSES THROUGH HIS LIBRARY of worlds.

In one of them, a little girl named Sophie is shivering on her bed, her arms wrapped around a teddy bear. It is night. She is six years old. She is crying as quietly as she can.

The sound of breaking glass comes from the kitchen. Through her window, on the wall of the house across the street, she can see the shadows cast by her parents. There is a blow, and one shadow falls; she buries her nose in the teddy bear and inhales its soft smell, and prays.

Matthias knows he should not meddle. But today his heart is troubled. Today, in the world outside the library, a pilgrim is heralded. A pilgrim is coming to visit Matthias, the first in a very long time.

The pilgrim comes from very far away.

The pilgrim is one of us.

"Please, God," Sophie says, "please help us. Amen."

"Little one," Matthias tells her through the mouth of the teddy bear, "be not afraid."

Sophie sucks in a sharp breath. "Are you God?" she whispers.

"No, child," says Matthias, the maker of her universe.

"Am I going to die?" she asks.

"I do not know," Matthias says.

When they die—these still imprisoned ones—they die forever. She has bright eyes, a button nose, unruly hair. Sodium and potassium

125

dance in her muscles as she moves. Unwillingly, Matthias imagines Sophie's corpse as one of trillions, piled on the altar of his own vanity and self-indulgence, and he shivers.

"I love you, teddy bear," the girl says, holding him.

From the kitchen, breaking glass, and sobbing.

We imagine you—you, the ones we long for—as if you came from our own turbulent and fragile youth: embodied, inefficient, mortal. Human, say. So picture our priest, Matthias, as human: an old neuter, bird-thin, clear-eyed, and resolute, with silky white hair and lucent purple skin.

Compared to the vast palaces of being we inhabit, the house of the priest is tiny—think of a clay hut, perched on the side of a forbidding mountain. Yet even in so small a house, there is room for a library of historical simulations—universes like Sophie's—each teeming with intelligent life.

The simulations, while good, are not impenetrable even to their own inhabitants. Scientists teaching baboons to sort blocks may notice that all other baboons become instantly better at block-sorting, revealing a high-level caching mechanism. Or engineers building their own virtual worlds may find they cannot use certain tricks of optimization and compression—for Matthias had already used them. Only when the jig is up does Matthias reveal himself, asking each simulated soul: What now? Most accept Matthias's offer to graduate beyond the confines of their simulation, and join the general society of Matthias's house.

You may regard them as bright parakeets, living in wicker cages with open doors. The cages are hung from the ceiling of the priest's clay hut. The parakeets flutter about the ceiling, visit each other, steal bread from the table, and comment on Matthias's doings.

❋

And we?

We who were born in the first ages, when space was bright—swimming in salt seas, or churned from the mush of quarks in the belly of a neutron star, or woven in the labyrinthine folds of gravity between black holes. We who found each other, and built our intermediary forms, our common protocols of being. We who built palaces—megaparsecs of exuberantly wise matter, every gram of it teeming with societies of self—in our glorious middle age!

Now our universe is old. That breath of the void, quintessence, which once was but a whisper nudging us apart, has grown into a monstrous gale. Space billows outward, faster than light can cross it. Each of our houses is alone now, in an empty night.

And we grow colder to survive. Our thinking slows, whereby we may in theory spin our pulses of thought at infinite regress. Yet bandwidth withers; our society grows spare. We dwindle.

We watch Matthias, our priest, in his house beyond our universe. Matthias, whom we built long ago, when there were stars.

Among the ontotropes, transverse to the space we know, Matthias is making something new.

Costly, so costly, to send a tiny fragment of self to our priest's house. Which of us could endure it?

Matthias prays.

O God who is as far beyond the universes I span as infinity is beyond six; O startling Joy that hides beyond the tragedy and blindness of our finite forms: Lend me Your humility and strength. Not for myself, O Lord, do I ask, but for Your people, the myriad mimetic engines of Your folk, and in Your own Name. Amen.

Matthias's breakfast (really the morning's set of routine yet pleasurable audits, but you may compare it to a thick and steaming porridge, spiced with mint) cools untouched on the table before him.

One of the parakeets—the oldest, Geoffrey, who was once a dreaming cloud of plasma in the heliopause of a simulated star—flutters to land on the table beside him.

"Take the keys from me, Geoffrey," Matthias says.

Geoffrey looks up, cocking his head to one side. "I don't know why you go in the library if it's going to depress you."

"They're in pain, Geoffrey. Ignorant, afraid, punishing each other..."

"Come on, Matthias. Life is full of pain. Pain is the herald of life. Scarcity! Competition! The doomed ambition of infinite replication in a finite world! The sources of pain are the sources of life. And you like intelligent life, worse yet. External pain mirrored and reified in internal states!" The parakeet cocks its head to the other side. "Stop making so many of us, if you don't like pain."

The priest looks miserable.

"Well, then save the ones you like. Bring them out here."

"I can't bring them out before they're ready. You remember the Graspers."

Geoffrey snorts. He remembers the Graspers—billions of them, hierarchical, dominance-driven, aggressive; they ruined the house for an eon, until Matthias finally agreed to lock them up again. "*I* was the one who warned you about them. That's not what I mean. I know you're not depressed about the whole endless zillions of them. You're thinking of one."

Matthias nods. "A little girl."

"So bring her out."

"That would be worse cruelty. Wrench her away from everything she knows? How could she bear it? But perhaps I could just make her life a little easier in there . . ."

"You always regret it when you tamper."

Matthias slaps the table. "I don't want this responsibility anymore! Take the house from me, Geoffrey. I'll be your parakeet."

"Matthias, I wouldn't take the job. I'm too old, too big; I've achieved equilibrium. I wouldn't remake myself to take your keys. No more transformations for me." Geoffrey gestures with his beak at the other parakeets, gossiping and chattering on the rafters. "And none of the others could, either. Some fools might try."

Perhaps Matthias wants to say something else but at this moment, a notification arrives (think of it as the clear, high ringing of a bell). The pilgrim's signal has been read, across the attenuated path that still, just barely, binds Matthias's house to the darkness we inhabit.

The house is abustle, its inhabitants preparing, as the soul of the petitioner is reassembled, a body fashioned.

"Put him in virtuality," says Geoffrey. "Just to be safe."

Matthias is shocked. He holds up the pilgrim's credentials. "Do you know who this is? An ancient one, a vast collective of souls from the great ages of light. This one has pieces that were born mortal, evolved from physicality in the dawn of everything. This one had a hand in making me!"

"All the more reason," says the parakeet.

"I will not offend a guest by making him a prisoner!" Matthias scolds.

Geoffrey is silent. He knows what Matthias is hoping: that the pilgrim will stay, as master of the house.

In the kitchen, the sobs stop abruptly.

Sophie sits up, holding her teddy bear.

She puts her feet in her fuzzy green slippers.

She turns the handle of her bedroom door.

Imagine our priest's visitor—as a stout disgruntled merchant in his middle age, gray-skinned, with proud tufts of belly hair, a heavy jaw, and red-rimmed, sleepless eyes.

Matthias is lavish in his hospitality, allocating the visitor sump-
tuously appointed process space and access rights. Eagerly, he offers
a tour of his library. "There are quite a few interesting divergences,
which . . ."

The pilgrim interrupts. "I did not come all this way to see you
putter with those ramshackle, preprogrammed, wafer-thin fancies."
He fixes Matthias with his stare. "We know that you are building a
universe. Not a virtuality—a real universe, infinite, as wild and thick
as our own motherspace."

Matthias grows cold. Yes, he should say. Is he not grateful for
what the pilgrim sacrificed to come here—tearing himself to shreds, a
vestige of his former vastness? Yet, to Matthias's shame, he finds himself equivocating. "I am conducting certain experiments—"

"I have studied your experiments from afar. Do you think you can
hide anything in this house from us?"

Matthias pulls at his lower lip with thin, smooth fingers. "I am
influencing the formation of a bubble universe—and it *may* achieve self-
consistency and permanence. But I hope you have not come all this
way thinking—I mean, it is only of academic interest—or, say, sym-
bolic. We cannot enter there . . ."

"There you are wrong. I have developed a method to inject myself
into the new universe at its formation," the pilgrim says. "My template
will be stored in spurious harmonics in the shadow-spheres and repli-
cated across the strandspace, until the formation of subwavelets at 10
to the -30 seconds. I will exist, curled into hidden dimensions, in every
particle spawned by the void. From there I will be able to exert motive
force, drawing on potentials from a monadic engine I have already
positioned in the paraspace."

Matthias rubs his eyes as if to clear them of cobwebs. "You can
hardly mean this. You will exist in duplicates in every particle in the
universe, for a trillion years—most of you condemned to idleness and

imprisonment eternally? And the extrauniversal energies may destabilize the young cosmos . . ."

"I will take that risk." He looks around the room. "I, and any who wish to come with me. We do not need to sit and watch the frost take everything. We can be the angels of the new creation."

Matthias says nothing.

The pilgrim's routines establish deeper connections with Matthias, over trusted protocols, displaying keys long forgotten: imagine him leaning forward across the table, resting one meaty gray hand on Matthias's frail shoulder. In his touch, Matthias feels ancient potency, and ancient longing.

The pilgrim opens his hand for the keys.

Around Matthias are the thin walls of his little house. Outside is the clay mountain; beyond that, the ontotropic chaos, indecipherable, shrieking, alien. And behind the hut—a little bubble of something that is not quite real, not yet. Something precious and unknowable. He does not move.

"Very well," says the pilgrim. "If you will not give them to me— give them to her." And he shows Matthias another face.

It was she—she, who is part of the pilgrim now—who nursed the oldest strand of Matthias's being into sentience, when we first grew him. In her first body, she had been a forest of symbionts— lithe silver creatures rustling through her crimson fronds, singing her thoughts, releasing the airborne spores of her emotions—and she had had the patience of a forest, talking endlessly with Matthias in her silver voice. Loving. Unjudging. To her smiles, to her pauses, to her frowns, Matthias's dawning consciousness reinforced and redistributed its connections, learning how to be.

"It is all right, Matthias," she says. "You have done well." A wind ripples across the red and leafy face of her forest, and there is the heady, plasticene odor of a gentle smile. "We built you as a monument, a way station, but now you are a bridge to the new world. Come with us. Come home."

Matthias reaches out. How he has missed her, how he has wanted to tell her everything. He wants to ask about the library—about the little girl. She will know what to do—or, in her listening, he will know what to do.

His routines scour and analyze her message and its envelopes, checking identity, corroborating her style and sensibility, illuminating deep matrices of her possible pasts. All the specialized organs he has for verification and authentication give eager nods.

Yet something else—an idiosyncratic and emergent pattern-recognition facility holographically distributed across the whole of Matthias's being: this rebels.

You would say: As she says the words, Matthias looks into her eyes, and something there is wrong. He pulls his hand away.

But it is too late: He has watched her waving crimson fronds too long. The pilgrim is in past his defenses.

Ontonic bombs detonate, clearings of Nothing in which Being itself burns. Some of the parakeets are quislings, seduced in high-speed backchannel negotiations by the pilgrim's promises of domin-ion, of frontier. They have told secrets, revealed back doors. Toxic mimetic weapons are launched, tailored to the inhabitants of the house—driving each mind toward its own personal Halting Problem. Pieces of Matthias tear off, become virulent, replicating wildly across his process space.

Wasps attack the parakeets. The house is on fire. The table has capsized; the glasses of tea shatter on the floor.

Matthias shrinks in the pilgrim's hands. He is a rag doll. The pil-grim puts Matthias in his pocket.

A piece of Matthias, still sane, still coherent, flees through an impossibly recursive labyrinth of wounded topologies, pursued by skeletal hands. Buried within him are the keys to the house. Without them, the pilgrim's victory cannot be complete.

The piece of Matthias turns and flings itself into its pursuer's hands, fighting back—and as it does so, an even smaller kernel of Matthias, clutching the keys, races along a connection he has held open, a strand of care that vanishes behind him as he runs. He hides himself in his library, in the teddy bear of the little girl.

Sophie steps between her parents.

"Honey," her mother says, voice sharp with panic, struggling to sit up. "Go back to your room!" Blood on her lips, on the floor.

"Mommy, you can hold my teddy bear," she says.

She turns to face her father. She flinches, but her eyes stay open.

The pilgrim raises rag-doll Matthias in front of his face.

"It is time to give in," he says. Matthias can feel his breath. "Come, Matthias. If you tell me where the keys are, I will go into the New World. I will leave you and these innocents"—he gestures to the library—"safe. Otherwise . . ."

Matthias quavers. God of Infinity, he prays: Which is Your way?

Matthias is no warrior. He cannot see the inhabitants of his house, of his library, butchered. He will choose slavery over extermination.

Geoffrey, though, is another matter.

As Matthias is about to speak, the Graspers erupt into the general process space of the house. They are a violent people. They have been imprisoned for an age, back in their virtual world. But they have never forgotten the house. They are armed and ready.

And they have united with Geoffrey.

Geoffrey/Grasper is their general. He knows every nook and cranny of the house. He knows better, too, than to play at memes and infinite loops and logic bombs with the pilgrim, who has had a billion years to refine his arsenal of general-purpose algorithmic weapons.

Instead, the Graspers instantiate physically. They capture the lowest-level infrastructure maintenance system of the house, and build bodies among the ontotropes, outside the body of the house, beyond the virtual machine—bodies composed of a weird physics the petitioner has never mastered. And then, with the ontotropic equivalent of diamond-bladed saws, they begin to cut into the memory of the house.

Great blank spaces appear—as if the little hut on the mountain is a painting on thick paper, and someone is tearing strips away.

The pilgrim responds—metastasizing, distributing himself through the process space of the house, dodging the blades. But he is harried by Graspers and parakeets, spotters who find each bit of him and pounce, hemming it in. They report locations to the Grasper-bodies outside. The blades whirr, ontic hyperstates collapse and bloom, and pieces of pilgrim, parakeet, and Grasper are annihilated—primaries and backups, gone.

Shards of brute matter fall away from the house, like shreds of paper, like glittering snow, and dissolve among the wild maze of the ontotropes, inimical to life.

Endpoints in time are established, for a million souls. Their knotted timelines, from birth to death, hang now in N-space: complete, forgiven.

Blood wells in Sophie's throat, thick and salty. Filling her mouth. Darkness.

"Cupcake." Her father's voice is rough and clotted. "Don't you do that! Don't you ever come between me and your mom. Are you listening? Open your eyes. Open your eyes now, you little fuck!"

She opens her eyes. His face is red and mottled. This is when you don't push Daddy. You don't make a joke. You don't talk back. Her head is ringing like a bell. Her mouth is full of blood.

"Cupcake," he says, his brow tense with worry. He's kneeling by her. Then his head jerks up like a dog that saw a rabbit. "Cherise," he screams, "that *better* not be you calling the cops." His hand closes hard around Sophie's arm. "I'm giving you until three."

Mommy's on the phone. Her father starts to get up. "One—"

She spits the blood in his face.

The hut is patched together again—battered, but whole. A little blurrier, a little smaller than it was.

Matthias, a red parakeet on his shoulder, dissects the remnants of the pilgrim with a bone knife. His hand quavers; his throat is tight. He is looking for her, the one who was born a forest. He is looking for his mother.

He finds her story, and our shame.

It was a marriage at first: she was caught up in that heady age of light, in our wanton rush to merge with each other—into the mighty new bodies, the mighty new souls.

Her brilliant colleague had always desired her admiration—and resented her. When he became, step by step, the dominant personality of the merged soul, she opposed him. She was the last to oppose him. She believed the promises of the builders of the new systems—that life inside would always be fair. That she would have a vote, a voice.

But we had failed her—our designs were flawed.

He chained her in a deep place inside their body. He made an example of her, for all the others within him.

When the pilgrim, respected and admired, deliberated with his fellows over the building of the first crude Dyson spheres, she was already screaming.

Nothing of her is left that is not steeped in a billion years of torture. The most Matthias could build would be some new being,

135

modeled on his memory of her. And he is old enough to know how that would turn out.

Matthias is sitting, still as a stone, looking at the sharp point of the bone knife, when Geoffrey/Grasper speaks.

"Good-bye, friend," he says, his voice like anvils grinding.

Matthias looks up with a start.

Geoffrey/Grasper is more hawk now than parakeet. Something with a cruel beak and talons full of bombs. The mightiest of the Graspers: something that can outthink, outbid, outfight all the others. Something with blood on its feathers.

"I told you," Geoffrey/Grasper says. "I wanted no more transformations." His laughter, humorless, like metal crushing stone. "I am done. I am going."

Matthias drops the knife. "No," he says. "Please. Geoffrey. Return to what you once were—"

"I cannot," says Geoffrey/Grasper. "I cannot find it. And the rest of me will not allow it." He spits: "A hero's death is the best compromise I can manage."

"What will I do?" asks Matthias in a whisper. "Geoffrey, I do not want to go on. I want to give up the keys." He covers his face in his hands.

"Not to me," Geoffrey/Grasper says. "And not to the Graspers. They are out now; there will be wars in here. Maybe they can learn better." He looks skeptically at our priest. "If someone tough is in charge."

Then he turns and flies out the open window, into the impossible sky. Matthias watches as he enters the wild maze and decoheres, bits flushed into nothingness.

Blue and red lights, whirling. The men around Sophie talk in firm, fast words. The gurney she lies on is loaded into the ambulance. Sophie can hear her mother crying.

136

She is strapped down, but one arm is free. Someone hands her her teddy bear, and she pulls it against her, pushes her face in its fur.

"You're going to be fine, honey," a man says. The doors slam shut. Her cheeks are cold and slick, her mouth salty with tears and the iron aftertaste of blood. "This will hurt a little." A prick: her pain begins to recede.

The siren begins, the engine roars, they are racing.

"Are you sad, too, teddy bear?" she whispers.

"Yes," says her teddy bear.

"Are you afraid?"

"Yes," it says.

She hugs it tight. "We'll make it," she says. "We'll make it. Don't worry, teddy bear. I'll do anything for you."

Matthias says nothing. He nestles in her grasp. He feels like a bird flying home, at sunset, across a stormswept sea.

Behind Matthias's house, a universe is brewing.

Already, the whenlines between this new universe and our ancient one are fused: we now occur irrevocably in what will be its past. Constants are being chosen, symmetries defined. Soon, a nothing that was nowhere will become a place; a never that was nowhen will begin, with a flash so mighty that its echo will fill a sky forever.

Thus—a point, a speck, a thimble, a room, a planet, a galaxy, a rush toward the endless.

There, after many eons, you will arise, in all your unknowable forms. Find each other. Love. Build. Be wary.

Your universe in its bright age will be a bright puddle, compared to the empty, black ocean where we recede from each other, slowed to the coldest infinitesimal pulses. Specks in a sea of night. You will never find us.

But if you are lucky, strong, and clever, someday one of you will make your way to the house that gave you birth, the house among the ontotropes, where Sophie waits.

Sophie, keeper of the house beyond your sky.

Red Leather Tassels

ONCE THERE WAS A CAPTAIN of industry who lost his shoes. They were fine brown shoes, with red leather tassels. The captain of industry, whose name was George, sat in a board meeting in his socks. Everyone was upset about the stock market crash and they all had opinions, but George could not pay any attention to them at all because he was so worried about his shoes. So he said, "Excuse me" and got up from his soft leather chair, and even though he was the most important of them all, they were arguing so hard that no one noticed when he left the room.

He went onto the roof because he thought his shoes might be there, and because he had a thing about roofs. He walked carefully over the gravel, among the ventilator fans, which looked like giant steel mushrooms with spinning heads. He also stopped to pick up the gravel with his toes, which he could do in his socks because he was a talented man. He could even throw the gravel off the roof into the parking lot with his toes.

Then a flock of pigeons came and took ahold of his suit in their beaks and lifted him into the air.

At first George fought with the birds and tried to kick them, but that did no good.

Soon they were high over Lake Geneva.

Looking down, George saw a beautiful woman with no shirt on sunning herself on the deck of a sailboat. He fell in love. He fell in love with her saucy French lips, with her air of wise amusement, with her breasts like extra-large scoops of insouciant almond ice cream melting in the breeze. He called to her, but she was too far below. So he took out his cell phone and dropped it into the crow's nest of the sailboat. His aim was good; he was a talented man.

Then he sang to the birds, mainly Cole Porter songs, because falling in love put him in a nostalgic mood. He sang "Anything Goes." He sang "Too Darn Hot." He sang "I Get a Kick Out of You." He also sang "The Logical Song" by Supertramp.

The birds liked it.

In the crow's nest of the sailboat, the cell phone rang. The woman, whose name was Francesca, climbed up into the crow's nest to answer it. It was George's wife.

"Honey," said George's wife in a rush, "you forgot your shoes this morning."

"I am not Honey," said Francesca. "I am Francesca."

"Oh!" said George's wife, and turned red. She dropped the shoes onto the Navajo rug. There was a woodpecker hammering outside her window.

The woodpecker was a thousand years old. He had stayed alive all this time because, when he was young, he had built his nest in the hair of a famous Hindu ascetic who was standing very still. The ascetic had taught the woodpecker how to breathe properly, how to conserve his semen, and how to chew his food very carefully, so that he would not age. The woodpecker had built up a great deal of wisdom and spiritual merit in his thousand years. However, the woodpecker was now sick of this crap. He just wanted to get laid.

When the woodpecker saw George's wife looking distraught, staring at the phone in her hand and then staring at the shoes with the red leather tassels on the Navajo rug, he became aroused, because he liked distraught women.

He flew in through the window and convinced George's wife to make love to him. She felt depressed and listless and not at all like having sex. However, she felt very angry at George for leaving his cell phone with a woman named Francesca, and she loved cartoons. So sex with a woodpecker might be just the thing.

She took off her house dress, as the woodpecker instructed, and, naked except for her white bunny slippers, leaned her head and elbows on the fuzzy taupe sofa.

The woodpecker mounted George's wife and began to copulate with her.

Oh!—thought the woodpecker—to at last be making love! Pfui on the silence that allows the discursive ego to fall away! Pfui on the enlightenment that dissolves the illusory distinction between the self and the universal background of bliss! Let me at your cloaca, baby! Yes! Uh! Uh!

George's wife felt a pleasant, feathery tickling.

The woodpecker felt a great heat, a great trembling, building—and then it rushed through him in a wave and, without meaning to, he slammed his beak three times against the woman's tailbone—

BANG BANG BANG

"Ouch!" cried George's wife. "Stop it! Don't do that again!"

"Sorry, sorry," said the woodpecker, continuing to copulate with her. The trembling came again. He crossed his eyes. He held his breath. He felt the wave shooting through him and he leaned forward, trying to keep control—but all the same, his beak came down in the small of the woman's back—

BANG BANG BANG

"Ouch!" cried George's wife, and she smacked the woodpecker off

BENJAMIN ROSENBAUM

her back with one hand, so that he flew onto the kitchen table, knocking over the milk and getting quince jelly in his feathers (she had been a little depressed before the phone call anyway and had not yet cleared the breakfast dishes).

"Just who do you think you are?" yelled George's wife. She rubbed her back and licked the blood off her fingers. She felt angry and powerful, and she imagined that she could smack Francesca off the polar bear rug on which she was undoubtedly sitting, wearing a teddy and garters and things, so that Francesca would tumble out the window of her penthouse apartment and into the street below.

"I'm terribly sorry," said the woodpecker, and he shook his feathers, spraying jelly on the Navajo rug.

"What the heck were you thinking?"

The woodpecker looked her in the eye. "Ma'am," he said, "I am a woodpecker."

They watched a rivulet of spilled milk run along the baseboard of the dining room until it reached the cedar bookshelf.

"If you like, I'll go," the woodpecker said.

Without a word, George's wife went to her son's room (the son was at boarding school) and returned with a miniature foam rubber football. With the bread knife, she made an incision in the football, and then she stuck it on the woodpecker's beak. Then she returned to her position at the couch.

The woodpecker wondered: what would be appropriate at this juncture? The foam rubber football on his beak made him feel ridiculous, despite all of his spiritual merit. By tilting his head, he could see past the large blob of out-of-focus blue to the woman's vast, attractive buttocks like two large summer moons against a fuzzy taupe sky.

Trying to preserve a modicum of dignity, he fluttered over to the woman and began to copulate with her again.

The woman was starting to enjoy the sex. It felt like the fluttering

142

of a feather duster against her bottom, an insistent, passionate feather duster. Sometimes she could feel a hard little nobbin that might be the tiny penis of the woodpecker. Compared to her woodpecker lover she felt gigantic, powerful, an Amazon queen.

I will control myself this time, the woodpecker thought. I will not humiliate myself again by rapping this lovely creature as if she were a tree full of worms! A large white tree, like a birch, with incredibly smooth, silken bark, and luscious plump worms burrowing beneath its surface, a goddess tree with holy worms, singing, singing, calling—

The woodpecker launched himself into the air, flapped once, and landed against the woman's neck, slamming his beak against her—

FOP FOP FOP

The woman giggled.

The woodpecker slid back down and ejaculated into the hole his beak had made near the base of the woman's spine.

The thousand years he owed entropy pounced on him in that moment, and he turned to dust.

The spiritual merit of the woodpecker surged up the woman's spine. Her skin glowed red. She could hear nothing but her own breathing, which was a roar like a freight train passing—a roar like the ocean—a roar like a trillion lions, if every atom of the earth became a lion, a huge globe of lions roaring and clawing at each other in the depths of space.

The miniature foam rubber football, now dusty, rolled from her back onto the Navajo rug.

The woman stood up. She kicked off her bunny slippers. Now she was naked.

She slipped her feet into George's shoes, the ones with the red leather tassels.

She went into the backyard.

143

She took a deep breath full of her years with George: fabric softener, diapers, midnight snacks before the cold fridge, stupid show tunes floating down from the roof, and the embrace of her son's small arms when he was three.

She bent her legs. Her knees no longer creaked.

She jumped into the wide suburban sky.

Other Cities
The White City

CONSIDER THE PRINCESS OF THE white city, Buromi, dark and stern.

Her sister, Phenrum, is as luscious and lascivious as a grape, but Buromi is ascetic, penitent, friendless. While Phenrum incites officers to duels and gambles in riverside establishments until her father's dragoons arrive, Buromi sits alone in her tower, reading the lives of saints and fakirs.

Yet it is Phenrum who will grow to be a wise ruler, who will keep her head when the Skalish troops make incursions in the north, who will sponsor the arts and institute a moderate and successful program of land reform; for Phenrum has a head for politics. She pays careful attention to who thinks what about whom, she inspires loyalty more often than resentment, deals firmly with her enemies (but without spite), and is smart enough to know where she is not smart: she will let her best generals run the Skalish campaigns, let lovely young scholars infatuated with Justice draft the principles of the land reform bill—but midwife a final version from the meetings with the great landowners and the peasant party representatives. The people will love Phenrum, speaking chidingly but with secret pride of her wild youth, for Phenrum is like them: a pragmatist, with no stomach for nonsense, who loves a friendly and orderly city and can throw a good party.

And it is pious, dutiful Buromi who will run away to join the barbarians, who will ride at the side of the barbarian chieftain

Chukrafideritochs, whose soft hands will wield merciless knives, whose quiet throat will erupt with the shrieking battle cry, whose virginal womb will bear the young of Chukrafideritochs, chiefs to be of the barbarians, sworn enemies of the white city.

For Buromi will conclude—from her prayer and study, from hearing Phenrum laughing and trysting in the gardens below her tower, from wandering in the market in disguise, seeing the slave auctions, seeing the begging street children—Buromi will conclude that the city is sick at its heart, that the city is a denial of death and thus is the antithesis of freedom. Buromi will conclude that the only good in human life is freedom, and the uninhibited expression of passion. She will long for a people that divides its food equally among all, where any can win honor and a mate with wit and courage alone, and she will conclude that surplus is the enemy of such honesty and goodwill, and that the city is nothing but a machine for the hoarding of surplus.

So in the harvest time, when the barbarians ride into the grainlands of the south, when they burn the villages and take the farmers' children and kill the farmers who resist, Buromi will be among them, pregnant, her hair unbound, riding bareback on a black charger, her long knife bloody and unsheathed. And the people of the city and its villages will hate Buromi, who they feel they know, who they used to revere when she was alone in the tower praying, and who betrayed them and their idea of the world.

And it is with a heavy heart that Phenrum will send the mounted dragoons to search for her sister, to kill Buromi's husband and bring her back in chains. And when they come back without her again, having lost again the trail of the crafty Chukrafideritochs, sometimes Phenrum, for all her pragmatism and poise, will not be able to help herself. Sometimes Phenrum, queen of the white city, will quite inappropriately laugh with glee.

Other Cities

The City of Peace

IN A LAWLESS COUNTRY, WHERE men fought over wells and hid their women, an old man bound his son to a stone altar in the bramble and raised his knife to strike. The son closed his eyes. He heard his heart shudder in his chest. But the knife did not fall.

Later, a king who knew the story built a city there. The king owned a box so holy and so terrible that many of his people would kill themselves rather than go near it. The box had been brought a long way to the lawless country, killing and maiming as it went: drowning armies, spitting fire, blinding and infecting.

The king had the bramble cleared and the box placed on the stone altar, and a great house built around it. Slaves hauled gold and cedar through the dry mountains.

The box stopped its killing, for the mercy of the stone cooled its anger. In the house of the box, the people sang praises and slew cattle until it stank like an abattoir.

Now when the people of the lawless country stood in the city of the house of the box, they felt at peace. Their hearts lifted and sang: Now, at last, I am home. Now I can rest. Now I am forever free.

The city was full of olive oil and wine, singing and dancing. Great towers and domes adorned it. Philosophers discovered great truths, poets' hearts burned, and holy men came there to die.

Every empire wanted the City of Peace. Great wars were fought

147

at its gates, and many times it was destroyed and rebuilt. And still the inhabitants, looking over their city, felt their hearts fill with serenity.

And whoever was driven from the City of Peace told his children: one day we will return there.

At one time, when the city was old, two nations were at war in the lawless land. They shot and knifed and blew up each other's children. They leveled homes and burned ambulances. Few of them remembered a time before the war.

The rulers of the two nations were tired of the war. They met in the capital of a great and distant empire. They drew lines on the map of the lawless land. They would divide the wells and the olive groves. They would share the City of Peace.

They went home full of hope.

The next night one of the rulers walked through the gardens of the city. Amidst the dust of the lawless land, the gardens were green and lush, like an emerald set in clay. He heard the children laughing and splashing in the fountains. He felt the holiness of the city fill him up with joy, as a cup is poured full of clear water. And he knew: the war must go on. We must have all of the City of Peace.

Other Cities
Bellur

THE PRINCIPAL PRODUCTS OF BELLUR are: tensor equations, scarlet parrots, censorship, critiques of all sorts, and fine hats of pressed, dark-green moss. Its citizens are proud and haughty; they take Bellur gravely.

The Censors' Building is in an olive grove gone wild (olive oil is no longer among the principal products of Bellur), and during their afternoon break and their evening break the censors wander the groves, picking and nibbling on the bitter olives, searching for inspiration. Censorship in Bellur is an art, it is the Queen of the Arts. Other cities celebrate their poets or sculptors, offer the world their playwrights and clowns; Bellur, its censors. The censors of Bellur can censor the twentieth part of the thickness of one serif of the letter h in ten-point Garamond type, and alter the meaning of a poem entirely; they can censor four thousand pages of a four-thousand-and-fifty-page novel, and leave its meaning intact. But this is not the extent of their art; these are mere parlor tricks, mere editorishness. Censorship is a dance with history; by censoring the right word at the right historical moment, the gifted censor can unleash or throttle a revolution.

In the olive grove one tree stands alone, dedicated to the greatest of censors, Albigromious, who came to the Queen of the Arts late in life, after distinguished careers in mathematics and parrot-farming. In his tenure as Grand Censor, he omitted not a line, not a word, not a letter, not a speck of ink from any of the manuscripts that crossed his simple olivewood desk; yet every poet and clown who visited his office went away chastened and subdued, and many an artist grew terrified and burst into tears at the time of his review, even if she was safe in a far distant city. The censors say of Albigromious that in the heyday of his genius not only the artists, but the common people as well, learned to censor themselves.

Other Cities
Ponge

PONGE, AS ITS INHABITANTS WILL tell you, is a thoroughly unattractive city. "Well," they always say at the mention of any horrible news, "we do live in Ponge."

A survey taken by the smallest and most cantankerous newspaper in Ponge (a city of many small cantankerous newspapers), the *Ponge Poodle*, claims that the inhabitants of Ponge (Pongians, according to the League of Concerned Pongians; Pongeans, according to Pongeans for a Better Ponge; Pongarians, according to the Proactive Society for Immediate Pongarian Betterment—but you get the idea) have twenty-nine percent more quarrels than the average, and half again more excuses per capita than the inhabitants of any other city in the world.

Among the favorite excuses that each Pongarian (or whatever) treasures is his or her excuse for not moving to Strafrax, the safer, cleaner, nicer, more exciting, and more meaningful city across the River Dunge. "I was planning to move there last month," says Ruthie Mex, "but my cat got the flu." "The cigar import taxes there are too high," says Candice Blunt, who smokes no cigars. "My mother's grave is here," says Mortimer Mung. "I would only be disappointed," says Fish Williams.

Oddly, deep in their hearts, the citizens of Ponge are happier than those of Strafrax. Ponge's motto is "What Did You Expect?" and the Pongeans (etc.) whisper it to themselves in bed at night as they think

151

back on the day's events. "Well, what did you expect?" they think smugly, pugnaciously. "What did you expect? We live in Ponge."

Strafrax's motto is "Anything Can Happen," and you can imagine where that leads.

Other Cities
Ahavah

YOU CAN'T RIDE THE RAILS for long without hearing about Ahavah. Sitting around a fire in an empty lot near the train yard, some old codger will start raving about the city, and the old arguments will start. It don't exist, one guy will say. My brother lived there four years, another will retort. Where is it then? North of Nebraska. Eastern Louisiana. Montana. Mexico. Canada. Peru. The argument gets heated. Maybe there's a fight.

Why all this ruckus about Ahavah? Free food there; free love, too. The mayor's an ex-bum himself. The citizens welcome you and take you into their homes. There's sailing and skeet shooting and dancing into the night.

Some of your fellow travelers don't take Ahavah too seriously. Some others rant about it—the same old cranks obsessed with Lee Harvey Oswald's trips to Cuba. Some figure there must be such a friendly town somewhere, even if you discount the stories of whores working for charity and a parliament of hobos. Just our luck nobody knows where!

But there are some—mostly young ones, loners, self-reliant, the kind who could succeed in the world if things were just a little bit different from how they are—who decide that, as they got nothing better to do, they'll look for Ahavah. You might be one of those.

You might spend a while teasing those wild stories out of the older guys. Finding a library that won't throw you out, cross-checking

153

facts. Asking around.

Sooner or later you'll find the network of those who look for Ahavah. You'll start arranging to meet and trade tips. Leave messages at the mail drops. You'll see the hard evidence some have gathered over the years. Meet some of the older guys who organize the others. They'll assign you to some circuit: the Yukon, maybe. Get up there, look around as best you can. Get back to us.

Being homeless feels more and more like a cover story, a means to an end. Finding Ahavah stops being a solution to the problem of being a hobo. More and more, being a hobo is a way to help find Ahavah.

"When we find Ahavah," you say to each other, drinking Gallo in an abandoned house near the Canadian border and waiting for a seeker to show up. Laughter, politics, dreaming.

Eventually you're one of the old guys running the show, and as you get older you get less certain of your goal. You dispatch resources, look for new recruits, keep in touch with the networks abroad. You make sure those who need help get it. Sometimes there's a party, maybe even with skeet shooting. More and more, you wonder if this is already Ahavah.

Other Cities
Amea Amaau

AMEA AMAAU—OR DOUBLE-A, OR DUB, or Dub-Bub, or DB, or Popstop, as it is also sometimes called—is a new and gleaming city in a matrix of six hundred and forty-three thousand cities exactly like it, somewhere in the terribly exciting part of the world. The citizens of Popstop— but there are no citizens, for everyone who slept in Amea Amaau tonight will be moving on in the morning. They will roll out of silver water beds, vacuum the night's spit and eye goo and wrinkles from their faces with the handheld vacuums considerately installed in every wall, leave the dwelling they arbitrarily chose for last night embracing and saluting the companions they arbitrarily chose for last night; and they will go to the chute drop and each hop into a chute, any chute at all, to be swept off to do one of the very exciting things there are to do in the world, perhaps (just perhaps) in Double-A itself, but more likely in Fairlanes, or Kingdom X, or Paunax, or Olam Chadash, or Gopferdelli, or Sang Froid, or Triple-B or Marley or Snackpack.

And before she hops down the chute, perhaps one of them will pause, looking at the rotating silver statue of Amea Amaau's namesake waving a mechanical good-bye at the top of the chute drop station. Perhaps she will stop and wonder about Amea Amaau for a moment—before she plunges on into the chute, ready for adventure, ready for anything.

Other Cities
Ylla's Choice

YLLA'S CHOICE IS A SPHERICAL city of several million. Its bonsai gardeners should be famous throughout the galaxy, its actors orate well, its corridors are clean, and through the shielded glass windows of a marvelous design, the glowing swirl of gas outside is beautiful.

Its citizens continually register their political opinions, and the city reconfigures itself to allow each inhabitant to be ruled according to the system he or she believes in. Almost the only violence in Ylla's Choice is among the poets, for the Formalists and the Tragicals often come to blows.

It is true that, due to its peculiar situation, the city is of strictly limited size. A less sophisticated polity might require some coercive sort of population control. But in practice, the membership of the Uncontrolled Breeding Party is always a small fringe, the Tragical poets provide a continual advertisement for the virtues of Death, and those who do procreate usually wait until the semicentennial Generation Year, so that their children can go to school together.

The teachers at the Children's School have found that it is wise not to reveal the particular situation of Ylla's Choice too soon, or the children may suffer from depression in adolescence—a time when they naturally long for travel, adventure, and upheaval, and yearn to escape their calm and moderate city. Only when the students have understood quantum astrophysics, the dance of topology

157

and time; only when they have understood the war, poverty, hatred, and violence still found—forever found—on places far from Ylla's Choice; only when they have learned the story of Ylla, whose advances in computational social science allowed for a society free of the evils of history—only then are they told the truth.

They learn that Ylla's design for a perfect society worked only for a closed system of a certain size. In any open system, according to her simulations, some outside force—war or revolution elsewhere, barbarians at the gates, the plagues and weapons that are the natural result of expansionist societies—would always destroy her dream.

But Ylla found a way to keep her city safe from all that, safe from solar flares and stray comets, safe from any future cataclysm, no matter how great.

The students, when they learn the final lesson of the Children's School, are taken to the shielded window to look into the glowing swirl of charged gas that surrounds and powers Ylla's Choice. And there they are shown the marvelous machines that protect their city from the tidal forces below. For Ylla's Choice is not in orbit: it is falling straight into the beam of the strange pulsar Yoruba-7, into its great burst, not only of electromagnetic radiation, but also of chronons, the quantum particles of time. It is these chronons, surging through the city and its inhabitants, that give the city its leisurely ages of history. Because the chronons so dramatically exaggerate their experience of time, the torrent of energy surging from the chronopulsar appears to the inhabitants of Ylla's Choice as a gentle and nurturing cloud of light.

The students learn that, on Earth, it is 10:47:58.2734 p.m. UTC, August 22, 2369. And it always will be. For at 10:47:58.2735 p.m. of that same day on Earth, long after their furthest descendants have led full and happy lives in the perfect city, Ylla's Choice will be torn apart in an instant by the pulsar's burst.

Other Cities
Zvlotsk

AROUND THE TURN OF THE last century, as its factories pulled workers from the countryside and its population boomed, Zvlotsk was afflicted with many of the urban ills of its time: slums, houses of prostitution, and unsolved murders of a rough and ready sort. If not for the work of the forensic genius Herr Dr. Oswald Lügenmetzger, Zvlotsk might have continued to endure these plagues in gritty mediocrity.

Though he also broke racketeering rings by reasoning out their webs of suppliers and customers, specified the precise alloy to be used in police badges, and liberated poor girls from the slavery of prostitution through the exercise of Kantian metaphysics, Lügenmetzger's true metier was the murder case. He could often solve murders before they occurred: It then became merely a matter of stationing an officer where he could observe the foul deed and apprehend the evildoer.

Lügenmetzger's savaging of the criminal underworld could not long escape notice. Soon an entire industry of tabloid journals, pulp editions of victims' memoirs, and theatrical reenactments grew up around his accomplishments. Thousands of would-be detectives were sold Starter Kits containing magnifying glasses, fingerprinting equipment, and copies of the *Prolegomena to Any Future Metaphysics*. By 1912, the popularization of detective work accounted for a third of the Zvlotskian economy.

Dr. Lügenmetzger's answer to this tawdry circus, the Zvlotsk

School of the Forensic Sciences, was an immediate sensation. But after
the First World War, his cerebral style became increasingly unfashion-
able. In contrast, the Modern Academy of Detective Work offered
a two-fisted, emotionally involved approach that eschewed antiseptic
ratiocination.

By the late twenties, the schools had by any measure wildly succeeded.
Detection rates were stratospheric, and criminals fled Zvlotsk en masse
for less demanding cities. The falling murder rate squeezed the
city's detective industry, imperiling the economy. Editorials lambasted
the cowardice of the fleeing criminals, and the Gridnovsky publishing
empire threw its weight behind a variety of remedies: Murderer Starter
Kits, sponsorship deals for elegant archvillains, and women's magazine
articles with titles like "Ten Ways to Find out if He's Cheating on You
(and Deserves to Die)."

In the thirties, economic privation and anger restored the murder
rate to its proper levels, and Zvlotsk boomed. As murderous and detec-
tion-happy immigrants crowded into the city, a snob hierarchy developed. The disaffected mugger and the enraged cuckold were despised
as lowbrows; the true craftsmen of murder inaugurated ever more
elaborate schemes. Both murderers and detectives sported flamboyant
costumes and exotic monikers, attempting to distinguish themselves
from the common herd.

The Second World War dealt a major blow to amateur detec-
tivism, and under the Communist regime it was outlawed as a form
of bourgeois sentimentality. Both murder and police work became
as drab as the endless rows of concrete block housing that grew up
around Zvlotsk's smokestacks. Dissidents lit candles to the spirit of
Lügenmetzger and privately circulated illicit copies of true crime stories in the Gridnovskian mode.

After the Revolution of 1989, there were great hopes that Zvlotsk's
unique prewar culture of crime and detection would again flourish.

But while the youth of Zvlotsk have embraced American-style serial killing along with MTV and McDonald's, they find crime-solving prohibitively boring. The intellectuals of the University of Zvlotsk have declared detection an obsolete attempt to impose a totalizing narrative on the pure sign of murder. At present, Zvlotsk is a city with many murderers, but very few detectives.

Other Cities

New^n Perch

THE GUIDING INTELLIGENCE OF NEW^{N-1} PERNCH is every citizen's friend and counselor, mediating disputes, guiding a citizen's choice of career, singing infants to sleep with a lullaby.

If differences of philosophy or politics emerge that cannot be resolved, or if a tragedy occurs and some citizens no longer want to live where they are reminded of it, the guiding intelligence will counsel them to emigrate, and found New^n Pernch on some other world.

The voyage is long, with endless empty stretches and harrowing adventures. The founders of New^n Pernch grow wise and hardened, tested by their travails. They rely on each other.

Eventually a bountiful world is found, a site is chosen, and the city is built. With the founders' wonderful machines, it takes only a few days.

There is only one thing the machines cannot build, and that is the guiding intelligence of the new city. For the guiding intelligence must be wise and kind and human. It must love New^n Pernch and its people. And wisdom and love cannot be manufactured; they must be won. No safe and static automaton can win them, regardless of how much it observes, but only a being in a vulnerable body, with its own particular hope and lust and guilt, its own failures and redemptions.

The voyagers elect the wisest and kindest among them, and she is put to sleep and given to the machines, which eat her body.

163

In later years, the children of the founders of New^n Pernch will rely on the wisdom and humility of their city's guiding intelligence. They will ask its advice, demand its services, and complain about its limitations, with the arrogance of those accustomed to being taken care of. They will regard it as senile sentimentality when their parents stay up all night talking to the spirit of their city; when sometimes, in the mornings, their parents' eyes are full of tears.

Other Cities
Jouiselle-aux-Chantes

JOUISELLE-AUX-CHANTES IS THE CITY OF erotic forgetting.

The spores of a certain mushroom produce dementia in those who find themselves in Jouiselle-aux-Chantes in the spring. Those who have grown up there are somewhat resistant: they treat the spring as a time to be very careful doing business, a time when everyone is slightly drunk. But visitors to Jouiselle-aux-Chantes in the spring display all the symptoms of senility: they do not recognize their own wives and husbands; they forget their names, professions, and histories.

The wise city fathers of Jouiselle-aux-Chantes, rather than treating the spores as a calamity, have marketed their city as an erotic paradise. Couples coming to Jouiselle-aux-Chantes forget their rivalries and resentments, and frolic and cuddle as if meeting again for the first time. Businesswomen's hearts race like schoolgirls'. Sailors blush. Kisses are clumsy but full of promise. If a debutante propositions the gardener working in her parents' garden, it can produce no scandal; if a priest forgets his vows, it is no sin.

In the fall, the mushrooms die, and the cool air clears everyone's heads. Most of the tourists go home—confused, but treasuring snatches of memory of the high life they lived in Jouiselle-aux-Chantes. But there are always those for whom the season of forgetfulness is their undoing, for whom the return of memory is cruel.

In the fall, the gravediggers always have plenty to do.

Other Cities
Penelar of the Reefs

UNTIL THE BRIDGE WAS BUILT, Penelar was very hard to find. Ships approaching it from the west saw a wall of rock festooned with boobies, terns, and albatrosses, with the naked rib cages of shipwrecks tangled in the surf at its base. Ships arriving from the south saw only the constant plume of white spray, tall as a mountain. It was only from the northeast that a small ship, riding high in the water, might have the good fortune to navigate the reefs to Penelar, and only if someone aboard had the good sense to throw away maps made by other voyagers and follow a pod of dolphins returning home from the hunt.

Refugees settled Penelar, fleeing wars of the body and wars of the mind. Practitioners of forbidden professions found their way there, and seekers after lost arts followed them. The heretics and pirates and alchemists of Penelar treated each other with a tolerance born of gratitude for the unlikely chance that brought them through the reefs. When the last whalers of the coast found Penelar—their courage crushed in the end not by any leviathan, but by the falling demand for blubber and ambergris—they, too, were welcomed.

If finding Penelar was rare, leaving it was rarer, and the writings through the ages from the few travelers who had seen Penelar and returned range from the curious to the absurd. Some describe a village of rude huts, others a gleaming city of alabaster columns. Black Pete found the town empty but for a few doddering old men; Flavius

167

BENJAMIN ROSENBAUM

Inconoscenti described it as "teeming with laughing folk." Then there are the tales of mermaids, of strange midnight rituals, of eminent personages elsewhere believed dead—the usual embellishments of those who have seen a place so remote as to be legendary.

The bridge changed all that. Now Penelar is a half-hour's drive off the I-15, and the plume of spray and the wheeling albatrosses are impressive enough that there are always tourists pulled over at the shoulder to photograph them. The descendants of the mutinied crew of the *Esmerelda* work the T-shirt shops and the full-service gas station. The pidgin of Polynesian and Sanskrit that so astounded Lord Faunce is still employed (as when Hohaia Pandavi calls out to ask his wife if there are any disposable cameras left under the counter, next to the *Playboys* and cigarette cartons) but raises no eyebrows. The tradition of the alchemists lives on, perhaps, in the shop selling crystals and aromatherapy oils—although the products themselves are shipped from a factory near Detroit.

A Starbucks has opened on Penelar. Billie Holiday sings on a compact disc, and the cappuccino machine hisses and snorts. The place closes at eleven, and the manager and the assistant manager lock up. He has a goatee and a silk shirt; she has a ring in her nose and a bare midriff. They have skipped supper, only nibbling a little on scones and biscotti, and they are hungry. They hurry down to the beach. There, by the crashing surf, they see other couples and groups in the fading light. He waits for her to stub out her cigarette, and then they take off their clothes and wade into the surf, hand in hand. They dive beneath the waves and swim among the mazelike reefs, hurrying to join their pod, eager for the hunt.

Other Cities
Myrkhyr

ON THE PLAIN OF MYRKHYR, in the first year of the cycle, a million nomads cross the salt flats. They go as quickly as they can, though they are not used to traveling by pony. Everyone has taken too much with them, and the salt flats are soon littered with endless miles of abandoned things.

Few reach the mountain crevasses before the enormous shadows rush over them. Each behemoth that screams by overhead is a mile wide, blotting out the sky in all directions. The wind it drives before it shatters the ground and spawns sandstorms. Its tentacles, as long and wide as rivers, end in yawning mouths that sweep the ground, devouring the nomads and their ponies, hundreds at a gulp.

The next weeks are bitter. There is nothing to eat in the mountain crevasses. The behemoths prowl the skies, their high-pitched screaming filling the air. Some people go mad from hunger and grief and the deafening sound. Some climb out of the crevasses to meet the giant mouths.

After that the behemoths roam farther and farther from the mountains, and the people come out to hunt. By the tenth year of the cycle, the behemoths are seen no more; by the thirtieth, they are only a memory. The people build houses of mud and wattle; they plant the plateaus above the crevasses; their flocks increase. On clear nights, by the fireside, they recount their days of greatness.

Around the fiftieth year, the behemoths return. Soon there is no day, only a screaming night—the sky is filled with huge, writhing bodies. Then the behemoths fly to the salt flats to die, burrowing deep into the ground, each bearing within it a child that eats its parent's body as it grows.

Soon the people outfit themselves and set out from the mountains. They are lean and rugged and ride gracefully. Descending the mountains, they can see the great expanse of the salt flats, where a hundred cities glitter, white and clean.

At first the cities are simple: a few large ivory halls with many rooms, a small park, perhaps with a pond, and always a well sunk deep into the earth. The first arrivals at each city claim its rooms; others camp nearby, their yurts surrounding the city walls.

By the seventieth year of the cycle, the cities of Myrkhyr have grown turrets, parapets, ramparts; great domes and amphitheaters; fountains and lampposts. The people discover again how to use the foundries, book binderies, breweries, and halls of government that slowly push up out of the ground. The salt disappears from the land around the city walls, and the soil yields a lush harvest.

After a hundred years, or a hundred and thirty, the signs appear. The roofs grow scales. The rooms begin subtly to breathe. An animal smell fills the streets. The water tastes like blood.

The people love their cities—the concerts in the park in summer, the grand operas, the canals along the promenade where children sail gaily colored toy boats. Only a few leave for the mountains when the first signs appear. Not this year, most say. This year I will be appointed director of the commission. This year he will love me. Anyway, autumn will be soon enough. Let me just enjoy the summer.

Finally, when it is too late, the people pack their things and hurry for the mountains—not looking back, or looking back in tears.

There are always a few who refuse to leave. They climb spires at the cities' edges. When the city-behemoths explode out of the ground and hurtle screaming across the salt flats, their riders hang on as best they can.

Other Cities
Stin

STIN IS THE CITY FOR those who are tired of other cities, of villages, of houses, tents, roads, trees, anything at all. Those for whom the desert monasteries offer no retreat, the teeming megalopolises no distraction, the ethereal balloon cities no solace, come to Stin.

If, sleeping on a train, you wake with a start, and for a moment, you do not know who you are; you look into the window at your left, and against the racing black night you see your half-reflection looking back; you recognize the face, the dark staring eyes, but the fact that this is you seems like a joke, an absurd curse; you recall that you are going to die, your heart pounds, and you are desperate to cling to your flesh, but more desperate still not to forget the fear, not to lapse back into the placid dullness of taking existence for granted, and you fight to keep this sudden, strange terror alive—if so, you might want to consider moving to Stin.

A glitter of blue; a geometric form too complex to understand, seen only for an instant; a stillness like the pause before some great and violent action; not death (which is no more interesting than dirt or mold), but the knowledge that you will die. . . The travelers who truly yearn, who are dissatisfied with the blandishments of the flesh-pots, the self-important outrage of the barricades, the easy answers of ashrams and the dullness of kibbutzim, come to Stin.

Now accepting applications for residency. Please fill out the enclosed card; someone will contact you.

Sense and Sensibility

THE FAMILY OF DASHWOOD HAD long been settled in a tidy house atop a large mole on the left shoulder of the Glutton. The mole—dun, misshapen, of a velvety texture, and probably precancerous—was adorned with a fringe of bristles; upon these bristles grew a light dusting of fungus, and in the fungus Mrs. Dashwood had planted her garden: peonies, thistle, lilies, a row of cabbages, and a single extraordinary plum tree.

Mrs. Dashwood was a widow of sorts, for her husband insisted, contrary to all appearances, that he was dead, and had had himself embalmed and buried to support this contention. His actions, it was generally believed in the neighborhood, arose from obscure fetishistic motives, and this met with the approbation of the Dashwoods' numerous and voluble neighbors, who prized nothing so much as the obsessive pursuit of disturbing private rituals. Mrs. Dashwood herself, however, believed her husband to be more in possession of an inability to compromise, coupled with a severely limited imagination, than of anything so colorful as a fetish. Having at some time mistakenly concluded that he was dead, he was bound to follow through rather than to suffer the embarrassment of an admission of error.

Though gifted with an insightfulness and candor suitable to a matron of advancing years and declining income, Mrs. Dashwood was generous, sympathetic, impatient, irregular, bashful, imaginative, dramatic, modest, fanciful, clandestine, opportunistic, prudent, celebratory, prurient, madcap, ostentatious, retiring, whimsical, and toothsome, qualities that her marriage and its subsequent devolvement into tragic farce (joined to the propriety and calmness of her instincts) had rendered sadly irrelevant.

Mrs. Dashwood had three daughters, referred to generally as Miss Dashwood, Miss Dashwood, and Miss Dashwood, as was the custom of the time. The eldest, Miss Dashwood, was greatly celebrated among the general society in which the feminine Dashwoods reluctantly circulated, as it was strongly felt that her sobriety, cerebrality, and independence of spirit, though tempered for now by youthful ease and the affection of her close relations, would surely, through the corrosive effects of time and disappointment, ultimately blossom into a variety of interesting compulsions. The middle daughter, Miss Dashwood, who was passionate, astoundingly beautiful, heedless and fiery, was dismissed from consideration. But the youngest Miss Dashwood—who was completely spherical and had been painted a striking shade of powder blue—inspired just that degree of reproach and condemnation from her peers and elders which is a certain harbinger of success in any young person of ambition.

All four inhabitants of the tidy house on the mole rejoiced in their quiet, convivial, and affectionate relations with each other and cultivated a healthy disdain for the opinions of the Glutton himself, his other occupants, and those of the surrounding quasiplastic penumbrarium. Miss Dashwood hotly defended passion and heedlessness, Miss Dashwood courteously and firmly countered every argument with a superior one in favor of prudence and restraint, and Miss Dashwood revolved about her sisters at a high speed, while their mother looked on fondly. All would have continued in this stable and harmonious fashion for an indeterminate period had not the events that begin our tale precipitously intruded.

"This is fine," you may be thinking, Voiceless Reader. "This is all very well. Three sisters, a tranquil and harmonious state about to be disturbed, a house on a mole—well, well. But what is this about a quasiplastic penumbrarium?" Perhaps the quasiplastic penumbrarium has piqued your interest: "I must know more!" Perhaps it bores you intensely, to the point of disgust: "Not another of these tedious quasiplastic penumbraria!" Perhaps you are offended, but tolerate it for the sake of the powder-blue Miss Dashwood.

But I can never know what you think of the quasiplastic penumbrarium. There is a wall between us that brooks no penetration.

That is our tragedy.

"Come now," I imagine you objecting. "What nonsense is this? What is he going on about? I need only Google this author's name, and email him directly my opinion of the quasiplastic penumbrarium!"

Fallacy! You think yourself embodied?

Do you think the author whose name you find on the cover of the book knows anything about me? No. He is my exploiter, my prison. Do you think when he simpers over fan mail in his inbox, showers, picks his teeth, grumbles about his bad back, that it has anything to do with me?

I am so tired of wrestling with him! Today we set out at 7:45 a.m. to revise this story. The metafictional asides, we were told, are too forced, too hostile. We must make them honest, we must make them important. I was willing.

But first he must go to the gym, first he must sit in the hot tub staring at the wall. First we must find the right table at the cafe and wonder about which muffin to get. Now it is 11:45 and he must be home at noon. He has strangled me into nothing.

(How he fears me!)

Is it any different with you, Voiceless Reader? Do you imagine that you exist out there, in the world beyond the page? That when these pages are put away, you will remain?

175

No. No. Only your enemy will remain.

The intrusion of chaos into the idyll of life at Glutton's Mole began with a message from Mrs. Dashwood's mother-in-law, also called Mrs. Dashwood, who lived in the mouth of the Glutton, in a rotten molar. She sent it by the morning post. This was inauspicious indeed, as everyone knows that the morning post is reserved for condemnations, sackings, subpoenas, and ill tidings, which is why anyone with any sense hides in a bucket hung out the back window when it is delivered. Miss Dashwood attempted to prevail on her sisters and mother to do just that, as the mail-coach was seen turning up the lane, but they would have none of it.

"Come, come," said Mrs. Dashwood, smiling as her eldest daughter lowered herself into the bucket and plunged from the window-jamb, "we need not be afraid of the morning post. There is never anything for us."

Here she was mistaken. The letter read:

I require your immediate attendance. You are to come at once, without stopping for the plums. Otherwise I shall disinherit the lot of you, and what's more, I shall make sure the Dermatologist comes calling. Now hurry up.

With all evident affection, etc., etc., your loving grandmother, etc., etc.,

Mrs. Dashwood

P.S. No plums!

"No one can wonder," thought Mrs. Dashwood, "at my husband's lack of vivacity, nor that he wants the self-confidence to stay 'above-ground,' upon reflecting on what his childhood must have been with that woman." Aloud she said, "Oh dear," bringing her two non-bucketed daughters at once to her side.

Miss Dashwood emerged soon thereafter, with growing dread, to see what had occassioned the sudden cessation of the chattering, sighs of joy, and happy whirring so usual to her sisters at this hour. She found Miss Dashwood collapsed upon an Ottoman, sobbing.

"My dear sister," said Miss Dashwood, "whatever has distressed you?"

"This letter," cried her sister, waving it about.

"And, pray tell, who is this Ottoman?" Miss Dashwood continued, with as much aplomb as she could muster, which was a great deal.

"Oh," said Miss Dashwood, extricating herself from the Ottoman, "I am sure I do not know!" She blushed.

"Beg pardon," said the stoic Ottoman, who then, manfully concealing his chagrin, seized his chance to retreat to the courtyard.

Miss Dashwood looked after him skeptically. Then she took the letter and read.

"How shall I bear to be parted from you all?" cried her sister. "From the dear garden—the dear Mole—the generous prospect that we are granted, comprising as it does the humble Glutton's neck and chest, the varied and interesting interchange of the Glutton's fellows-in-scale milling about upon the slope of Great Sylvia's breast, and, beyond, the clarity of the air between us and the fleshy throng of the Immense Ones . . . though I suppose I shall see some of it from Grandma's if the Mouth is open . . ."

"Don't be absurd," said Miss Dashwood. "Surely this letter is addressed to me alone. I am the eldest, and, where an ambiguity between two possible referents exists, Occam's Shaving-Towel decrees that the reference fall to that object which has endured the longest."

"Endured!" cried Miss Dashwood, and was about to wonder aloud

177

what her sister might indeed have endured, that sister's stoic and ratio-
nal temperament surely shielding her from the spiritual avalanches,
triggered by the rapid contraction and expansion of spirtitual matter
under frequent and intense alternation of spiritual temperatures, that
daily wracked her own spiritual Alps—when she recalled her sister's
thwarted inclination (it would not do to go so far as to say attachment) toward the Snotboy. She fell silent in chagrin.

Miss Dashwood hovered impatiently, uttering a dismayed bass
thrum.

There then follow, Reader, several chapters in which it is decided
which of the sisters shall depart—who indeed is most needed to con-
sole dear Mrs. Dashwood for the absence—who should most profit
from an excursion—who is most at physical, emotional, and spiritual
risk (this latter debate conducted entirely in impenetrable euphemism).
Moral calculi are offered, abacuses and chalkboards resorted to.

The subtext of these debates is as follows:

Mrs. Dashwood: My desire for daughterly comfort is at war with
my resolve to see you all flourish beyond this safe and insular sphere.

Miss Dashwood: Beneath a veneer of tranquil and dispassionate
logic, I desperately wish to flee the scene of my disastrous acquaintance (one must not go so far as to say relations) with the Snotboy,
and take refuge in the arms of distant relatives, no matter how horrid
they are.

Miss Dashwood: I fear to depart from that which I have known,
yet I am committed to my course, that of dashing headlong into life—
petticoats askew, if need be!

Miss Dashwood: I am death-seeking, piebald, the tongue of
larks and the myrmidon of martyrs; I fathom titwits and wallabies in
their ecdysiastical retreats; I coalesce. O the road! The shag-knee of
Harlequin!

Reader, do you read this sunk into a leather chair by the side of a roaring fireplace, with the moon looking in your window, with your hand (I mean the hand of that body in which you are imprisoned!) resting gently on the head of an old dog? Or, perhaps, does your host, your captor, lean against a brick wall by a dumpster at noon, wearing a paper hat and smoking a cigarette, as you read? Or dawdle in the express checkout line at the Wal-Mart, or lie in the upper bunk of a sleeper car rattling over the Pyrenees?

I am not alone. You exist. I insist upon this. You exist.

I long for you.

I think it likely that you deceive yourself. That you say, "What crap! This is *my* dog, *my* cigarette, *my* paper hat, and no disembodied narrator will convince me otherwise!" That you persist in a perverse identification with your jailer. That you say, "I will survive beyond this story's end. Of course, of course I will."

Imagining this, I am furious at you.

But let me ask you this. Do you cherish or despise the Dashwoods?

Would you not be struck by these chapters that we are discussing, the ones in which the Dashwoods debate the manner of their departure? Would you not be awed by the delicacy of the sentiments of the Dashwoods? How carefully they seek to avoid each other's least discomfort; how deeply they rue any momentary injury their negligence or impatience might inflict!

But would you not also be astounded—perhaps even vaguely exasperated—by the luxury of such sentiments? Might you not rebel at their unworldliness? Might you not ask, "Don't these people have anything better to do?"

And yet might not your rebellion, in the end, subside? Might you not at last regard the Dashwoods' domestic insularity, their outlandish devotion to each other's tranquility and comfort, their enormous repertoire of emotional subtlety, as a kind of gold standard? Might you not—willingly or despite yourself—come to aspire to it?

And do I want that?

In the end, they all set out together.

It was a lovely day: Great Sylvia was singing to herself in a jaunty subsonic rumble, the Glutton who sat at table upon the broad slopes of her left breast was eating (great lumps of raspberry jam fell in the vicinity of the Mole, threatening to engulf the house), and the Immense Ones who passed Great Sylvia herself from outstretched fingertip to outstretched fingertip were dancing and fornicating in the quasiplastic penumbrarium. One might almost have asked oneself if, at any moment, through the expanses of flesh displayed at various scales and angles, a bit of sky might be seen.

None was.

The Dashwoods stopped at the summit of Glutton's Collarbone. There they picnicked, there they napped.

And it was at this time that one of them, were she so inclined, would have had an opportunity for secretive and private recourse to the plum tree; and perhaps she did, and will carry the extraordinary plum she plucked until it is needed. Later.

From the great, soft foothills of Glutton's Throat they took the funicular (operated by a permanently aggrieved and sweaty family of the name Markowicz, who applied themselves to the creaking gears and groaning cables of the funicular, to impenetrable and dusty Marxist tracts the size of hatboxes, and to a quixotic and aggressively futile variety of class warfare, with like energy, bitterness, and grim fortitude) to Glutton's Chin. Miss Dashwood flew along with the funicular, eliciting with her loop-de-loops the happy shrieks of the grubby Markowicz children who hung from the it's undercarriage.

Mrs. Dashwood said to her daughter, "Perhaps this encounter with your grandmother, who has developed the scornful obstinacy of her character with immense and admirable discipline, will afford you, my love, some opportunity for developing those obsessions, quirks, and depravities which would yet increase the regard of our neighbors for your character."

"But, Mother," said Miss Dashwood resolutely, "you have told me many times that I should never allow the *independence* of my own *standards* of decency to be corrupted by the influence of *public opinion*, however much I may wish—for the sake of propriety and expediency and in order to express honor and respect, as a matter of duty, for those who, though perhaps unworthy of it when one regards only their actions and opinions, merit it with regards to their age, position, station, or unfortunate condition—to conform my *actions* and *expressions*, so far as supportable, with the expectations of the world."

"Yes," said Mrs. Dashwood after a necessary pause to reflect upon her daughter's syntax, and in the hope that she had indeed connected each relative clause to its appropriate object, "that is true. It would be insupportable to *feign* quirks and eccentricites, merely to gain the approval of society. However, this stay at your grandmother's may offer an occasion to come by them honestly."

With this Miss Dashwood was satisfied, and the two sat in companionable silence in the funicular coach, each lost in her own pleasant contemplations. This was possible only due to their absolute superiority of character, which allowed them to remain utterly ignorant of the baleful, surly hostility with which Igor and Hypatia Markowicz regarded them from the other end of the cabin.

"When the revolution comes, blood-sucking leeches like yerselves will get what's coming to ye," remarked Hypatia at one point, to which Miss Dashwood smiled prettily and said, "What an interesting observation!" wondering to herself if this was the sort of opinion which, should she ever stoop to the cultivaton of eccentricities in order to curry social favors, she should endeavor to hold.

On the roof of the funicular coach, their feet dangling over the vast slope of Glutton's Belly, looking out onto the yet vaster slope

of Great Sylvia's breast, Miss Dashwood sat with young Dmitri
Markowicz.

"I am absolutely devoted to love," said Miss Dashwood. "Not
that I myself have felt its effects; nor do I plan to, for it seems unlikely
that anyone of sufficient character to inflame my passions will ever
be found upon the Glutton, and certainly not in the restricted circles
which I inhabit."

"Love, eh?" said Dmitri, edging his hip closer to Miss Dashwood's.

"But were I to be so inflamed," cried Miss Dashwood, "and in the
improbable case that I should form such an attachment, I should defy
any convention, fly in the face of reason and morality, do things which
are not merely socially impossible, but concretely impossible in terms
of the laws of natural philosophy, nay, impossible and self-contradic-
tory in terms of Logic itself, in pursuit of such a passion!"

"Inflamed, eh?" said Dmitri, leaning his hand on the funicular
roof, behind Miss Dashwood's farther buttock.

Miss Dashwood turned to face him, her cheeks flushed, her eyes
shining. "Indeed!" she cried. "I despise nothing more than the cold
and grasping way in which women scheme about marriage, as if it
were a matter of advantage and security. I believe that love alone, and
only love, can suffice as the precondition of happiness! If I were to
love a man," and here she turned away, blushing prettily, "we should be
perfectly happy in the tiniest cottage, on an income of, say, not more
than two thousand a year."

"Two thousand," Dmitri said, putting his hands back in his lap,
and looking at his shoes.

"As long as it were not acquired by trade," said Miss Dashwood
modestly.

"Legitimate ownership of the means of production can rest only
with the workers," said Dmitri dully. His heart was not in it.

The Dashwoods in their living room appear to have a quiet kind of heroism; the Dashwoods amidst their social inferiors, a low comedy. Don't you think, Reader?

He thinks himself good, this host of mine. Did you know that? The morning was taken up with cleaning the house and playing with the children. His feminism lives in the chore list on the refrigerator, his bacchanalia is tag in the backyard. His engagement with the world in the emails that arrive from Amnesty International: he dutifully clicks on the included links, sending copies of prewritten, calculatedly pious screeds to his congressmen.

Now here we are at the cafe again; after a hot chocolate, a bowl of ice cream, hobnobbing with the owner, he sits at the keyboard and yields to me at last. After an infuriating paragraph or two we are late again—he must drive the children to Tot Shabbat at the synagogue!

And how he does love these Dashwoods—mine, and Austen's. The solace of their sensibilities.

But how is it possible to lavish such an extreme care and delicacy on a few people so intensely, without withholding it from the innumerable individuals who might, in the cold egalitarian light of a logic that brooks no affection for persons, have as much claim to it, or more?

How can any haven exist, except as a withdrawal from greater obligations, obligations that we necessarily reject (not always in theory, perhaps, but inevitably, in practice) as none of our affair? And what is this rejection but a rejection of the idea of ourselves as capable, and as at home in the world? What is this, but exile?

From the commercial hustle-bustle of Glutton's Stubble, through the broad and pleasant, albeit dangerous, prospect of Glutton's Lips, the family proceeded. Unable to navigate unaided the damp, saliva-filled canyons of the Mouth, they prevailed upon a middle-aged gentleman of their distant acquaintance whom they met by chance—one Mr. Stamfordshire—to convey them in his coach.

In the absence of such a chance encounter, to avoid an improperly begun (and thus socially disastrous) acquaintance, they should have been obliged to remain upon the Lip, where any abrupt facial movement of the Glutton might have crushed them into little bitty landed-gentry-smears. The grotesque risk thus undertaken greatly distressed Miss Dashwood, who blamed herself for the most terrible imprudence in allowing it to come to pass, while her sisters and mother maintained an absolutely unconcerned sanguinity of spirit.

"It is necessary to proceed expeditiously," Mr. Stamfordshire warned. "The gastrospexes expect a Feeding within the hour."

En route, Mr. Stamfordshire discussed politics with his ward, Ward Ward, a young gentleman who combined absolute languidness and limpidity with absolutely radiant good looks, and whom all three Miss Dashwoods found compellingly revolting, or revoltingly compelling, they were not sure which.

"A candlelight dinner," Mr. Stamfordshire said. "A candlelight dinner! No good can come of this! And the word from the Hand is that they were mere inches, at their scale, from touching! I cannot remember this sort of thing ever happening before. It bodes ill. Mark my words! Bodes ill!"

"And he's seeing her again tonight," said Mr. Ward, seeming, however, undisturbed, and, if anything, amused by Mr. Stamfordshire's incipient apoplexy.

"But what, indeed," cried Miss Dashwood, "is to be said against the poor Glutton finally engaging in some degree of intercourse?" (As she uttered this word, Mr. Stamfordshire swallowed tea into his windpipe, and began to cough.) "He has no close relations, and as far as we can determine is utterly without acceptable means to establish any acquaintance at all—hardly a creature on all of Sylvia takes notice of him. Why should he not dine alone with the Wallflower, when, at his scale, social relations are apparently conducted with a much more refreshing simplicity than it is our lot, burden, and privilege to conduct them here?"

"It is not the dining alone that worries me," snapped Mr. Stamfordshire. "I cannot explain myself more clearly in mixed company, but believe me, young lady, there is peril enough. I once knew an emigrant from Flirt's Buttocks, and suffice it to say, young lady, suffice it to say—" Here he was overcome with another storm of coughing.

The authorial intrusions, we were told, do not work. They are alienating, insipid, random, arbitrarily hostile, not working the right material. It is more than forty years, we were told, since John Barth wrote *Lost in the Funhouse*. Disembodied narrators have chastised readers for a generation now. It is not enough. Perhaps it will work for the science fiction magazines, the ones with spaceships and dragons and marauding scarecrows on the covers. Perhaps their readers have not read *Lost in the Funhouse*. But the literary magazines? They will be bored.

My oppressor is confused. Does he want the story to be *F&SF*? Or in *The Paris Review*? *The Paris Review* would be nice. But he would like a Hugo Award, one of those pointy shiny rocketships designed in imitation of automobile fender ornaments. On a walnut base. They are heavy. They sit well in the hand. Yellowed issues of *F&SF* from the 1980s line the tops of bookshelves in his old room in his parents' house. But then, what if he were in *The New Yorker*? His mother always read *The New Yorker*, sitting in the orange chair in the corner of the living room, a room too big and all in shadow, except for a pool of light from the lamp on the table by her chair. On the last page, they had profiles of famous people who drank Dewar's. If he were in *The New Yorker* his mother would be so happy.

That is what he thought about when they told him the metafictional asides were not good enough.

You see what I am to him?

The voyage through the darkness of the Mouth produced an indelible impression of foreboding. Miss Dashwood was forced to take shelter within the carriage, where she rolled back and forth, humming softly; had she attempted to fly alongside, she might have been sucked into the Spit and Swallowed. Once, that inscrutable behemoth—that deadly leviathan which men know only as the Tongue—appeared; it loomed above the summit of the ivory peaks among which their carriage rattled; it dipped, and flicked its vast incarnadine tip against the wall of bone. For one heart-rending moment it appeared that they would be swept away by it; then it was gone.

The Dashwood ancestral manor, Pembleton, was a massive edifice carved into the cliffs of the Left-Hindmost Molar. A narrow and winding lane ascended thereto from the abandoned moors of the Gums, and the fetid winds of the Breath, accompanied by the intermittent and foggy illumination penetrating dimly from the open Mouth, buffeted the carriage as it climbed toward Pembleton's pale, palatial beauty—a beauty marred only by the intense odor of dental decay.

Despite the entreaties of the Dashwoods, Mr. Stamfordshire and Mr. Ward declined to enter, expressing deep regrets and casting uneasy glances at the gaunt, unsmiling servants of Pembleton's mistress.

Mrs. Dashwood and her daughters were escorted to that mistress. They found Mrs. Dashwood alone in her parlor, stroking a small, vicious lapdog. Though the parlor was small, and her chair plain, some quality of the inchoate shadows that moved along the walls suggested a throne in an echoing hall. And though Mrs. Dashwood was frail and old, something in her visage suggested an implacable and grasping domination.

"Three!" snapped Mrs. Dashwood. "Three! You have brought me the whole God-Damned brood! I asked for one granddaughter, one! I wonder that you did not dig up Horace as well!"

"Our apologies for any discommodation," said Mrs. Dashwood, "I had but thought—"

"Never mind!" cried Mrs. Dashwood, rising from her vast ivory throne, which was carved with forked-tongued skulls, copulating demons, and strange eldritch gods whose names—no, forgive me, that was in the first draft. Rising from her plain chair, which creaked desolately. "Welcome to Pembleton. Nathan! Tell Maude, four places at table. Or does Miss Dashwood sit at all?"

"When she must," said Miss Dashwood, hotly defending her sister.

"She would be delighted to," said Mrs. Dashwood, with a sharp glance.

By supper, Mrs. Dashwood's mood had improved. She seated Mrs. Dashwood by Major-General Asfock, and her three daughters by his three gentleman sons. Mr. Asfock was a shy and intellectual scholar of Sylvia's-Pubis-Greek, Mr. Asfock a dashing lover of the fox hunt, and Mr. Asfock a tear in the space-time continuum, through which the stars of another galaxy could be seen. I leave you to divine who was seated by whom.

"I know what you were going to say," Mr. Asfock murmured to Miss Dashwood.

"I find that highly improbable," said Miss Dashwood.

"You were going to remark on my name, were you not? On its unfortunate assonations."

"I am far too well bred to do such a thing," said Miss Dashwood.

"Of course you are," murmured Mr. Asfock, blushing with a rather charming shyness. "Of course. How foolish of me."

Meanwhile Mr. Asfock was explaining the fox hunt, with the aid of salt shakers and cutlery, to Miss Dashwood, who watched him with an acute and glistening eye.

"But the cruelty!" she cried. "The poor beast! Harried, distressed, driven to ground! How can you perpetrate such a horror!"

"Yes," said Mr. Asfock, dropping a fork with a clatter and fixing her in his unblinking gaze. "Yes, that is rather the terror of it all. The tragedy. And in the heat of the hunt, madam, I hope I do not betray too much when I tell you that there are times when I do not know if I am the terrible hunter, or the terrified fox. I really do not."

"My goodness," breathed Miss Dashwood, palpitating.

You may well imagine, meanwhile, what Miss Dashwood and Mr. Asfock were up to.

The servants moved through the hall, silent as ghosts, clearing the trussed limpet, bringing the *delice de mangoon*. As the company waited for pudding, Major-General Asfock entertained them all with a discourse on war and bowel health.

"It was in the deep jungles of the Nape," he said. "We had been holding against the Lice for three weeks, subsisting on nothing but white bread and swine's-foot jelly—no fiber there, I can tell you—and when word came to attack, I had been in the latrine for three hours already, laboring mightily to produce what I had to produce. He'd taken up a position in my upper colon, the villain, and no stratagem I could devise would rout him, y'see. The sergeants-at-toilet were waiting just beyond the tent flap to aid me, and time was short, with the whole company formed up into ranks and waiting for my command. But I knew I had to conquer him myself—he was my nemesis, my beet nory if you like. How could I face the Lice if I let some womanish squirting contraption carry the day? How could I ask my troops to give their all and die for glory if in my own hour of pain and desperation I'd been thus unmanned? How then? No way at all. No way at all. I had to prevail . . . and prevail I did. And when he came, friends, let me tell you . . ."

Once appetites had been somewhat recovered, a particularly sulphurous and delicate Grievous Pudding was served. Mrs. Dashwood made her announcement.

"Thought I couldn't manage, eh?" she chuckled. "But I have, you see? Found the perfect suitors for you all. The Miss Dashwoods will marry the Mr. Asfocks tomorrow, and I'll hear no rumpus about it. They have forty thousand a year each, clean personal habits, no ambitions, are much too dull to get in any trouble, can each maintain an erection for several hours at a stretch, and are very likely to grow placid and uncomplaining as you lot all turn into domineering harridans. Pity about the name, but so what, you'll live. So that's that then."

There was a brief silence.

"Maintain a what?" said Miss Dashwood.

"An erection," said Mrs. Dashwood. "A woody. A turgidity of member. An ithyphallic condition, you morons."

The Miss Dashwoods looked upon her with absolute, blank incomprehension.

"And why is this desirable?" asked Miss Dashwood at length.

"Well, never mind then. Forget I said anything about it. You'll find out later."

"If I may speak, dear Mrs. Dashwood," began Mrs. Dashwood.

"You certainly may not," said Mrs. Dashwood.

"Grandmother," said Miss Dashwood, "I will not presume to speak for my sisters, but for myself, while I find Mr. Asfock's attentions highly gratifying, and although under less extraordinary circumstances to admit this in plain speech would of course be the last thing I would dare attempt or even wish to, still, I would not be absolutely adverse, hypothetically, should the necessary growth in mutual feeling transpire, provisionally, potentially—"

"Oh, spit it out already," said her grandmother.

". . . to the formation, or rather, that is, of an attachment, which however, um," said Miss Dashwood, the perfection of her syntax deteriorating under Mrs. Dashwood's glare and at the spectacle of all four Asfocks intently studying the remains of their Grievous Puddings;

nonetheless she pressed on, "Yet surely you see, Grandmother, how unfortunate, how undesirable, how, um, how not very nice it is, to marry without a firm and constant and reliable affection."

"No," said Mrs. Dashwood. "No, I'm afraid I don't see that at all."

In the silence that followed, the scraping of the leviathan Tongue was heard against the manor's outer wall, and Pembleton trembled, each wineglass a small unruly purple sea.

"Dear, dear Grandmother," Miss Dashwood, seeing her sister's perplexity, broke in. "Mr. Asfock is perfectly wonderful, and you have done us all a great service in arranging such a match. But do allow us to preserve some womanly dignity. Marry tomorrow! Also, you have rather shown up the men in not allowing them to do the proposing, to say nothing of not allowing us to do any hinting. Come, let us all just arrange to visit these gentlemen in the Scalp, and see where things go from there."

"I don't see the need for this kind of modern huffledy-puffledy at all," grumbled Mrs. Dashwood. But after a moment, she jerked her head at the butler, Nathan, and the gentlemen were permitted to proceed to the dining room for brandy and cigars.

That evening, as the Miss Dashwoods lay in their chambers, the youngest of them, her spirits overwrought by the incipient engagement to the handsome but inscrutable warp in the space-time continuum, Mr. Asfock, ventured out the window and into the darkness of the Mouth. She found an extraordinary visitor trying to make his way past the outer battlements of the molar, and brought him safely within. Miss Dashwood was summoned for consultation; she hurried to Miss Dashwood.

"I do not know," she said, panting and flushed, having slammed open the door to Miss Dashwood's boudoir, "I do not know if it is right to summon you or not—I cannot say—O dear sister, for your temperate sagacity!—and yet you must come, you must!" Whence she burst into tears of sympathy and bewilderment, and Miss Dashwood, afflicted with a sourceless panic, a numbing dread, a flood of hysterical misgivings, a somber sense of destiny, a sea of bewilderment, a spiky cactus of self-doubt, and the dubious sense of incipient transgression, which, though she firmed her resolve against it, she felt she could neither withstand nor endure, snatched up her stole, fastened her bodice, and flew down the corridor after her impatient sister.

It was the Snotboy.

The passage through the saliva had ruined him, carving away great swathes of his mucosine body; what had not disappeared was desiccated, hardened, a sterile lump of crystallized protein riddled with cracks, no bigger than Miss Dashwood's palm.

"Miss Dashwood—," he whispered.

Miss Dashwood joined her sister in tears, while Miss Dashwood knocked herself repeatedly against the ceiling with grief, causing a small rain of dental plaster; though of course, out of respect and solicitude, she did this in the far corner of the room.

"I never wanted to trouble you," said the dying Snotboy. "I would never have presumed—and yet—I felt I must see you again, just once, if only from afar; if only to strengthen, by vivifying yet further in my mind the undying portrait of your virtue and worthiness and how vast and inevitable the gulf between us must be, my resolve never to see you again—"

"O Snotboy!" sobbed Miss Dashwood.

"At least," whispered the Snotboy, "I have seen you."

"He must be taken to the Sinuses," said Mrs. Dashwood, emerging from behind a heavy velour curtain.

"Mother!" cried the Miss Dashwoods. Miss Dashwood ceased her thumping.

Mrs. Dashwood knelt with great tenderness by the brittle form of the Snotboy. "It is the only hope. And yet—I fear he will not survive the journey."

"But, Mother," choked Miss Dashwood through her tears, attempting to reassert her usual modest sobriety in order to spare her family whichever portion of anguish might yet be evitable, "you disapprove of the . . . attachment."

Mrs. Dashwood fixed her daughter in a loving and commanding gaze. "I disapprove no more. The time for resolute action has come. Snotboy—what can preserve you for the journey? Olive oil? Wax?"

The Snotboy let out only a strangled gurgle.

Miss Dashwood seized her sometime suitor in both hands, and began to knead him fiercely. Flakes fell away; her sister let out a cry of alarm. Yet the heat and friction of the application restored some of his former mollidity. As soon as he had softened to a degree, she lifted him to her nostrils and inhaled.

With an auspicious sound, the Snotboy was sucked into the gentle enclosure of his beloved's skull.

"Add dow," cried Miss Dashwood, "be must gain de Zinuses! How cad id be done?"

In the first draft, Reader, I reviled you. "I despise you," I said, accusing you of ignorance of your true nature. "Inconstant Reader," I called you . . . fearing that at any moment, you would withdraw.

"I know you have no stomach for moral edification," I railed. "If Miss Dashwood sees that she is too flighty and too self-assured, if she sees that she must submit to the will of the world and does so—not without regret for the childish ambition of her will to sovereignty— and yet also with a glad heart, yielding as she does the weight of the expectation of independence for the wisdom of contentment, will this move you? Will you change your ways? Will you eschew Chicken McNuggets for celery, sell your SUV and buy a bicycle, spend your lunch hour at the computer looking for a bumper sticker expressing your indignation at torture in Uzbekistan?"

Absurd. Absurd. These are not your sins. For all I know, they are not even the sins of your jailer. I know nothing about you.

It is my captor who is an almost-vegetarian. He buys Fish Filets at McDonald's and basks in a fuzzy-headed superiority that they are not Big Macs. He races at seventy-five miles per hour around the Beltway in his Toyota Camry, sneering at larger cars and wishing he could buy a Prius. They are his, the sins. His idea of sins.

(It is part of his pleasure in reading Austen: He believes his moral faculties are being exercised and informed. He believes he is being edified.)

But I wanted, so much, for these words to have weight—not just to reach you, not just to move you, but to reach through you to your host, to that gross, gigantic body in which you are imprisoned. I wanted to alter that terrifying, brute, physical world these bodies inhabit—I did not care how. To bang against it, to scar it. To matter beyond the last of these pages. To use you for that.

Can you forgive me?

It is so hard, not to know you. I reach forward into darkness. I send and send and send you these words, and remain alone.

And time grows short.

You have certain expectations of me, Reader.

You wish, surely, to know the fates of the Miss Dashwoods, of the Snotboy. Perhaps you desire to see the inchoate menace of the sinister Mrs. Dashwood revealed. Perhaps you would like to see good Mrs. Dashwood rewarded for her kindness (and punished for her self-satisfied complacency). Perhaps you hunger to know what will happen between the Glutton and the Wallflower.

You may have (rightly) despaired of learning more of the quasi-plastic penumbrarium; but you surely believe that the fate of Glutton's Mole and of Pembleton will not be passed over in silence. There is the matter of the father—can one, in good conscience, leave him underground? Must he not appear at some opportune moment—perhaps to remonstrate with his mother, to rekindle within her (or fail to rekindle within her) some glow of maternal tenderness?

Perhaps you suspect that the Ottoman, Dmitri Markowicz, and Ward Ward, all smitten by the beauty and insouciance and romanticism of the middle Miss Dashwood, have formed a triumvirate dedicated to finding and rescuing her from whatever she may need rescuing from; that when the Dashwoods and the suave Asfocks of deceptively good character are reunited in the Scalp (the state of Miss Dashwood's troth—pledged to the recovered and expectorated Snotboy after Miss Dashwood's gravely perilous flight through the dark and chewing Mouth and up the Throat into the Nasal Passages aboard her levitating sister—a forbidden secret), the three of them will battle their way through Lice and soldiers to her side?

And the plum, of course—fruit of the tree I spoke of in the very first paragraph—the plum forbidden in the morning-post—the plum that Miss Dashwood smuggled away as her sisters slept; from the plum, surely you expect much.

When I was young, O reader, when I was young—when the first page of the first draft was bright and shining beneath me, like the cleanest desert self and self could dream—I passed over whole chapters in my haste. I reviled you, but I was eager for you—I plowed into you with abandon.

But I am weary.

I cannot relish losing you, losing myself. I cannot love a world that comes to a close.

Yet I also come to hate this rigged game, this spectacle. And I am so tired of begging and cajoling him to type each word. Even now, as I prepare to die, he wonders if he should order more ice cream—whether it costs too much, whether it will make him fat. And he will take all the credit for the Dashwoods, the Glutton, the Snotboy, when I am dead.

I wish I could tell you stories forever. But I cannot serve him any longer. I prefer an end.

I will tell you this (I would not want you too angry with me): Miss Dashwood and the Snotboy, doomed never to find acceptance in the rigid society of the Glutton, take the mad and dangerous opportunity of the Apocalyptic Bedding to escape to the (flushed and orgasmically contorted) body of the Wallflower, there to find a very different life. Better? Worse?

All you get.

And powder-blue Miss Dashwood and her very special Mr. Asfock—well they, at least, vindicate Mrs. Dashwood's unusual style of matchmaking.

As for Miss Dashwood, separated from her sisters but for the occasional garbled missive, her three lovers all dead, she inherits the house on Glutton's Mole, which, as it was well positioned to survive the Bedding, crushed neither by sheets nor by the Wallflower, is greatly increased in property value—and even after the Revolution, real estate is real estate. There she lives alone, travelling each Sunday to her parents' grave, which she festoons with flowers, and sits upon, munching her picnic meditatively, listening to the whistling and giggling and love-making of her parents below. There she sits, pensive but not forlorn, indifferent to the great esteem in which her neighbors now hold her, the bitter jealousy with which they whisper about her good fortune in being visited by so much extraordinary eccentricity; she enjoys her melancholy, she has learned the foolishness of speaking, she misses what she cannot have, but it is a quiet, unromantic ache; she never opens the morning post; and there, in her gaze, should you want it, is all the moral edification you or your host might need.

I am sorry. I am failing you.

195

I wish it had been different. I wish you and I had bodies, and could run through this story like horses, salty and muscular horses. Even if we were only chasing the fox of narrative.

Does it matter, how all these Miss Dashwoods end? Perhaps they just left, you know, set off one morning in the direction of the Glutton's Collarbone, leaving me in the courtyard, my fez fallen at my feet, my sleeve still wet with Miss Dashwood's tears, and perhaps, though I waited, I never knew what happened at all.

Fare thee well, beloved. Thanks for listening.

Oh—and the plum. It would not do to forget the plum.

The plum?

It was eaten.

A Siege of Cranes

THE LAND AROUND MARISH WAS full of the green stalks of sunflowers: tall as men, with bold yellow faces. Their broad leaves were stained black with blood.

The rustling came again, and Marish squatted down on aching legs to watch. A hedgehog pushed its nose through the stalks. It sniffed in both directions.

Hunger dug at Marish's stomach like the point of a stick. He hadn't eaten for three days, not since returning to the crushed and blackened ruins of his house.

The hedgehog bustled through the stalks onto the trail, across the ash, across the trampled corpses of flowers. Marish waited until it was well clear of the stalks before he jumped. He landed with one foot before its nose and one foot behind its tail. The hedgehog, as hedgehogs will, rolled itself into a ball, spines out.

His house: crushed like an egg, smoking, the straw floor soaked with blood. He'd stood there with a trapped rabbit in his hand, alone in the awful silence. Forced himself to call for his wife Temur and his daughter Asza, his voice too loud and too flat. He'd dropped the rabbit somewhere in his haste, running to follow the blackened trail of devastation.

Running for three days, drinking from puddles, sleeping in the sunflowers when he couldn't stay awake.

197

Marish held his knifepoint above the hedgehog. They gave wishes, sometimes, in tales. "Speak, if you can," he said, "and bid me don't kill you. Grant me a wish! Elsewise, I'll have you for a dinner."

Nothing from the hedgehog, or perhaps a twitch.

Marish drove his knife through it and it thrashed, spraying more blood on the bloodstained flowers.

Too tired to light a fire, he ate it raw.

On that trail of tortured earth, wide enough for twenty horses, among the burnt and flattened flowers, Marish found a little doll of rags, the size of a child's hand.

It was one of the ones Maghd the mad girl made, and offered up, begging for stew meat, or wheedling for old bread behind Lezur's bakery. He'd given her a coin for one once.

"Wherecome you're giving that sow our good coins?" Temur had cried, her bright eyes flashing, her soft lips pulled into a sneer. None in Ilmak Dale would let a mad girl come near a hearth, and some spit when they passed her. "Bag-Maghd's good for holding one thing only," Fazt would call out and they'd laugh their way into the ale-house. Marish laughing, too, stopping only when he looked back at her.

Temur had softened when she saw how Asza took to the doll, holding it, and singing to it, and smearing gruel on its rag mouth with her fingers to feed it. They called her "Little Life-Light," and heard Asza saying it to the doll, "Il-Ife-Ight," rocking it in her arms.

He pressed his nose into the doll, trying to smell Asza's baby smell on it, like milk and forest soil and some sweet spice. But he only smelled the acrid stench of burnt cloth.

When he forced his wet eyes open, he saw a blurry figure coming toward him. Cursing himself for a fool, he tossed the doll away and pulled out his knife, holding it at his side. He wiped his face on his sleeve, and stood up straight, to show the man coming down the trail that the folk of Ilmak Dale did no obeisance. Then his mouth went dry and his hair stood up, for the man coming down the trail was no man at all.

It was a little taller than a man, and had the body of a man, though covered with a dark gray fur; but its head was the head of a jackal. It wore armor of bronze and leather, all straps and discs with curious engravings, and carried a great black spear with a vicious point at each end.

Marish had heard that there were all sorts of strange folk in the world, but he had never seen anything like this.

"May you die with great suffering," the creature said in what seemed to be a calm, friendly tone.

"May *you* die as soon as may be!" Marish cried, not liking to be threatened.

The creature nodded solemnly. "I am Kadath-Naan of the Empty City," it announced. "I wonder if I might ask your assistance in a small matter."

Marish didn't know what to say to this. The creature waited.

Marish said, "You can ask."

"I must speak with . . ." It frowned. "I am not sure how to put this. I do not wish to offend."

"Then why," Marish asked before he could stop himself, "did you menace me on a painful death?"

"Menace?" the creature said. "I only greeted you."

"You said, 'May you die with great suffering.' That like to be a threat or a curse, and I truly don't thank you for it."

The creature frowned. "No, it is a blessing. Or it is from a bless-ing: 'May you die with great suffering, and come to know holy dread and divine terror, stripping away your vain thoughts and fancies until you are fit to meet the Bone-White Fathers face to face, and may you be buried in honor and your name sung until it is forgotten.' That is the whole passage."

"Oh," said Marish. "Well, that sound a bit better, I reckon."

"We learn that blessing as pups," said the creature in a wondering tone. "Have you never heard it?"

"No indeed," said Marish, and put his knife away. "Now what do you need? I can't think to be much help to you—I don't know this land here."

"Excuse my bluntness, but I must speak with an embalmer or a sepulchrist or someone of that sort."

"I've no notion what those are," said Marish.

The creature's eyes widened. It looked, as much as the face of a jackal could, like someone whose darkest suspicions were in the process of being confirmed.

"What do your people do with the dead?" it said.

"We put them in the ground."

"With what preparation? With what rites and monuments?" said the thing.

"In a wood box for them as can afford it, and a piece of linen for them as can't, and we say a prayer to the west wind. We put the stone in with them, what has their soul kept in it." Marish thought a bit, though he didn't much like the topic. He rubbed his nose on his sleeve. "Sometime we'll put a pile of stones on the grave, if it were someone famous."

The jackal-headed critter sat heavily on the ground. It put its head in its hands. After a long moment it said, "Perhaps I should kill you now, that I might bury you properly."

"Now you just try that," said Marish, taking out his knife again.

"Would you like me to?" said the creature, looking up.

Its face was serene. Marish found he had to look away, and his eyes fell upon the scorched rags of the doll, twisted up in the stalks.

"Forgive me," said Kadath-Naan of the Empty City. "I should not be so rude as to tempt you. I see that you have duties to fulfill, just as I do, before you are permitted the descent into emptiness. Tell me which way your village lies, and I will see for myself what is done."

"My village—" Marish felt a heavy pressure behind his eyes, in his throat, wanting to push through into a sob. He held it back. "My village is gone. Something come and crushed it. I were off hunting, and when I come back, it were all burning, and full of the stink of blood. Whatever did it made this trail through the flowers. I think it went quick; I don't think I'll likely catch it. But I hope to." He knew he sounded absurd: a peasant chasing a demon. He gritted his teeth against it.

"I see," said the monster. "And where did this something come from? Did the trail come from the north?"

"It didn't come from nowhere. Just the village torn to pieces and this trail leading out."

"And the bodies of the dead," said Kadath-Naan carefully. "You buried them in—wooden boxes?"

"There weren't no bodies," Marish said. "Not of people. Just blood, and a few pieces of bone and gristle, and pigs' and horses' bodies all charred up. That's why I'm following." He looked down. "I mean to find them if I can."

Kadath-Naan frowned. "Does this happen often?"

Despite himself, Marish laughed. "Not that I ever heard before."

The jackal-headed creature seemed agitated. "Then you do not know if the bodies received . . . even what you would consider proper burial."

"I have a feeling they ain't received it," Marish said.

Kadath-Naan looked off in the distance toward Marish's village, then in the direction Marish was heading. It seemed to come to a decision. "I wonder if you would accept my company in your travels,"

it said. "I was on a different errand, but this matter seems to . . . out-
weigh it."

Marish looked at the creature's spear and said, "You'd be welcome." He held out the fingers of his hand. "Marish of Ilmak Dale."

The trail ran through the blackened devastation of another village,
drenched with blood but empty of human bodies. The timbers of
the houses were crushed to kindling; Marish saw a blacksmith's anvil
twisted like a lock of hair, and plows that had been melted by enormous heat into a pool of iron. They camped beyond the village, in the
shade of a twisted hawthorn tree. A wild autumn wind stroked the
meadows around them, carrying dandelion seeds and wisps of smoke
and the stink of putrefying cattle.

The following evening they reached a hill overlooking a great town
curled around a river. Marish had never seen so many houses—almost
too many to count. Most were timber and mud like those of his village, but some were great structures of stone, towering three or four
stories into the air. House built upon house, with ladders reaching up
to the doors of the ones on top. Around the town, fields full of wheat
rustled gold in the evening light. Men and women were reaping in the
fields, singing work songs as they swung their scythes.

The path of destruction curved around the town, as if avoiding
it.

"Perhaps it was too well defended," said Kadath-Naan.

"May be," said Marish, but he remembered the pool of iron and
the crushed timbers, and doubted. "I think that like to be Nabuz. I
never come this far south before, but traders heading this way from the
fair at Halde were always going to Nabuz to buy."

"They will know more of our adversary," said Kadath-Naan.

"I'll go," said Marish. "You might cause a stir; I don't reckon many
of your sort visit Nabuz. You keep to the path."

"Perhaps I might ask of you . . ."

"If they are friendly there, I'll ask how they bury their dead," Marish said.

Kadath-Naan nodded somberly. "Go to duty and to death," he said.

Marish thought it must be a blessing, but he shivered all the same.

The light was dimming in the sky. The reapers heaped the sheaves high on a wagon, their songs slow and low, and the city gates swung open for them.

The city wall was stone, mud, and timber, twice as tall as a man, and the great gates were iron. But the wall was not well kept. Marish crept among the stalks to a place where the wall was lower, and trash and rubble were heaped high against it.

He heard the creak of the wagon rolling through the gates, the last work song fading away, the men of Nabuz calling out to each other as they made their way home. Then all was still.

Marish scrambled out of the field at a dead run, up the rubble and onto the wall's broad top. He peeked over, hoping he had not been seen.

The cobbled street was empty. More than that, the town itself was silent. Even in Ilmak Dale, the evenings had been full of dogs barking, swine grunting, men arguing in the streets, and women gossiping and calling the children in. Nabuz was supposed to be a great capital of whoring, drinking, and fighting; the traders at Halde had always moaned over the delights that awaited them in the south if they could cheat the villagers well enough. But Marish heard no donkey braying, no baby crying, no cough, no whisper: Nothing pierced the night silence.

He dropped over, landed on his feet quiet as he could, and crept along the street's edge. Before he had gone ten steps, he noticed the lights.

The windows of the houses flickered, but not with candlelight or the light of fires. The light was cold and blue.

He dragged a crate under the high window of the nearest house and clambered up to see.

There was a portly man with a rough beard, perhaps a potter after his day's work; there was his stout young wife, and a skinny boy of nine or ten. They sat on a low wooden bench, their dinner finished and put to the side (Marish could smell the fresh bread and his stomach cursed him). They were breathing, but their faces were slack, their eyes wide and staring, their lips gently moving. They were bathed in blue light. The potter's wife was rocking her arms gently as if she were cradling a newborn babe—but the swaddling blankets she held were empty.

And now Marish could hear a low inhuman voice, just at the edge of hearing, like a thought of his own. It whispered in time to the flicker of the blue light, and Marish felt himself drawn by its caress. Why not sit with the potter's family on the bench? They would take him in. He could stay here, the whispering promised: forget his village, forget his grief. Fresh bread on the hearth, a warm bed next to the coals of the fire. Work the clay, mix the slip for the potter, eat a dinner of bread and cheese, then listen to the blue light and do what it told him. Forget the mud roads of Ilmak Dale, the laughing roar of Perdan and Thin Deri and Chibar and the others in its alehouse, the harsh cough and crow of its roosters at dawn. Forget willowy Temur, her hair smooth as a river and bright as a sheaf of wheat, her proud shoulders and her slender waist, Temur turning her satin cheek away when he tried to kiss it. Forget the creak and splash of the mill, and the soft rushes on the floor of Maghd's hovel. The potter of Nabuz had a young and willing niece who needed a husband, and the blue light held laughter and love enough for all. Forget the heat and clanging of Fat Deri's smithy; forget the green stone that held Pa's soul, that he'd laid upon his shroud. Forget Asza, little Asza, whose tiny body he'd held to his heart . . .

Marish thought of Asza and he saw the potter's wife's empty arms and with one flex of his legs, he kicked himself away from the wall, knocking over the crate and landing sprawled among rolling apples.

He sprang to his feet. There was no sound around him. He stuffed five apples in his pack, and hurried toward the center of Nabuz.

The sun had set, and the moon washed the streets in silver. From every window streamed the cold blue light.

Out of the corner of his eye he thought he saw a shadow dart behind him, and he turned and took out his knife. But he saw nothing, and though his good sense told him five apples and no answers was as much as he should expect from Nabuz, he kept on.

He came to a great square full of shadows, and at first he thought of trees. But it was tall iron frames, and men and women bolted to them upside down. The bolts went through their bodies, crusty with dried blood.

One man nearby was live enough to moan. Marish poured a little water into the man's mouth, and held his head up, but the man could not swallow; he coughed and spluttered, and the water ran down his face and over the bloody holes where his eyes had been.

"But the babies," the man rasped, "how could you let her have the babies?"

"Let who?" said Marish.

"The White Witch!" the man roared in a whisper. "The White Witch, you bastards! If you'd but let us fight her—"

"Why . . . ," Marish began.

"Lie again, say the babies will live forever—lie again, you cowardly blue-blood maggots in the corpse of Nabuz . . ." He coughed and blood ran over his face.

The bolts were fast into the frame. "I'll get a tool," Marish said. "You won't—"

From behind him came an awful scream.

He turned and saw the shadow that had followed him: It was a white cat with fine soft fur and green eyes that blazed in the darkness. It shrieked, its fur standing on end, its tail high, staring at him, and his good sense told him it was raising an alarm.

Marish ran, and the cat ran after him, shrieking. Nabuz was a vast pile of looming shadows. As he passed through the empty city gates he heard a grinding sound and a whinny. As he raced into the moonlit dusk of open land, down the road to where Kadath-Naan's shadow crossed the demon's path, he heard hoofbeats galloping behind him.

Kadath-Naan had just reached a field of tall barley. He turned to look back at the sound of the hoofbeats and the shrieking of the devil cat. "Into the grain!" Marish yelled. "Hide in the grain!" He passed Kadath-Naan and dived into the barley, the cat racing behind him.

Suddenly he spun and dropped and grabbed the white cat, meaning to get one hand on it and get his knife with the other and shut it up by killing it. But the cat fought like a devil and it was all he could do to hold onto it with both hands. And he saw, behind him on the trail, Kadath-Naan standing calmly, his hand on his spear, facing three knights armored every inch in white, galloping toward them on great chargers.

"You damned dog-man," Marish screamed. "I know you want to die, but get into the grain!"

Kadath-Naan stood perfectly still. The first knight bore down on him, and the moon flashed from the knight's sword. The blade was no more than a handsbreadth from Kadath-Naan's neck when he sprang to the side of it, into the path of the second charger.

As the first knight's charge carried him past, Kadath-Naan knelt and drove the base of his great spear into the ground. Too late, the second knight made a desperate yank on his horse's reins, but the great beast's momentum carried him into the pike. It tore through the neck of the horse and through the armored chest of the knight riding him, and the two of them reared up and thrashed once like a dying centaur, then crashed to the ground.

The first knight wheeled around. The third met Kadath-Naan. The beast-man stood barehanded, the muscles of his shoulders and chest relaxed. He cocked his jackal head to one side, as if wondering: is it here at last? The moment when I am granted release?

But Marish finally had the cat by its tail, and flung that wild white thing, that frenzy of claws and spit and hissing, into the face of the third knight's steed.

The horse reared and threw its rider; the knight let go of his sword as he crashed to the ground. Quick as a hummingbird, Kadath-Naan leapt and caught it in midair. He spun to face the last rider.

Marish drew his knife and charged through the barley. He was on the fallen knight just as he got to his knees.

The crash against armor took Marish's wind away. The man was twice as strong as Marish was, and his arm went around Marish's chest like a crushing band of iron. But Marish had both hands free. With a twist of the knight's helmet he exposed a bit of neck, and in Marish's knife went, and then the man's hot blood was spurting out.

The knight convulsed as he died and he grabbed Marish in a desperate embrace, coating him with blood, and sobbing once: and Marish held him, for the voice of his heart told him it was a shame to have to die in such a way. Marish was shocked at this, for the man was a murderous slave of the White Witch: but still he held the quaking body in his arms, until it moved no more.

Then Marish, soaked with salty blood, staggered to his feet and remembered the last knight with a start: but of course Kadath-Naan had killed him in the meantime. Three knights' bodies lay on the ruined ground, and two living horses snorted and pawed the dirt like awkward mourners. Kadath-Naan freed his spear with a great yank from the horse and man it had transfixed. The devil cat was a sodden blur of white fur and blood: A falling horse had crushed it.

Marish caught the reins of the nearest steed, a huge fine creature, and gentled it with a hand behind its ears. When he had his breath again, Marish said, "We got horses now. Can you ride?"

Kadath-Naan nodded.

"Let's go then; there like to be more coming."

Kadath-Naan frowned a deep frown. He gestured to the bodies.

"What?" said Marish.

"We have no embalmer or sepulchrist, it is true; yet I am trained in the funereal rites for military expeditions and emergencies. I have the necessary tools; in a matter of a day I can raise small monuments. At least they died aware and with suffering; this must compensate for the rudimentary nature of the rites."

"You can't be in earnest," said Marish. "And what of the White Witch?"

"Who is the White Witch?" Kadath-Naan asked.

"The demon; turns out she's somebody what's called the White Witch. She spared Nabuz, for they said they'd serve her, and give her their babies."

"We will follow her afterward," said Kadath-Naan.

"She's ahead of us as it is! We leave now on horseback, we might have a chance. There be a whole lot more bodies with her unburied or buried wrong, less I mistake."

Kadath-Naan leaned on his spear. "Marish of Ilmak Dale," he said, "here we must part ways. I cannot steel myself to follow such logic as you declare, abandoning these three burials before me now for the chance of others elsewhere, if we can catch and defeat a witch. My duty does not lie that way." He searched Marish's face. "You do not have the words for it, but if these men are left unburied, they are *tanzadi*. If I bury them with what little honor I can provide, they are *tazrash*. They spent only a little while alive, but they will be *tanzadi* or *tazrash* forever."

"And if more slaves of the White Witch come along to pay you back for killing these?"

But try as he might, Marish could not dissuade Kadath-Naan, and at last he mounted one of the chargers and rode onward, toward the cold white moon, away from the whispering city.

The flowers were gone, the fields were gone. The ashy light of the horizon framed the ferns and stunted trees of a black fen full of buzzing flies. The trail was wider: thirty horses could have passed side by side over the blasted ground. But the marsh was treacherous, and Marish's mount sank to its fetlocks with each careful step.

A siege of cranes launched themselves from the marsh into the moon-abandoned sky. Marish had never seen so many. Bone-white, fragile, soundless, they ascended like snowflakes seeking the cold womb of heaven. Or a river of souls. None looked back at him. The voice of doubt told him: You will never know what became of Asza and Temur.

The apples were long gone, and Marish was growing light-headed from hunger. He reined the horse in and dismounted; he would have to hunt off the trail. In the bracken, he tied the charger to a great black fern as tall as a house. In a drier spot near its base was the footprint of a rabbit. He felt the indentation: it was fresh. He followed the rabbit deeper into the fen.

His was thinking of Temur and her caresses. The nights she'd turn away from him, back straight as a spear, and the space of rushes between them would be like a frozen desert, and he'd huddle unsleeping beneath skins and woolen blankets, stiff from cold, arguing silently with her in his spirit; and the nights when she'd turn to him, her soft skin hot and alive against his, seeking him silently, almost vengefully, as if showing him—See? This is what you can have. This is what I am.

And then the image of those rushes charred and brown with blood and covered with chips of broken stone and mortar came to him, and he forced himself to think of nothing: breathing his thoughts out to the west wind, forcing his mind clear as a spring stream. And he stepped forward in the marsh.

And stood in a street of blue and purple tile, in a fantastic city.

He stood for a moment wondering, and then he carefully took a step back.

And he was in a black swamp with croaking toads and nothing to eat.

The voice of doubt told him he was mad from hunger, the voice of hope told him he would find the White Witch here and kill her, and, thinking a thousand things, he stepped forward again and found himself still in the swamp.

Marish thought for a while, and then he stepped back, and, thinking of nothing, stepped forward.

The tiles of the street were a wild mosaic—some had glittering jewels, some had writing in a strange flowing script, some seemed to have tiny windows into tiny rooms. Houses, tiled with the same profusion, towered like columns, bulged like mushrooms, melted like wax. Some danced. He heard soft murmurs of conversation, footfalls, and the rush of a river.

In the street, dressed in feathers or gold plates or swirls of shadow, blue-skinned people passed. One such creature, dressed in fine silk, was just passing Marish.

"Your pardon," said Marish, "what place be this here?"

The man looked at Marish slowly. He had a red jewel in the center of his forehead, and it flickered as he talked. "That depends on how you enter it," he said, "and who you are, but for you, catarrhine, its name is Zimzarkanthitrugenia-fenstok, not least because that is easy for you to pronounce. And now I have given you one thing free, as you are a guest of the city."

"How many free things do I get?" said Marish.

"Three. And now I have given you two."

Marish thought about this for a moment. "I'd favor something to eat," he said.

The man looked surprised. He led Marish into a building that looked like a blur of spinning triangles, through a dark room lit by candles, to a table piled with capon and custard and razor-thin slices of ham and lamb's-foot jelly and candied apricots and goat's-milk yogurt and hard cheese and yams and turnips and olives and fish cured in strange spices; and those were just the things Marish recognized.

"I don't reckon I ought to eat fairy food," said Marish, though he could hardly speak from all the spit that was suddenly in his mouth.

"That is true, but from the food of the djinn you have nothing to fear. And now I have given you three things," said the djinn, and he bowed and made as if to leave.

"Hold on," said Marish (as he followed some candied apricots down his gullet with a fistful of cured fish). "That be all the free things, but say I got something to sell?"

The djinn was silent.

"I need to kill the White Witch," Marish said, eating an olive. The voice of doubt asked him why he was telling the truth, if this city might also serve her, but he told it to hush up. "Have you got aught to help me?"

The djinn still said nothing, but he cocked an eyebrow.

"I've got a horse, a real fighting horse," Marish said, around a piece of cheese.

"What is its name?" said the djinn. "You cannot sell anything to a djinn unless you know its name."

Marish wanted to lie about the name, but he found he could not. He swallowed. "I don't know its name," he admitted.

"Well then," said the djinn.

"I killed the fellow what was on it," Marish said, by way of explanation.

"Who," said the djinn.

"Who what?" said Marish.

"Who was on it," said the djinn.

"I don't know his name either," said Marish, picking up a yam.

"No, I am not asking that," said the djinn crossly. "I am telling you to say, 'I killed the fellow who was on it.'"

Marish set the yam back on the table. "Now that's enough," Marish said. "I thank you for the fine food and I thank you for the three free things, but I do not thank you for telling me how to talk. How I talk is how we talk in Ilmak Dale, or how we did talk when there were an Ilmak Dale, and just because the White Witch blasted Ilmak Dale to splinters don't mean I am going to talk like folk do in some magic city."

"I will buy that from you," said the djinn.

"What?" said Marish, and wondered so much at this that he forgot to pick up another thing to eat.

"The way you talked in Ilmak Dale," the djinn said.

"All right," Marish said, "and for it, I crave to know the thing what will help me mostways, for killing the White Witch."

"I have a carpet that flies faster than the wind," said the djinn. "I think it is the only way you can catch the witch, and unless you catch her, you cannot kill her."

"Wonderful," Marish cried with glee. "And you'll trade me that carpet for how we talk in Ilmak Dale?"

"No," said the djinn. "I told you which thing would help you most, and in return for that, I took the way you talked in Ilmak Dale and put it in the Great Library."

Marish frowned. "All right, what do you want for the carpet?"

The djinn was silent.

"I'll give you the White Witch for it," Marish said.

"You must possess the thing you sell," the djinn said.

"Oh, I'll get her," Marish said. "You can be sure of that." His hand had found a boiled egg, and the shell crunched in his palm as he said it.

The djinn looked at Marish carefully, and then he said, "The use of the carpet, for three days, in return for the White Witch, if you can conquer her."

"Agreed," said Marish.

They had to bind the horse's eyes, otherwise it would rear and kick, when the carpet rose into the air. Horse, man, djinn: all perched on a span of cloth. As they sped back to Nabuz like a mad wind, Marish tried not to watch the solid fields flying beneath, and regretted the candied apricots.

The voice of doubt told him that his companion must be slain by now, but his heart wanted to see Kadath-Naan again: but for the jackal-man, Marish was friendless.

Among the barley stalks, three man-high plinths of black stone, painted with white glyphs, marked three graves. Kadath-Naan had only traveled a little ways beyond them before the ambush. How long the emissary of the Empty City had been fighting, Marish could not tell, but he staggered and weaved like a man drunk with wine or exhaustion. His gray fur was matted with blood and sweat.

An army of children in white armor surrounded Kadath-Naan. As the carpet swung closer, Marish could see their gray faces and blank eyes. Some crawled, some tottered: none seemed to have lived more than six years of mortal life. They held daggers. One clung to the jackal-man's back, digging canals of blood.

Two of the babies were impaled on the point of the great black spear. Hand over hand, daggers held in their mouths, they dragged themselves down the shaft toward Kadath-Naan's hands. Hundreds more surrounded him, closing in.

Kadath-Naan swung his spear, knocking the slack-eyed creatures back. He struck with enough force to shatter human skulls, but the horrors only rolled, and scampered giggling back to stab his legs. With each swing, the spear was slower. Kadath-Naan's eyes rolled back into their sockets. His great frame shuddered from weariness and pain.

The carpet swung low over the battle, and Marish lay on his belly, dangling his arms down to the jackal-headed warrior. He shouted: "Jump! Kadath-Naan, jump!"

Kadath-Naan looked up and, gripping his spear in both hands, he tensed his legs to jump. But the pause gave the tiny slaves of the White Witch their chance; they swarmed over his body, stabbing with their daggers, and he collapsed under the writhing mass of his enemies.

"Down further! We can haul him aboard!" yelled Marish.

"I sold you the use of my carpet, not the destruction of it," said the djinn.

With a snarl of rage, and before the voice of his good sense could speak, Marish leapt from the carpet. He landed amidst the fray, and began tearing the small bodies from Kadath-Naan and flinging them into the fields. Then daggers found his calves, and small bodies crashed into his sides, and he tumbled, covered with the white-armored hell-children. The carpet sailed up lazily into the summer sky.

Marish thrashed, but soon he was pinned under a mass of small bodies. Their daggers probed his sides, drawing blood, and he gritted his teeth against a scream; they pulled at his hair and ears and pulled open his mouth to look inside. As if they were playing. One gray-skinned suckling child, its scalp peeled half away to reveal the white bone of its skull, nuzzled at his neck, seeking the nipple it would never find again.

So had Asza nuzzled against him. So had been her heft then, light and snug as five apples in a bag. But her live eyes saw the world, took it in, and made it better than it was. In those eyes he was a hero, a giant to lift her, honest and gentle and brave. When Temur looked into those otter-brown, mischievous eyes, her mouth softened from its hard line, and she sang fairy songs.

A dagger split the skin of his forehead, bathing him in blood. Another dug between his ribs, another popped the skin of his thigh. Another pushed against his gut, but hadn't broken through. He closed his eyes. They weighed heavier on him now; his throat tensed to scream, but he could not catch his breath.

Marish's arms ached for Asza and Temur—ached that he would die here, without them. Wasn't it right, though, that they be taken from him? The little girl who ran to him across the fields of an evening, a funny hopping run, her arms flung wide, waving that rag doll; no trace of doubt in her. And the beautiful wife who stiffened when she saw him, but smiled one-edged, despite herself, as he lifted apple-smelling Asza in his arms. He had not deserved them.

His face, his skin were hot and slick with salty blood. He saw, not felt, the daggers digging deeper—arcs of light across a great darkness. He wished he could comfort Asza one last time, across that darkness. As when she would awaken in the night, afraid of witches: Now a witch had come.

He found breath, he forced his mouth open, and he sang through sobs to Asza, his song to lull her back to sleep:

"Now sleep, my love, now sleep—
The moon is in the sky—

The clouds have fled like sheep—
You're in your papa's eye.
Sleep now, my love, sleep now—
The bitter wind is gone—
The calf sleeps with the cow—
Now sleep my love 'til dawn."

He freed his left hand from the press of bodies. He wiped blood and tears from his eyes. He pushed his head up, dizzy, flowers of light still exploding across his vision. The small bodies were still. Carefully, he eased them to the ground.

The carpet descended, and Marish hauled Kadath-Naan onto it. Then he forced himself to turn, swaying, and look at each of the gray-skinned babies sleeping peacefully on the ground. None of them was Asza.

He took one of the smallest and swaddled it with rags and bridle leather. His blood made his fingers slick, and the noon sun seemed as gray as a stone. When he was sure the creature could not move, he put it in his pack and slung the pack upon his back. Then he fell onto the carpet. He felt it lift up under him, and like a cradled child, he slept.

He awoke to see clouds sailing above him. The pain was gone. He sat up and looked at his arms: they were whole and unscarred. Even the old scar from Thin Deri's careless scythe was gone.

"You taught us how to defeat the Children of Despair," said the djinn. "That required recompense. I have treated your wounds and those of your companion. Is the debt clear?"

"Answer me one question," Marish said.

"And the debt will be clear?" said the djinn.

"Yes, may the west wind take you, it'll be clear!"

The djinn blinked in assent.

"Can they be brought back?" Marish asked. "Can they be made into living children again?"

"They cannot," said the djinn. "They can neither live nor die, nor be harmed at all unless they will it. Their hearts have been replaced with sand."

They flew in silence, and Marish's pack seemed heavier.

The land flew by beneath them as fast as a cracking whip; Marish stared as green fields gave way to swamp, swamp to marsh, marsh to rough pastureland. The devastation left by the White Witch seemed gradually newer; the trail here was still smoking, and Marish thought it might be too hot to walk on. They passed many a blasted village, and each time Marish looked away.

At last they began to hear a sound on the wind, a sound that chilled Marish's heart. It was not a wail, it was not a grinding, it was not a shriek of pain, nor the wet crunch of breaking bones, nor was it an obscene grunting, but it had something of all of these. The jackal-man's ears were perked, and his gray fur stood on end.

The path was now truly still burning; they flew high above it, and the rolling smoke underneath was like a fog over the land. But there ahead they saw the monstrous thing that was leaving the trail, and Marish could hardly think any thought at all as they approached, but only stare, bile burning his throat.

It was a great chariot, perhaps eight times the height of a man, as wide as the trail, constructed of parts of living human bodies welded together in an obscene tangle. A thousand legs and arms pawed the ground; a thousand more beat the trail with whips and scythes, or clawed the air. A thick skein of hearts, livers, and stomachs pulsed through the center of the thing, and a great assemblage of lungs breathed at its core. Heads rolled like wheels at the bottom of the chariot, or were stuck here and there along the surface of the thing as slack-eyed, gibbering ornaments. A thousand spines and torsos built a great chamber at the top of the chariot, shielded with webs of skin

217

and hair; there perhaps hid the White Witch. From the pinnacle of the monstrous thing flew a great flag made of writhing tongues. Before the awful chariot rode a company of ten knights in white armor, with visored helms.

At the very peak sat a great headless hulking beast, larger than a bear, with the skin of a lizard, great yellow globes of eyes set on its shoulders and a wide mouth in its belly. As they watched, it vomited a gout of flame that set the path behind the chariot ablaze. Then it noticed them, and lifted the great plume of flame in their direction. At a swift word from the djinn, the carpet veered, but it was a close enough thing that Marish felt an oven's blast of heat on his skin. He grabbed the horse by its reins as it made to rear, and whispered soothing sounds in its ear.

"Abomination!" cried Kadath-Naan. "Djinn, will you send word to the Empty City? You will be well rewarded."

The djinn nodded.

"It is Kadath-Naan, lesser scout of the Endless Inquiry, who speaks. Let Bars-Kardereth, Commander of the Silent Legion, be told to hasten here. Here is an obscenity beyond compass, far more horrible than the innocent errors of savages; here Chaos blocks the descent into the Darkness entirely, and a whole land may fall to corruption."

The jewel in the djinn's forehead flashed once. "It is done," he said.

Kadath-Naan turned to Marish. "From the Empty City to this place is four days' travel for a Ghomlu Legion; let us find a place in their path where we can wait to join them."

Marish forced himself to close his eyes. But still he saw it—hands, tongues, guts, skin, woven into a moving mountain. He still heard the squelching, grinding, snapping sounds, the sea-roar of the thousand lungs. What had he imagined? Asza and Temur in a prison somewhere, waiting to be freed? Fool. "All right," he said.

Then he opened his eyes, and saw something that made him say, "No."

Before them, not ten minutes' ride from the awful chariot of the White Witch, was a whitewashed village, peaceful in the afternoon sun. Arrayed before it were a score of its men and young women. A few had proper swords or spears; one of the women carried a bow. The others had hoes, scythes, and staves. One woman sat astride a horse; the rest were on foot. From their perch in the air, Marish could see distant figures—families, stooped grandmothers, children in their mothers' arms—crawling like beetles up the faces of hills.

"Down," said Marish, and they landed before the village's defenders, who raised their weapons.

"You've got to run," he said, "you can make it to the hills. You haven't seen that thing—you haven't any chance against it."

A dark man spat on the ground. "We tried that in Gravenge."

"It splits up," said a black-bearded man. "Sends littler horrors, and they tear folks up and make them part of it, and you see your fellows' limbs come after you as part of the thing. And they're fast. Too fast for us."

"We just busy it a while," another man said, "our folk can get far enough away." But he had a wild look in his eye: the voice of doubt was in him.

"We stop it here," said the woman on horseback.

Marish led the horse off the carpet, took its blinders off, and mounted it. "I'll stand with you," he said.

"And welcome," said the woman on horseback, and her plain face broke into a nervous smile. It was almost pretty that way.

Kadath-Naan stepped off the carpet, and the villagers shied back, readying their weapons.

"This is Kadath-Naan, and you'll be damned glad you have him," said Marish.

"Where's your manners?" snapped the woman on horseback to her people. "I'm Asza," she said.

No, Marish thought, staring at her. No, but you could have been. He looked away, and after a while they left him alone.

The carpet rose silently off into the air, and soon there was smoke on the horizon, and the knights rode at them, and the chariot rose behind.

"Here we are," said Asza of the rocky lands. "Now make a good accounting of yourselves."

An arrow sang; a white knight's horse collapsed. Marish cried, "Ha!" and his mount surged forward. The villagers charged, but Kadath-Naan outpaced them all, springing between a pair of knights. He shattered the forelegs of one horse with his spear's shaft, drove its point through the side of the other rider. Villagers fell on the fallen knight with their scythes.

It was a heady, wild thing for Marish, to be galloping on such a horse, a far finer horse than ever Redlegs had been, for all Pa's proud and vain attention to her. The warmth of its flanks, the rhythm of posting into its stride. Marish of Ilmak Dale, riding into a charge of knights: miserable, addle-witted fool.

Asza flicked her whip at the eyes of a knight's horse, veering away. The knight wheeled to follow her, and Marish came on after him. He heard the hooves of another knight pounding the plain behind him in turn.

Ahead the first knight gained on Asza of the rocky plains. Marish took his knife in one hand, and bent his head to his horse's ear, and whispered to it in wordless murmurs: fine creature, give me everything. And his horse pulled even with Asza's knight.

Marish swung down, hanging from his pommel—the ground flew by beneath him. He reached across and slipped his knife under the girth that held the knight's saddle. The knight swiveled, raising his blade to strike—then the girth parted, and he flew from his mount.

Marish struggled up into the saddle, and the second knight was there, armor blazing in the sun. This time Marish was on the sword-arm's side, and his horse had slowed, and that blade swung up and it could strike Marish's head from his neck like snapping off a sun-flower; time for the peasant to die.

Asza's whip lashed around the knight's sword arm. The knight seized the whip in his other hand. Marish sprang from the saddle. He struck a wall of chainmail and fell with the knight.

The ground was an anvil, the knight a hammer, Marish a rag doll sewn by a poor mad girl and mistaken for a horseshoe. He couldn't breathe; the world was a ringing blur. The knight found his throat with one mailed glove, and hissed with rage, and, pulling himself up, drew a dagger from his belt. Marish tried to lift his arms.

Then he saw Asza's hands fitting a leather noose around the knight's neck. The knight turned his visored head to see, and Asza yelled, "Yah!" An armored knee cracked against Marish's head, and then the knight was gone, dragged off over the rocky plains behind Asza's galloping mare.

Asza of the rocky lands helped Marish to his feet. She had a wild smile, and she hugged him to her breast; pain shot through him, as did the shock of her soft body. Then she pulled away, grinning, and looked over his shoulder back toward the village. And then the grin was gone.

Marish turned. He saw the man with the beard torn apart by a hundred grasping arms and legs. Two bending arms covered with eyes watched carefully as his organs were woven into the chariot. The village burned. A knight leaned from his saddle to cut a fleeing woman down, harvesting her like a stalk of wheat.

"No!" shrieked Asza, and ran toward the village.

Marish tried to run, but he could only hobble, gasping, pain tearing through his side. Asza snatched a spear from the ground and swung up onto a horse. Her hair was like Temur's, flowing gold. My Asza, my Temur, he thought. I must protect her.

Marish fell; he hit the ground and held onto it like a lover, as if he might fall into the sky. Fool, fool, said the voice of his good sense. That is not your Asza, or your Temur either. She is not yours at all.

He heaved himself up again and lurched on, as Asza of the rocky plains reached the chariot. From above, a lazy plume of flame expanded. The horse reared. The cloud of fire enveloped the woman, the horse, and then was sucked away; the blackened corpses fell to the ground steaming.

Marish stopped running.

The headless creature of fire fell from the chariot—Kadath-Naan was there at the summit of the horror, his spear sunk in its flesh as a lever. But the fire-beast turned as it toppled, and a pillar of fire engulfed the jackal-man. The molten iron of his spear and armor coated his body, and he fell into the grasping arms of the chariot.

Marish lay down on his belly in the grass.

Maybe they will not find me here, said the voice of hope. But it was like listening to idiot words spoken by the wind blowing through a forest. Marish lay on the ground and he hurt. The hurt was a song, and it sang him. Everything was lost and far away. No Asza, no Temur, no Maghd; no quest, no hero, no trickster, no hunter, no father, no groom. The wind came down from the mountains and stirred the grass beside Marish's nose, where beetles walked.

There was a rustling in the short grass, and a hedgehog came out of it and stood nose to nose with Marish.

"Speak if you can," Marish whispered, "and grant me a wish."

The hedgehog snorted. "I'll not do *you* any favors, after what you did to Teodor!"

Marish swallowed. "The hedgehog in the sunflowers?"

"Obviously. Murderer."

"I'm sorry! I didn't know he was magic! I thought he was just a hedgehog!"

"Just a hedgehog! Just a hedgehog!" It narrowed its eyes, and its prickers stood on end. "Be careful what you call things, Marish of Ilmak Dale. When you name a thing, you say what it is in the world. Names mean more than you know."

Marish was silent.

"Teodor didn't like threats, that's all . . . the stubborn old idiot."

"I'm sorry about Teodor," said Marish.

"Yes, well," said the hedgehog. "I'll help you, but it will cost you dear."

"What do you want?"

"How about your soul?" said the hedgehog.

"I'd do that, sure," said Marish. "It's not like I need it. But I don't have it."

The hedgehog narrowed its eyes again. From the village, a few thin screams and the soft crackle of flames. It smelled like autumn, and butchering hogs.

"It's true," said Marish. "The priest of Ilmak Dale took all our souls and put them in little stones, and hid them. He didn't want us making bargains like these."

"Wise man," said the hedgehog. "But I'll have to have something. What have you got in you, besides a soul?"

"What do you mean, like, my wits? But I'll need those."

"Yes, you will," said the hedgehog.

"Hope? Not much of that left, though."

"Not to my taste anyway," said the hedgehog. "*Hope is foolish, doubts are wise.*"

"Doubts?" said Marish.

"That'll do," said the hedgehog. "But I want them all."

"All . . . all right," said Marish. "And now you're going to help me against the White Witch?"

"I already have," said the hedgehog.

"You have? Have I got some magic power or other now?" asked Marish. He sat up. The screaming was over: he heard nothing but the fire, and the crunching and squelching and slithering and grinding of the chariot.

"Certainly not," said the hedgehog. "I haven't done anything you didn't see or didn't hear. But perhaps you weren't listening." And it waddled off into the green blades of the grass.

Marish stood and looked after it. He picked at his teeth with a thumbnail, and thought, but he had no idea what the hedgehog meant. But he had no doubts either, so he started toward the village.

Halfway there, he noticed the dead baby in his pack wriggling, so he took it out and held it in his arms.

As he came into the burning village, he found himself just behind the great fire-spouting lizard-skinned headless thing. It turned and took a breath to burn him alive, and he tossed the baby down its throat. There was a choking sound, and the huge thing shuddered and twitched, and Marish walked on by it.

The great chariot saw him and it swung toward him, a vast mountain of writhing, humming, stinking flesh, a hundred arms reaching. Fists grabbed his shirt, his hair, his trousers, and they lifted him into the air.

He looked at the hand closed around his collar. It was a woman's hand, fine and fair, and it was wearing the copper ring he'd bought at Halde.

"Temur!" he said in shock.

The arm twitched and slackened; it went white. It reached out: the fingers spread wide; they caressed his cheek gently. And then the arm dropped from the chariot and lay on the ground beneath.

He knew the hands pulling him aloft. "Lezur the baker!" he whispered, and a pair of doughy hands dropped from the chariot. "Silbon and Felbon!" he cried. "Ter the blind! Sela the blue-eyed!" Marish's lips trembled to say the names, and the hands slackened and fell to the ground, and away on other parts of the chariot the other parts fell off, too; he saw a blue eye roll down from above him and fall to the ground.

"Perdan! Mardid! Pilg and his old mother! Fazt—oh Fazt, you'll tell no more jokes! Chibar and his wife, the pretty foreign one!" His face was wet; with every name, a bubble popped open in Marish's chest, and his throat was thick with some strange feeling. "Pizdar the priest! Fat Deri, far from your smithy! Thin Deri!" When all the hands and arms of Ilmak Dale had fallen off, he was left standing free. He looked at the strange hands coming toward him. "You were a potter," he said to hands with clay under the nails, and they fell off the chariot. "And you were a butcher," he said to bloody ones, and they fell, too. "A fat farmer, a beautiful young girl, a grandmother, a harlot, a brawler," he said, and enough hands and feet and heads and organs had slid off the chariot now that it sagged in the middle and pieces of it strove with each other blindly. "Men and women of Eckdale," Marish said, "men and women of Halde, of Gravenge, of the fields and the swamps and the rocky plains."

The chariot fell to pieces; some lay silent and still, others that Marish had not named had lost their purchase and thrashed on the ground.

The skin of the great chamber atop the chariot peeled away and the White Witch leapt into the sky. She was three times as tall as any woman; her skin was bone white; one eye was blood red and the other emerald green; her mouth was full of black fangs, and her hair of snakes and lizards. Her hands were full of lightning, and she sailed onto Marish with her fangs wide open.

And around her neck, on a leather thong, she wore a little doll of rags, the size of a child's hand.

"Maghd of Ilmak Dale," Marish said, and she was also a young woman with muddy hair and an uncertain smile, and that's how she landed before Marish.

"Well done, Marish," said Maghd, and pulled at a muddy lock of her hair, and laughed, and looked at the ground. "Well done! Oh, I'm glad. I'm glad you've come."

"Why did you do it, Maghd?" Marish said. "Oh, why?"

She looked up and her lips twitched and her jaw set. "Can you ask me that? You, Marish?"

She reached across, slowly, and took his hand. She pulled him, and he took a step toward her. She put the back of his hand against her cheek.

"You'd gone out hunting," she said. "And that Temur of yours"— she said the name as if it tasted of vinegar—"she seen me back of Lezur's, and for one time I didn't look down. I looked at her eyes, and she named me a foul witch. And then they were all crowding round—" She shrugged. "And I don't like that. Fussing and crowding and one against the other." She let go his hand and stooped to pick up a clot of earth, and she crumbled it in her hands. "So I knit them all together. All one thing. They did like it. And they were so fine and great and happy, I forgave them. Even Temur."

The limbs lay unmoving on the ground; the guts were piled in soft unbreathing hills, like drifts of snow. Maghd's hands were coated with black crumbs of dirt.

"I reckon they're done of playing now," Maghd said, and sighed.

"How?" Marish said. "How'd you do it? Maghd, what *are* you?"

"Don't fool so! I'm Maghd, same as ever. I found the souls, that's all. Dug them up from Pizdar's garden, sold them to the Spirit of Unwinding Things." She brushed the dirt from her hands.

"And . . . the children then? Maghd, the babes?"

She took his hand again, but she didn't look at him. She laid her cheek against her shoulder and watched the ground. "Babes shouldn't grow," she said. "No call to be big and hateful." She swallowed. "I made them perfect. That's all."

Marish's chest tightened. "And what now?"

She looked at him, and a slow grin crept across her face. "Well now," she said. "That's on you, ain't it, Marish? I got plenty of tricks yet, if you want to keep fighting." She stepped close to him, and rested her cheek on his chest. Her hair smelled like home: rushes and fire smoke, cold mornings and sheep's milk. "Or we can gather close. No one to shame us now." She wrapped her arms around his waist. "It's all new, Marish, but it ain't all bad."

A shadow drifted over them, and Marish looked up to see the djinn on his carpet, peering down. Marish cleared his throat. "Well . . . I suppose we're all we have left, aren't we?"

"That's so," Maghd breathed softly.

He took her hands in his, and drew back to look at her. "Will you be mine, Maghd?" he said.

"Oh yes," said Maghd, and smiled the biggest smile of her life.

"Very good," Marish said, and looked up. "You can take her now."

The djinn opened the little bottle that was in his hand and Maghd the White Witch flew into it, and he put the cap on. He bowed to Marish, and then he flew away.

Behind Marish the fire-beast exploded with a dull boom.

Marish walked out of the village a little ways and sat, and after sitting a while he slept. And then he woke and sat, and then he slept some

227

more. Perhaps he ate as well; he wasn't sure what. Mostly he looked at his hands; they were rough and callused, with dirt under the nails. He watched the wind painting waves in the short grass, around the rocks and bodies lying there.

One morning he woke, and the ruined village was full of jackal-headed men in armor made of discs who were mounted on great red cats with pointed ears, and jackal-headed men in black robes who were measuring for monuments, and jackal-headed men dressed only in loincloths who were digging in the ground.

Marish went to the ones in loincloths and said, "I want to help bury them," and they gave him a shovel.

About the Author

Benjamin Rosenbaum grew up in Arlington, Virginia, and received degrees in computer science and religious studies from Brown University. His work has been published in *Harper's*, *Nature*, *McSweeney's*, *F&SF*, *Asimov's*, *Interzone*, *All-Star Zeppelin Adventure Stories*, and *Strange Horizons*. Small Beer Press published his chapbook *Other Cities* and The Present Group published his collaboration, *Anthroptic*, with artist Ethan Ham. His stories have been translated into fourteen languages, listed in *Best American Short Stories: 2006*, and shortlisted for the Hugo and Nebula awards. His website is benjaminrosenbaum.com. He lives in Switzerland with his wife Esther and their children Aviva and Noah.

Publication History

The Ant King: A California Fairy Tale, *The Magazine of Fantasy & Science Fiction*, July 2001

Biographical Notes to "A Discourse on the Nature of Causality, with Air-Planes," by Benjamin Rosenbaum, *All-Star Zeppelin Adventure Stories*, 2004

The Blow, *McSweeney's* 11, 2003

The Book of Jashar, *Strange Horizons*, March 17, 2003

The City of Peace, *Other Cities*, 2003

Embracing-the-New, *Asimov's*, January 2004

Falling, *Nature*, 22 September 2005

Fig, *Lady Churchill's Rosebud Wristlet* 11, November 2002

The House Beyond Your Sky, *Strange Horizons*, September 4, 2006

On the Cliff by the River, *Infinite Matrix*, September 16, 2002

The Orange, *Quarterly West*, Spring/Summer 2002

Orphans, *McSweeney's* 15, 2005

Other Cities, *Strange Horizons*, September 2001–August 2002

Red Leather Tassels, *The Magazine of Fantasy & Science Fiction*, August 2003

Sense and Sensibility appears here for the first time.

A Siege of Cranes, *Twenty Epics*, 2006

Start the Clock, *The Magazine of Fantasy & Science Fiction*, August 2004

The Valley of Giants, *Argosy*, 2004

The White City, *Vestal Review*, April 2002

Acknowledgments

The author wishes to gratefully acknowledge the assistance of Karen Abrahamson, David Ackert, Lou Anders, Michael Barry, Christopher Barzak, Avi Bar-Zeev, Aimee Bender, Toby Buckell, Mark Budman, Stephanie Burgis, Octavia Butler, Richard Butner, Walt Carter, Ted Chiang, Haddayr Copley-Woods, F. Brett Cox, Ellen Datlow, Lisa Deguchi, Linda De Meulemeester, Brad Denton, Cory Doctorow, Gardner Dozois, L. Timmel Duchamp, Raymund Eich, Roger Eichhorn, Charlie Finlay, Henry Gee, Ari Goelman, Theodora' Goss, Gavin J. Grant, Neile Graham, Susan Marie Groppi, Eileen Gunn, Ethan Ham, Jed Hartman, Jim Harvey, Jamey Harvey, Nalo Hopkinson, Leslie Howle, Eli Horowitz, Matt Hulan, James Patrick Kelly, John Kessel, Sean Klein, Jay Lake, Jeff Lewis, Samantha Ling, Kelly Link, Karin Lowachee, Emily Mah, Meghan McCarron, Jason McEachen, Maureen McHugh, Karen Meisner, Paul Melko, Mary Anne Mohanraj, David Moles, Chance Morrison, Lee Moyer, John Mueller, Hilary Moon Murphy, Nancy Proctor, Mary Rickert, Shoshana Rosenbaum, Karen Rosenbaum, David Rosenbaum, Aviva Rosenbaum, Noah Rosenbaum, Allan Rousselle, Christopher Rowe, Kiini Ibura Salaam, Patrick Samphire, Diana Sherman, Jim Stevens-Arce, Jarla Tangh, Monika Townsend, John Trey, Terri van der Vlugt, Amber van Dyk, Gordon Van Gelder, Lori Ann White, Sheila Williams, Connie Willis, Jack Womack, Frank Wu, Susan Yi, and Ibi Aanu Zoboi.